'I hope I find you well, Miss Aveton.'

Elizabeth looked startled. 'Great heavens, Dan, what is this? This is our own dear Judith. Had you forgot?'

'I have forgotten nothing.' He laid no stress upon his words, but Judith understood. The wound had gone too deep. She had killed his love through no fault of her own. She would not be given an opportunity to explain, and perhaps it was better not to try.

After living in southern Spain for many years, **Meg Alexander** now lives in Kent, although, having been born in Lancashire, she feels that her roots are in the north of England. Meg's career has encompassed a wide variety of roles, from professional cook to assistant director of a conference centre. She has always been a voracious reader, and loves to write. Other loves include history, cats, gardening, cooking and travel. She has a son and two grandchildren.

Recent titles by the same author:

THE MERRY GENTLEMAN
THE LOVE CHILD

THE PASSIONATE FRIENDS

Meg Alexander

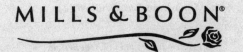

MILLS & BOON®

All the characters in this book have no existence outside the imagination of the author, and have no relation whatsoever to anyone bearing the same name or names. They are not even distantly inspired by any individual known or unknown to the author, and all the incidents are pure invention.

First published in Great Britain 1998
Harlequin Mills & Boon Limited,
Eton House, 18-24 Paradise Road, Richmond, Surrey TW9 1SR

© Meg Alexander 1998

ISBN 0 263 81232 4

Set in Times Roman 10½ on 12 pt.
04-9810-72779 C1

Printed and bound in Great Britain
by Caledonian International Book Manufacturing Ltd, Glasgow

Chapter One

1802

Elizabeth Wentworth gasped in dismay. 'Judith, you can't mean it! Do you tell us that you have agreed to marry Truscott? I won't believe you!'

A slight cough from the third member of the trio of ladies seated in the salon of the house in Mount Street checked a further outburst for the moment.

Elizabeth looked at her sister-in-law in a mute appeal for support, but Lady Wentworth refused to catch her eye.

In the twelve years since her marriage, Prudence had mellowed, learning to control her temper. Hasty words could never be recalled, however much one might regret them later.

Now, heavily pregnant with her fourth child, she struggled to sit upright on the sofa, smiling at their visitor as she did so.

'When did this happen, Judith? How you have surprised us! We had no idea…' Her voice was gentle, and the look she gave her friend was full of affection.

This effort to soften the impropriety of Elizabeth's reaction to Judith's news did not succeed. The younger girl jumped to her feet, and began to pace the room.

'Why did you accept him?' she cried. 'Oh, Judith, he won't make you happy. Why, the man is a charlatan, a mountebank! I know that he is all the rage at present, with his fashionable sermons, but he doesn't believe a word of them. For all his talk of hellfire and damnation, he likes nothing better than to mix with the very society which he affects to despise.'

'Elizabeth, you go too far!' Prudence said sternly. 'Pray allow Judith to speak at least one word. You might also pay her the compliment of believing that she knows her own mind.'

Elizabeth looked mutinous, but she held her tongue as she flung herself into a chair.

'Pru, don't scold,' Judith said quietly. 'I knew that this must come as a shock to both of you. After all, the Reverend Truscott has never given me reason to believe that he had noticed me...that is, until these last few weeks.'

Elizabeth tensed, and seemed about to speak, but a glance from Prudence silenced her. Each knew what the other was thinking. It was less than a month since Judith had learned of her handsome inheritance from her mother's brother. Nothing had been expected from the elderly recluse, but he had surprised the Polite World by leaving his vast wealth to his only niece.

'I was surprised myself,' Judith continued in her gentle way. She gave her listeners a faint smile. 'I am no beauty, as you know, and I don't shine in society. I find it hard to chat to people I don't know, and as for being witty…?' She pulled a wry face at the thought of her own shortcomings.

'Dearest Judith, you underestimate yourself,' Elizabeth exclaimed with warmth. 'Confess it! You have a wicked sense of humour. Why, on occasion have we not been helpless, all three of us, when you have been telling us your tales?'

'That's because I know you well, and I feel easy in your company. Your family has been so good to me… I still miss the Dowager Duchess dreadfully.'

'And she was fond of you.' Elizabeth returned to the attack. 'What would she have said, I wonder, had she known of your decision?'

'She always wished me to marry,' Judith said mildly. 'She was so happy for both her sons when they chose you and Prudence. She longed for the same joy for me.'

'That was different!' Elizabeth said firmly. 'Judith, will you tell us that you have a *tendre* for this man?'

Judith coloured. 'Perhaps not everyone can hope to be as fortunate as you were yourselves…to find the one person in the world for whom you'd give your life.'

'Then wait!' Elizabeth cried in an agony of mind. 'You are still young. There must be a dozen men more suitable than Truscott. Few could be less so. You haven't given yourself a chance.'

'I'm twenty-five, and I've had several Seasons. How many men have offered for me? No, don't bother to reply. You know that I didn't take, as the saying goes.'

'That's because you are so quiet. You don't give

anyone a chance to know you. Dearest, we all love you. At one time we had hoped that you and Dan—'

'Elizabeth, that is quite enough!' At the mention of her adopted son, Prudence felt it wise to put an end to Elizabeth's incautious remarks.

Six years ago she too had hoped that Judith and Dan might make a match of it. She'd welcomed the growing friendship between the two young people, so different from her own fiery relationship with Sebastian, or Elizabeth and Perry's stormy wooing.

Judith and Dan would sit for hours, exchanging few words but evidently content in each other's company, as Dan drew his designs for improvements to the warships of the British Fleet, and Judith put her thoughts on paper.

Only with friends could she be persuaded to read her words aloud, but they were worth waiting for. Her pithy little vignettes describing the foibles of the world about her reduced her tiny audience to tears of laughter.

Now, at the mention of Dan's name, Judith started and turned her head. Naked emotion showed for an instant on her face, but it was quickly banished.

'How is Dan?' she asked in an even voice. Not for a second must she betray the wrenching agony of that final interview six years ago. These loving friends must never know how bitterly she regretted her decision to refuse the man she loved. They loved him too, and they would not forgive her.

'He's home at last,' Elizabeth said with satisfaction. 'He's changed, of course—quite the elegant man about town now that he is grown so tall and broad—but beneath it all he is still the same old Dan.'

Judith felt a twinge of panic. She must not see him, especially now when she had steeled herself to wed the Reverend Truscott. That would be a refinement of torture. She rose to take her leave.

'Do stay!' Elizabeth begged. 'The men will be home quite soon. Perry and Sebastian will be sorry to miss you, and you haven't seen Dan for years—'

'Judith may have other appointments,' Prudence broke in swiftly. She was well aware of what had happened all those years ago. Had she not spent months listening to an inconsolable Dan? How she'd struggled to provide him with diversions, but nothing had served to comfort him. In the end it was Sebastian who had suggested a solution. Dan had been accepted as a chartmaker on a trip to the Antipodes. To part with the boy she'd first known as a terrified nine-year-old foundling had been a wrench, but Dan had welcomed the suggestion, and therefore she'd agreed to it.

Judith would not be swayed. She drew on her gloves with what she hoped was not unseemly haste. Then she looked down at the anxious faces of her friends.

'My dears, you must not worry about me,' she said quietly. 'I am persuaded that this is for the best. I shall have my own home, and hopefully a family. That must count for something...' Her smile wavered only a very little.

Judith's expression cut Elizabeth to the heart. She flung her arms about her friend.

'Promise me one thing,' she cried. 'Don't set your wedding date just yet! Give yourself time to consider...'

'I have considered,' Judith replied. 'We are to wed in four weeks' time…'

'Oh, no—!' Whatever Elizabeth had been about to add to this unfortunate remark was stilled as the door to the salon opened, and three gentlemen entered the room.

It was obvious at once that two of them were brothers. The family resemblance between Sebastian, Lord Wentworth, and the younger figure of Peregrine was strong. Both men were well above the middle height, and powerfully built, though Peregrine topped his brother by an inch or two. They had the same dark eyes, strong features, and a decided air of authority. Perhaps it was something in the clean lines of the jaw, or a certain firmness in the mobile lips which did not invite argument.

Now both men were smiling as they led their companion towards Judith.

'Here is an old friend come to greet you,' Peregrine announced cheerfully. 'He is grown so large that I shall not wonder if you do not recognise him.'

Judith was forced to proffer a trembling hand, but she could not meet Dan's eyes. Then the familiar head, topped with a mass of red-gold curls, bent to salute her fingertips. Dan stopped just short of pressing his lips against her skin. The gesture was all that courtesy demanded, but the touch of his hand was enough to set her senses reeling.

She drew her own away as if she had been stung, but Dan did not appear to notice.

'I hope I find you well, Miss Aveton,' he said with cool formality.

Elizabeth looked startled. 'Great heavens, Dan,

what is this? You are grown mighty high in the instep since you lived among the aborigines. This is our own dear Judith. Have you forgot?'

'I have forgotten nothing.' He laid no stress upon his words, but Judith understood. The wound had gone too deep. She would not be given an opportunity to explain, and perhaps it was better not to try. They must go their separate ways, though the thought of her own future filled her with despair.

Later she could not remember how she got herself out of the room and into her carriage. She had some vague recollections of promising another visit, but her head was spinning. It was all she could do to take her leave with an exchange of mechanical civilities, struggling for self-control until she could be alone.

As the door closed behind her, Peregrine looked at his wife.

'Well, my love, had you not best tell us all about it? I know that look of old. Something has happened to distress you—'

'Judith is going to be wed,' Elizabeth said flatly.

Sebastian smiled at her. 'That, surely, is a matter for congratulation, is it not?'

'No, it isn't!' Elizabeth cried. 'Oh, Perry, you won't believe it! She is to marry that awful creature, the Reverend Truscott.'

'My darling, I hope that you did not tell her of your views. It must have been her own decision, and hardly your concern.'

'It *is* my concern. Judith is my friend. I can't bear to see her throw herself away on that…that snake!'

'These are strong words, Elizabeth.' Sebastian's

smile had vanished. 'The man is a well-known preacher. Why have you taken him in such dislike?'

Elizabeth glanced at her husband, and knew that she must speak with caution. Perry's temper was as hasty as her own. She must not mention the leering looks with which the preacher always greeted her, the silky murmurings in her ear with offers to counsel her alone, or the fact that the Reverend Truscott always held her hand for much longer than courtesy demanded.

'I don't quite know,' she murmured. 'I find him sinister. There is something of the night about him.'

'It must be your imagination, dearest.' Perry took Elizabeth's hand. 'I suspect that you have no wish to lose your friend to anyone.'

Sebastian looked at Prudence. 'You are very quiet, my love. Have you no opinions on this matter?'

Prudence was struggling with her own emotions. She knew Dan's heart almost as well as she knew her own.

Dan had stiffened for just a moment at Elizabeth's news, but when she forced herself to glance at him his expression was carefully neutral.

'Judith's announcement came as a shock to us,' she said lightly. 'We had no idea, you see, that Mr Truscott thought of Judith, or she of him. He gave no indication of any special attachment to her.'

'Until she became an heiress,' Elizabeth cried fiercely. 'Can you be in any doubt of the reason for this sudden offer?'

'My darling, that is unfair,' Perry protested at once. 'We all love Judith for her special qualities. I wonder only that she had not wed before.'

It was at this point that Dan excused himself, with

a muttered explanation of a forgotten engagement. He had grown so pale that the freckles stood out sharply against his fair skin, and there was a strange, lost look in his blue eyes.

'Everyone is behaving so strangely today,' Elizabeth complained. 'What ails Dan? Have I said something to upset him?'

'Perhaps he doesn't care to listen to gossip,' Prudence soothed. 'He is still out of things as yet. He doesn't know the people of whom we speak.'

'He knows Judith. I should have thought that he'd like to know about the man whom she is to wed. Oh, Prudence, now that he is back, do you think that she will change her mind?'

'I doubt it. She seemed quite determined.'

'Then something must have happened to persuade her. I'd lay odds that her frightful stepmother is behind all this. That woman should have been drowned at birth!'

Prudence felt unable to argue. She was well aware that it was Mrs Aveton's violent opposition to Dan's suit which had caused so much unhappiness between the two young lovers all those years ago. The woman had conducted a campaign of hate, telling all her acquaintances that Dan was naught but a penniless foundling, sprung from who knew what vile slum in the industrial north of England.

Her venomous tongue had done its work. Dan had been cut dead by certain members of the *ton* on more than one occasion. His friendships fell away, and Prudence had been surprised to find that he was no longer included in the invitations which reached her daily.

She had made it her business to find out why, and

when she had discovered the truth she confronted
Mrs Aveton. It had been an unpleasant interview,
with protestations of innocence on the lady's part,
and Prudence in such a towering rage that Mrs
Aveton was forced to retract her slanderous remarks.

By then the damage was done, and Judith could
bear it no longer. Though it broke her heart to do so,
she had sent Dan away, vowing as she did so that
no other man for whom she felt the least affection
would be subjected to such inhuman treatment.

Dan had fought her decision with everything in his
power, but she would not be swayed. His honour and
his good name were at stake.

She placed no reliance on Mrs Aveton's promise
not to return to the attack. Her stepmother's machi-
nations might become more subtle, but they would
not cease.

Now, as Judith was borne back to the house which
she shared with her two half sisters and their mother,
she regretted the impulse which had taken her to
Mount Street that day. Prudence and Elizabeth had
been shocked by the news of her betrothal. That
much was clear. How could she explain the reasons
which had led to her decision?

The news of her inheritance had caused uproar
within the Aveton family, though the money was to
be held in trust for her unless she married. True, she
might use the income from it as she wished, but she
might not touch the capital.

Mrs Aveton had spared no pains to discover if it
was possible to break the terms of the old man's will.
When Judith's lawyers explained that this could not
be done, the girl had been subjected to a series of

merciless attacks. They had continued until Judith began to fear for her own sanity.

There was nothing she could do. A woman of her age might not set up her own establishment, even had she the means to do so. The constant quarrelling caused her to retreat even further into her shell. Until today she believed that she'd succeeded in crushing her emotions to the point where nothing mattered any more.

Yet it wasn't entirely out of desperation that she'd accepted the Reverend Truscott's offer for her hand. She'd been moved by his kindly interest in her, and the way he took her part against her stepmother.

Mrs Aveton had seemed a little afraid of him. Certainly the preacher's tall cadaverous figure was imposing. Dressed always in funereal black, when he thundered forth his exhortations from the pulpit the deep-set eyes held all the fire of a fanatic.

Yet, to Judith's surprise, Mrs Aveton had welcomed his suit. Perhaps she welcomed the opportunity to be rid of a girl who was a constant irritation to her.

Judith walked across the hall, intending to seek the sanctuary of her own room. Her thoughts were in turmoil. The sight of Dan had brought the agony of her loss flooding back again. She had deceived herself into thinking that she had succeeded in forgetting him. Her present pain was as raw as it had been six years ago.

A footman stopped her before she reached the staircase.

'Madam has asked to see you, miss, as soon as you returned.'

With lagging steps, Judith entered the salon, to find Mrs Aveton at her writing desk.

'There you are at last.' There was no note of welcome in her stepmother's voice. 'Selfish as always! Had you no thought of helping me to write these invitations?'

'I'm sorry, ma'am. Had you mentioned it, I would have stayed behind.' Judith glanced at the pile of cards. 'So many? I thought we had agreed upon a quiet wedding.'

'Nonsense! The Reverend Truscott is a man of note. His marriage cannot be seen as some hole-and-corner affair. It is to take place in his own church, and he tells me that you are to be married by the bishop.'

'He called today?'

'He did, and he was not best pleased to miss you. One might have thought that you would wait for him. What an oddity you are, to be sure! You take no interest in arrangements for the reception, the food, the musicians, or even in your trousseau.'

'I shall need very little,' Judith told her quietly. 'Ma'am, who is to pay for all this? I would not put you to so much expense.'

An unbecoming flush stained Mrs Aveton's cheeks. 'The expense must fall upon the bride and her family, naturally. When you are wed, your husband will control your fortune. The creditors will wait until then.'

'I see.' Judith realised that she herself was to pay. 'Shall I finish the invitations for you?'

'You may continue. Dear me, there is so much to do. My girls, at least, are pleased with their new gowns.'

Judith was silent, glancing down at the list of names upon the bureau. An exclamation escaped her lips.

'Well, what is it now?' her stepmother cried impatiently.

'The Wentworths, ma'am? Lady Wentworth is with child. She won't be able to accept.'

'I know that well enough. It need not prevent us sending her an invitation. I detest the woman, and that uppish sister-in-law of hers, but we must not be lacking in our attentions to Lord Wentworth and his family. I have included the Earl and Countess of Brandon, of course. My dear Amelia will be certain to attend.' With this pronouncement she swept from the room.

As Judith walked upstairs she permitted herself a wry smile, knowing full well that Amelia, Countess of Brandon, would be furious to hear herself described in such familiar terms. Mrs Aveton was her toady, tolerated only for her well-known propensity for gossip.

Judith sighed. She liked the Earl of Brandon. As head of the Wentworth family and a highly placed member of the Government she knew him only slightly, but he had always treated her with courtesy and kindness. His wife was a cross which he bore with fortitude.

She removed her coat and bonnet and then returned to the salon. There she sat dreaming for some time, the pile of invitations forgotten. Her life might have been so different had she and Dan been allowed to wed. Now it was all too late.

'Great heavens, Judith! You have not got on at all.'

The door opened to admit the Reverend Charles Truscott, with Mrs Aveton by his side.

'Now, ma'am, you shall not scold my little bride. If I forgive her, I am sure that you may do so too.' The preacher rested a benevolent hand upon Judith's hair, as if in blessing.

It was all she could do not to jerk her head away. She rose to her feet and turned to face him, but she could not summon up a smile.

'So grave, my love? Well, it is to be expected. Marriage is a serious step, but given to us by the Lord especially for the procreation of children. Better to marry than to burn, as the saying goes.'

Judith had the odd impression that he was almost licking his lips. Revulsion overwhelmed her. How could she let him touch her? Her flesh crawled at the thought. For an instant she was tempted to cry out that it had all been a mistake, that she had changed her mind and no longer wished to wed him, but he and Mrs Aveton had moved away. Now they were deep in conversation by the window. She could not hear what they were saying.

'The arrangement stands?' Mrs Aveton asked in a low voice.

'I gave you my word, dear lady. When the money is in my hands, you will receive your share.' The preacher glanced across at his bride-to-be. 'I shall earn mine, I think. Your stepdaughter is the oddest creature. Half the time I have no idea what she is thinking.'

'That need not concern you, sir. Give her enough children, and you will keep her occupied, but you must bear down hard upon her radical notions. She likes to read, and she even writes a little, I believe.'

'Both most unsuitable occupations for a woman, but she will be taught to forget that nonsense.'

The Reverend Truscott glanced at his betrothed. There was much else that he would teach her. Judith was no beauty. The brown hair, grave grey eyes, and delicate colouring were not to his taste at all, but her figure was spectacular. Tall and slender, he guessed that his hands would span her waist, but the swelling hips and splendid bosom promised untold pleasures.

His eyes kindled at the thought, but the prospect of controlling her inheritance gave him even greater joy. He banished his lascivious expression and looked down at the list of guests upon the bureau, noticing at once that there were no ticks against the names of the Wentworth family.

'My dear child, you must not forget to invite your friends,' he chided. 'I know how much you think of them, and I must learn to know them better.'

'I could well do without the ladies of the family,' Mrs Aveton snapped. 'Lady Wentworth is mighty free with her opinions, and as for the Honourable Mrs Peregrine Wentworth...? Words fail me!'

'A little...er...sprightly, perhaps? The privilege of rank, dear lady. After all, we must speak with charity of our fellow-creatures. And, you are friendly with the Countess of Brandon, are you not?'

'She thinks no better of them than I do myself...'

Judith made an unsuccessful attempt to hide her amusement. The animosity was mutual.

'There now, we have made our dear Judith smile at last! Believe me, my love, your friends will always be welcome at our home.'

Judith gave him a grateful look. Perhaps he would be kind. It was fortunate that she could not read his mind. The Reverend Truscott knew an enemy when he met one, and Prudence, Lady Wentworth, had left him in no doubt of her own opinion.

He'd seen her look of disgust as he moved about among his congregation, fawning on the women, and flattering the men. She had surprised him once, when he'd cornered one of his young parishioners beside the vestry. He'd gone too far on that occasion, and the girl was looking distressed.

Her ladyship had not addressed him, but her dagger-glance was enough to persuade him to hurry away, leaving the girl to rearrange her bodice as best she could.

Mrs Peregrine was quite another matter. She was a beauty, that one, and he'd sensed the fire beneath the Madonna-like appearance. She hated and despised him. That much was clear. He could not mistake the expression in her huge, dark eyes, but her dislike only served to whet his appetite. He'd conquered such women before, with his talk of love and salvation. It would be a pleasure to add her to his list of victims.

Looking up, he caught sight of his reflection in the mirror, and felt his usual sense of satisfaction. His looks were the only thing for which he had to thank his actress mother and his unknown father.

Was he growing too gaunt? He thought not. His tall, spare figure and the dark head with the deep-set eyes and narrow jaw had just a touch of the fanatic. It was no bad thing. A certain air of the vulpine had served him well in his chosen profession. Who could resist him when he thundered forth his message from the pulpit?

He sensed that Judith was watching him.

'Forgive me, my dear,' he said easily. 'I should not have come to you looking as I do. My duties with parishioners have kept me out all day. You must think me sadly dishevelled, but I could not resist the temptation to call upon you.'

'Judith thinks nothing of the kind,' Mrs Aveton interposed. 'It is good of you to call again, when this foolish girl was not here to greet you earlier in the day.'

'Perhaps she believes that absence makes the heart grow fonder,' the preacher chuckled. With many protestations of devotion he took his leave of them.

'You had best get on with the invitations, Judith. There is little time to spare before your marriage, and I suppose we must do something about your trousseau. Tomorrow we had best go into Bond Street.'

Judith nodded her agreement.

However, on the following day, her stepmother lost all patience with her lack of interest in the garments offered for her inspection.

'Do pay attention!' she cried sharply. 'Nothing will make you into a beauty, but you owe it to your husband to appear respectable.'

'Miss has a perfect figure,' the modiste encouraged. 'She would look well in any of these wedding gowns.'

'Hold your tongue!' Mrs Aveton glared at her. Her own daughters were both short and dumpy. 'I will decide upon a suitable garment.' She settled upon a dull lavender which did nothing for Judith's colouring.

'This will do! And now I have the headache, thanks to your stupidity. The rest of your things you may choose for yourself whenever you wish. I have no time to accompany you again.'

Judith said nothing, though she felt relieved. The excuse to complete her shopping alone would get her out of the house, and away from the constant carping and criticism. She must take her maid, of course, but the girl was her only friend within the household, and she understood her quiet mistress well.

This fact had not escaped Mrs Aveton's notice. She had already spoken to the Reverend Truscott on the subject.

On the following day she confronted Judith.

'You are grown too familiar with that girl,' she said. 'You had best make it clear that she should be looking for another position after you are married. Your husband will not care to find you being friendly with a servant.'

'I had hoped to take her with me. She is the daughter of my father's housekeeper, and I've known her all my life.'

'Your father has been dead these many years. I should have dismissed her long ago.'

A lump came into Judith's throat, but she did not argue further. Her husband-to-be might view the girl more kindly.

Mrs Aveton glanced through the window. 'It may be coming on to rain,' she said. 'I shall need the carriage myself this morning. You may walk to Bond Street. There is plenty of shelter on the way.'

Judith didn't care if it poured. She could use a shower as an excuse to stay out for as long as possible. She left the house as quickly as possible, and walked along the street with Bessie beside her.

'Miss Judith, it's spitting already. You'll get drenched. Must you go out today?'

'I think so, Bessie. Have you got the list?'

'It's in my pocket, miss, but it's coming on heavier than ever. Won't you step into this doorway?'

The wind was already sweeping the rain into their faces, and both girls ran for shelter. Half-blinded by the shower, Judith did not notice the hackney carriage until it stopped beside them. Then a strong hand gripped her elbow.

'Get in!' Dan said. 'I want to talk to you.'

Chapter Two

Judith was too startled to do other than obey him. It was only when she was seated in a corner of the carriage that she realised the folly of her action.

She glanced up, a protest ready on her lips, but Dan was smiling at Bessie.

'I hope I see you well,' he said kindly. 'It's Bessie, isn't it? Do you remember me?'

'You haven't changed, Mr Dan. I'd know you anywhere.'

He grinned at that. 'Once seen, never forgotten? It's my carroty top that gives me away.'

'Dan, please! I'm sorry, but we have so much to do this morning. I am to go to Bond Street. Bessie has a list...' Judith felt that she was babbling inanities. What did her shopping matter?

'Then Bessie can do your shopping for you. Your credit is good, I take it? She may order your things to be delivered...'

'No, she can't! I mean, that would not do at all. I am to choose...at least...' Her voice tailed away.

'Bessie, will you do this for us? I must speak to your mistress.'

'No, you must not! Bessie, I forbid you...'

Bessie took not the slightest notice of her pleas. She was beaming at Dan, who had always been a favourite with her.

'I'll be happy to do it, Mr Dan.'

'Then we'll pick you up on the corner of Piccadilly. Shall we say in two hours' time?'

'Dan, I can't! Please set us down. We shall be missed, and then there will be trouble.'

'Nonsense! Prudence informs me that shopping takes an age. Besides, I can't wait outside your door indefinitely, hoping to catch you on your own.'

'We might have met again in Mount Street,' she protested.

Dan gave her a quizzical look. 'Yesterday I had the impression that you didn't plan to visit your friends for some little time.'

They had reached Bond Street, and he rapped on the roof of the carriage to stop the driver. Bessie sprang down, but when Judith tried to follow her he barred the way.

'Hear me out!' he begged. 'It is little enough to ask of you.'

Sensing his determination, Judith sank back into the corner. She had no wish to create a scene in public, and if he followed them someone of her acquaintance might see them together, and draw the wrong conclusions.

'This is folly!' she told him quietly. 'You should not have sought me out.'

'Folly?' Dan's smile vanished. 'What of your own? What do you know of the man you plan to marry?'

Judith turned her face away. 'He has been kind to

me, and he stands up to Mrs Aveton. In his presence she is not so cruel.'

'And that is enough for you? You have not asked yourself why they deal so well together? What a pair! The man is a monster, Judith! He is a charlatan…a womaniser—'

'Stop!' Judith's nerves were at breaking point. 'You must not…you have no right to say such things to me…'

'Long ago I thought I had the right to tell you all that was in my heart. That is past, I know. I can't deny that our feelings for each other must have changed, but I may still stand your friend, I hope?'

'You have a strange way of showing it. Did Prudence and Elizabeth send you to me? I may tell you that I don't care to have my affairs discussed behind my back.'

'No one sent me. I came of my own accord. They spoke of you, of course…'

'And obviously of Mr Truscott too. They are both prejudiced against him, but why, I can't imagine.'

'Perhaps they see another side to his character. You meet him at his best, but how long will that last? If you become his wife you will be powerless against him.'

'Dan, you are making him out to be an ogre. Oh, I know you mean it for the best, and I am grateful…'

'I don't want your gratitude,' he muttered. 'Like all your friends, I wish only for your happiness.'

'Then believe me, you must say no more. You are but recently returned to England. How can you judge a man of whom you have no knowledge?'

'I trust Prudence, and Elizabeth too. They love you dearly, Judith. Would they stand in the way of your happiness? Both of them have hearts of gold. Neither would be so set against this man without some sound basis for their feelings.'

'I have made my choice.' Her face was set.

'Have you? Or have others made it for you? Forgive me, I don't mean to suggest that you are easily swayed. I know you better than that. You will always do what you think right.'

'Then why won't you believe me?'

Dan leaned back and folded his arms. 'You haven't told me why you wish to marry Truscott. I am told that he is all the rage among the *ton*, but that won't weigh with you, I know. To capture him might be a feather in some other woman's cap, but not in yours.'

'At least you don't insult me by suggesting it.'

'Kindness then, and protection from your stepmother? It seems poor enough reason to accept him.'

For once Judith lost her temper. 'You don't know what my life has been! How could you? It was bad enough before, but my uncle's money has become a curse. You heard of my inheritance?'

Dan nodded.

'I thought I would go mad,' she told him simply. 'I was allowed no rest until I agreed to try to break the trust. It couldn't be done. Then matters grew much worse. Marriage seemed to be the only answer.'

Dan laid a sympathetic hand upon her own, but she snatched it away at once.

'I don't want sympathy,' she cried in anguish. 'That only makes things worse...'

'Oh, Judith, was there no one else? Someone who might have made you happy?'

Judith felt like screaming at him. Of course there was someone else. Why could he not see it? Her situation was so different now. Years ago, when they were both penniless they could have no hope of marriage. Now she could offer him her fortune. It was a vain hope. Knowing him as she did, the money would prove to be an even greater barrier, even if he loved her still.

He didn't. Had he not mentioned that their feelings must have changed during their years of separation? His present concern stemmed only from the memory of past friendship, urged on, no doubt, by Prudence and Elizabeth, in spite of his denials.

She could not know of the discussion which had taken place the previous evening in the Wentworth home. In her forthright way, Prudence had tackled Dan outright, sweeping away his initial refusal to seek out Judith.

'Don't try to gammon me,' she'd said. 'I know that you still love her. You gave yourself away this afternoon. Will you stand by and let her throw herself away upon a man who will condemn her to a life of misery?'

'Pru, I can't. She would see it as a piece of gross impertinence on my part, and she would be right.'

'Stuff and nonsense! I think at least that you should try to persuade her to reconsider. Elizabeth and I can do no good with her. She seems bent on self-destruction.'

'And you think that I will fare better?'

'She loves you, Dan. She always has. I know Judith well. Once given, her affections will not change. If you were to offer for her now, all might yet be well.'

She was dismayed to see the bitterness in his normally cheerful face.

'Would you have me add to my tarnished reputation? Must I be considered a fortune-hunter too?'

'So you will sacrifice your love for pride? I had thought better of you. Mrs Aveton's evil words were forgotten long ago.'

'They would be recalled if I did as you suggest. Judith suffered enough before. This time I doubt if she could bear more slurs. I did not think her looking well at all.'

'She isn't happy, Dan. At least see her. If nothing more you might persuade her to delay the ceremony. Truscott may yet betray himself.' Prudence rose to her feet, pressing her hands against her aching back, and Dan gave her an anxious look.

'You shall not worry,' he said. 'It can't be good for you, especially at this present time. I'll do as you say if it will comfort you, though I think you are mistaken in what you say. Judith no longer cares for me.'

Prudence let that pass. No words of hers would convince him. Dan must find out for himself. She smiled at him in gratitude.

'I think I must be carrying twins,' she joked. 'By the start of the seventh month I was not as large as this with my other children.'

'Then you must take extra care. Shall you stay in London for the birth?'

'I don't know yet. It can be very hot and noisy in the summer months. Sebastian thinks that we should go down to Hallwood.' She reached out a hand to him. 'Dearest Dan, I've missed you so. It is so good

to have you home again. As for Judith, I knew that
you wouldn't fail me.'

'Don't expect too much,' he warned. 'My powers
of persuasion aren't as great as yours.'

He found that he was right. Judith would not be
swayed.

'At least postpone the ceremony,' he urged. 'It
would give us time to make enquiries.'

Her voice grew cold. 'Are you suggesting that you
intend to spy on my betrothed?'

'Judith, the man appeared from nowhere. I can't
find a soul who knows anything of his background
or his antecedents—' He stopped, and looked at her
set face. 'Forgive me! I, of all people, have no right
to say such things. My own background is sneered
at by the *ton*.'

Judith fired up at that. 'I hope you are not suddenly
ashamed of it. Your mother and father were good
country folk, as Prudence and Sebastian soon discovered.' For the first time she gave him a faint
smile. 'Your skills must have come from some-
where…'

'Sadly, they haven't yet made my fortune but,
Judith, we were not discussing my affairs…'

'Believe me, I prefer that you say no more of
mine. Dan, it must be late. Is it not time to pick up
Bessie?'

'Not yet. We still have a few moments. Will you
promise me one thing?'

'If I can.'

'Don't cut yourself off from your friends for these
next few weeks. Come to Mount Street. The change
will do you good. It will be like old times.'

Her lips began to tremble. 'I'm tired,' she said. 'I can't fight my friends as well as Mrs Aveton.'

'Then they shall say nothing to distress you. I'll guarantee it. Do you promise?'

'I'll try.' With an effort she regained a little of her self-control. 'You've told me nothing of your own concerns. This voyage has been of some advantage to you?'

Wisely, Dan accepted the change of subject.

'I learned much about the operation of a sailing ship, and other vessels too, even to the handling of an outrigger canoe in the South Seas. All are designed to take advantage of certain conditions of wind and weather.'

'And your own designs? You were always inventing something.'

'I have a thick sheaf of them. Some I sent back to England for the attention of my Lords of the Admiralty, but I have heard nothing.'

'Wouldn't the Earl of Brandon mention your work?' she suggested shyly. 'If Lord Wentworth were to ask him...?'

'I don't want patronage. My work must stand on its own merit, or not at all.'

'You'll get there one day,' she encouraged. 'You have plenty of time.'

'Have I?' His lip curled. 'I am twenty-six already.'

'A very great age indeed,' she twinkled.

'Pitt was younger when he first became a Member of Parliament...'

Judith gave him a droll look. 'I didn't know that you had the ambition to become a politician.'

She'd hoped to cheer him, and was rewarded with a grin.

'I haven't, and well you know it.'

Judith smiled back at him. 'That's a relief! I was beginning to tremble for the future of the country. Oh, there is Bessie! I must leave you now.'

'Not yet!' he begged. He tried to take her hand but she shook her head. With a sigh he stopped the coachman, and prepared to take up Bessie.

'We shall walk,' Judith told him hurriedly. 'The rain has cleared—'

'I won't hear of it. Get in, Bessie!' He rapped on the roof of the carriage to tell the man to drive on. As they entered the street where he had found them, Judith turned to him.

'Pray set us down here,' she said. 'If I am seen in your company there may be trouble.'

When Dan returned to Mount Street it was to report the failure of his mission.

'Well, I, for one, will not give up,' Elizabeth cried at once. 'Will Judith come to us today?'

'I doubt it. She fears you will return to the attack.' Dan's smile robbed his words of all offence.

'And so I shall.'

'No, you will not, my darling.' Perry gave his wife an affectionate look. 'Subtlety is needed here. You cannot gain your way with confrontation.'

His words brought a roar of laughter from each member of his family.

'Subtlety, Perry? Since when are you a master of the art?'

Perry took Sebastian's teasing in good part.

'I can be devious when I choose,' he replied in airy tones. 'I may surprise you yet.'

'You have already done so. I was never more

astonished in my life. Tell me, how is this subtle approach to be accomplished?'

'I haven't decided yet, but I'll think of something.'

'Perry, there is so little time.' Elizabeth's eyes were anxious. 'The days go by so quickly, and Judith's wedding will be upon us before we know it.'

Sebastian's eyes were resting upon his wife's face, and when he began to speak he chose his words with care.

'Let us consider this matter sensibly. We have no proof that the Reverend Truscott is other than he claims to be.'

'We could find out,' Dan said quickly.

Sebastian held up a hand for silence. 'Hear me out. Prudence and Elizabeth both dislike and distrust him. They may be right, but if they are mistaken I must point out to you that Judith's happiness is at stake. Any interference on our part would be a serious matter.'

'Sebastian, we have no wish to injure her.' Prudence gave him a pitiful look.

'Dearest, I know that well enough, but Judith has had an unhappy time since her father died. We must be careful not to make things worse.'

'They would be much worse if she married that dreadful creature!' Elizabeth was unrepentant.

'Quiet! The oracle is speaking!' Perry laid a finger against his wife's lips.

Sebastian laughed at that. 'I'm no oracle, but we must do nothing foolish.'

'Then what *can* we do? She may be walking blind-fold into a life of misery. I won't stand by and let that happen.' Dan ran his fingers through his flaming hair. 'I'll abduct her first.'

'You will do no such thing!' Sebastian's tone was cutting. 'Would you expose her to scandal? Her life would be ruined; she would be cut by society, unable to see her friends and received by none. Let us hear no more of such nonsense.'

'There's no need to cut up rough at Dan, old chap. What do you suggest?'

'There can be no harm in making a few enquiries. I'll see what I can do.'

'And I can ask around,' Perry broke in cheerfully. 'I ain't much of a one for church-going, but I could mingle with the Reverend's congregation and question a few people.'

'With your well-known subtlety?' His brother's tone was ironic. 'I can hear you now. Would it not be something on the following lines, "We think your preacher is a rogue. What do you know against him?"'

Even Perry was forced to join in the laughter.

'Perhaps you're right,' he admitted. 'I'd best leave it to you.'

'I think you had. It should not take above a day or two.'

'Don't be too sure,' Elizabeth warned. 'That snake will cover his tracks.'

'Yet even snakes may be trapped and destroyed, my dear.' With these words from Sebastian the rest of the company had to be content.

Unwittingly, Elizabeth had hit upon the truth, but the past life which the preacher had been at such pains to conceal was, at that moment, in danger of being revealed to the world.

* * *

Truscott had, that very morning, been approached by a filthy urchin in his own church.

'Out!' He'd eyed the ragged figure with distaste. The child was little better than a scarecrow. 'You'll get no charity here.'

'Don't want none, mester. I been paid. I wuz to give you this.' The child held out a grimy scrap of paper, but his eyes were wary. He kept his distance, as if ready to dodge a blow.

'What's it about?'

'Dunno. I was to fetch you with me.'

A discreet cough drew the preacher's attention to a small group of ladies advancing down the nave towards him.

'My dear sir, do you never rest?' one of them asked tenderly. 'We'd hoped that you'd take tea with us today. We are raising funds for the Foundling Hospital.'

'God bless you! Sadly, this little chap is in some kind of trouble.' The Reverend Truscott considered resting a benevolent hand upon the urchin's spiky hair, but he thought better of it.

'You ain't read the note,' the child accused.

'My little man, you have given me no time to do so.' With the eyes of the ladies upon him, he was forced to open the paper. Drat the child! Had they been alone he would have been well rewarded for his impertinence.

The words were ill-spelt, and formed in an illiterate hand, but the message was all too clear. As its full enormity sank into his consciousness the colour drained from his face. He swayed, and held himself upright only by clutching at the back of the nearest pew.

'Bad news? Mr Truscott, you must sit down. Let me get you a glass of water.'

He could have struck the speaker. What he needed at that moment was a glass of brandy. If only these ridiculous old biddies would go away! He raised a hand to cover his eyes.

'Thank you, pray don't trouble yourself,' he murmured. 'This is but a momentary faintness.'

'It is exhaustion, sir. You do too much. This child must not trouble you today.' She tried to shoo the boy away. 'Your bride-to-be will scold you.'

'Let him be! The Lord will sustain me in his work. I will accompany the child. I fear it is to a deathbed.'

If only it were, he thought savagely. So many of his problems would be solved. With a brave smile he ushered the ladies from the church. Then he returned to the vestry to draw on a voluminous cloak, and cram a wide-brimmed hat low on his brow.

The boy's eyes never left him. A child indeed! There was cynicism in that look, and a quick intelligence which, he knew well enough, stemmed from a life of survival on the streets.

He spared no sympathy for the lad. The strong survived, and the weak went under. He'd been lucky. No, that wasn't true! Luck had played no part in his rise to fame. Say rather that a ruthless streak had helped him climb the ladder to success.

And was he to lose it now? The words of the message burned in his brain like letters of fire.

''My friend seen your notice in the paper, Charlie. Time yore pore old mother had a share. The boy will fetch you to me. Best come, or you'll be sorry.''

It was unsigned, but no signature was needed. The

letter was authentic. Only his mother had ever called him Charlie.

'Is it far?' He spat out the question to the boy.

'Not far. I allus walks it, rain or shine.' The child inspected him with critical eyes. 'Best hide that ticker, guv'nor, and the chain. You'll lose it, certain sure.'

The preacher said nothing. He never walked abroad without his knife, a long and narrow blade, honed to razor sharpness. As a child, he'd learned to take care of himself. His lips drew back in a snarl. He was more than a match for any ruffian.

Now anger threatened to choke him. It was sheer ill-luck that had revealed his whereabouts. The *Gazette*, which had carried the announcement of his betrothal, was unlikely to fall into his mother's hands. In any case, she could not read. He'd thought himself safe. Yet some cruel trick of fate had given her a friend who was sharper than herself.

He glanced about him, and was not surprised to find that he was being led towards the parish of St Giles. He knew the area well, but he had not thought to enter it again.

Preoccupied with the scarce-veiled threat contained in the message, he was unaware that he was being followed. Even so, he pulled his cloak close, sinking the lower part of his face deep within its folds. Then he glanced about him before he entered the maze of alleys which led far into that part of London known as 'The Rookery'.

Behind him, Dan prepared to follow, but his way was blocked by a thick-set individual wearing a slouch hat and a rough jacket out-at-elbows.

'Not in there, sir, if you please! You wouldn't come out alive.'

Dan stared at the man. He was an unprepossessing individual. His broken nose and battered ears suggested a previous career as a pugilist. When he smiled his missing teeth confirmed it.

'Out of my way, man!' Dan snapped impatiently. The figure of the Reverend Truscott had already disappeared.

'Now, sir, you wouldn't want me to plant you a facer, as I must do if you intend to be a foolish gentleman? I has my orders from his lordship...'

'Who are you?'

'A Redbreast, sir.'

'You mean you are a Bow Street Runner?'

The man threw his eyes to heaven, and dragged Dan into a doorway. 'Not so loud!' he begged. 'You'll get my throat slit.'

'I'll go with you.'

'No, you won't, young sir. You'll slow me down. This ain't the place for you. Now be a good gentleman, and leave this job to me.' His tone was respectful, but extremely firm.

Dan thought of pushing past him, but the Runner was already on his toes, ready for any sudden move. 'We're wasting time,' he said significantly.

'Then I'll wait for you here.'

'Best go back to Mount Street, sir. I may be some time.' He turned quickly and disappeared into an alley way.

Wild with frustration, Dan retraced his steps. The delay had lost him his quarry.

Damn Sebastian! Why must he always be one step ahead? Then common sense returned. At least his lordship had wasted no time in setting enquiries afoot. The Runner had seemed competent enough. His very appearance would make him inconspicuous in that nefarious area.

Dan himself was unarmed. It hadn't occurred to him to carry a weapon. Now, on reflection, he knew that the Runner had been right to stop him.

Always a poor parish, in the previous century the Church Lane rookery had reached the depths of squalor with its population of hawkers, beggars and thieves. Every fourth building was a gin shop, where the verminous inhabitants could drink themselves into oblivion for a copper or two. Stupefied with liquor, they could forget the filthy decaying lodging houses in which they lived under wretched conditions.

The narrow warrens and dimly lit courts had always attracted a transient population. Overcrowding was rife, and it was easy enough for the worst of criminals to cover their tracks, hiding in perfect safety among the teeming masses. They issued forth only to rob the unwary, and murder was a commonplace.

Dan shuddered. He didn't lack courage, but, unarmed, he'd be no match for a mob. He'd been a fool to think of entering that slum alone. His very appearance made him a tempting target. An attack might, at best, have left him injured. He could be of no possible service to Judith then.

Meantime, the Reverend Charles Truscott had penetrated to the very heart of the thieves' den. As a child he'd grown accustomed to the sight of the tumbledown hovels, the piles of rotting garbage in the streets, and the all-pervading stench.

Now he had grown fastidious, and the smell which assailed his nostrils made him want to gag. Then his guide pushed open a door which swung drunkenly on its broken hinges, and beckoned him inside.

'Up there!' The boy jerked a thumb towards a rickety flight of stairs and vanished.

The preacher found that his stomach was churning, and he could taste bile in his throat. He was tempted to turn and flee, but he dared not risk the loss of all that had been so hard-won.

He schooled his features into an expression of smooth benevolence, mounted the stairs, and knocked at the door which faced him.

It swung open at his touch, and for a moment he thought the room was empty. He looked about him in disgust. He'd seen squalor in his time, but this was beyond all. Flies swarmed over a broken bowl of half-eaten food, and looking down, he saw that they had laid their eggs. The place was bare, except for a single chair without a back, and a battered wooden crate. A heap of rags lay upon the floor, but there was neither bed nor mattress.

'Well, Charlie, how do you like it? A regular palace, ain't it?' A face peered out at him from beneath the heap of rags.

The preacher stared at his mother without affection.

'What are you doing here?' he asked. 'I thought you'd be long gone.'

'In a wooden box? That would have suited you...'

He was in full agreement with this sentiment, but he must not antagonise her.

'I meant only that I thought you would have found a better place.'

'Ho, yus? Look at me, Charlie!' With a swift movement she thrust aside the rags, and staggered to her feet. He was aware of the strong smell of gin.

'You're drunk,' he accused.

'Drunk for a penny, dead drunk for twopence,' she jeered. 'Well, son, how would you like to see me on a stage?' She thrust her face so close to his that the stench was overpowering.

He hadn't seen her for years, and now the raddled features shocked him. Nellie Truscott had been a beauty. Her looks were all she had had to offer in the marketplace. Now she was painfully thin, her hair grey and unkempt, and her face bloated with excess.

He tried without success to hide his feelings, and his expression roused her to fury.

'Quite the fine gentleman, ain't you? Ashamed of your poor old mother? You done nothing to help me, Charlie. Now it's time to pay.'

'Don't be a fool,' he told her roughly. 'I'm naught but a poor parson.'

'And on the way to being a rich one. You was always smooth, my lad. Now your lady wife will help me.'

His face grew dark and the look in his eyes was frightening. She cowered away from him.

'You'll stay away from her,' he said softly. 'Shall I remind you how I serve those who cross me?'

She made a feeble attempt to placate him. 'I shan't do nothing you don't like, but I must have money, Charlie. Even the men round here don't want me now I'm sick...'

The preacher had been about to grip her wrist. A reminder of his capacity for inflicting pain would have done no harm, but now he shrank back. Thank

God he hadn't touched her. He had no difficulty in guessing at the disease from which she suffered. It was a common cause of death in prostitutes.

'Here!' He threw a handful of coins on to the wooden chest. 'This is all I have with me.'

'It ain't much, Charlie. Can you come tomorrow?'

'No, I can't.' He was about to say more when a man and a woman entered the room.

'It's no matter, Nellie. Tomorrow we'll all go up town to hear the Reverend preach. I hear it's a rare treat.' The woman laughed, and even her companion smiled. They had him in their power and they knew it.

The preacher ground his teeth, but he knew when he was beaten. With a sudden access of native cunning his mother had used her newfound knowledge of his coming fortune to surround herself with friends. She must have promised them a share.

'I'll come at the same time,' he said.

Chapter Three

Judith was puzzled. She'd promised to accompany the Reverend Truscott to the charity tea in aid of the foundling children. When he didn't arrive she decided that she must have mistaken his instructions. Eventually, she went alone, only to discover that he had been called away on parish business.

The next day, at her stepmother's insistence, she stayed indoors to wait for his usual daily visit, but he did not arrive. That evening, a note was delivered to her, explaining that he would be away for several days in connection with a family matter. This did not trouble her unduly. In fact, it was something of a relief to be spared the need to agree with his sententious remarks.

She took herself to task for this unworthy thought. No one was perfect, least of all herself, and if her betrothed seemed, at times, to be a little pompous, it was easy to forgive his didactic manner. He was a good man. That she believed with all her heart.

She stayed in her sitting-room all morning, conscious of her own failings. She had not been entirely truthful with the man she was to marry. What would he say when he learned that she was actually writing a novel? It could not be considered a suitable occupation for a preacher's wife, but the story begged to be written. Throughout each day she found herself composing further snatches of dialogue, or planning yet another scene.

She was not destined to be left in peace for long. At nuncheon that day, Mrs Aveton made her displeasure clear.

'Must I tell you yet again?' she cried. 'You have not bought above one half of the items on your list. You put me out of all patience, Judith. Peace will return to this household only when you are wed and gone from here.'

Judith doubted the truth of this statement. Mrs Aveton's daughters were as ill-tempered as she was herself, and the servants were treated frequently to the sound of quarrelling, screams, and wild hysterics. Neither of the girls had yet been sought in marriage. They had neither fortunes, nor a pleasant disposition to recommend them.

'Must I go back to Bond Street, ma'am?' she asked hopefully. She welcomed any excuse to get her out of the house.

'I see no other way of obtaining your necessary purchases,' came the sarcastic reply.

'And I may take the carriage?'

'I suppose so. At least you will be there and back more quickly than you were the other day. You must watch this habit of dawdling, Judith. It cannot please your husband.'

Judith felt a tiny spurt of rebellion. Was everything she did now to be directed to that desirable end? Her face grew wooden. She'd buy those last items as quickly as possible. Then she'd pay a visit to Mount Street. Perhaps it was folly. She suspected that it was, but at that moment she longed to be with those who loved her.

With Bessie in attendance, she hurried through her shopping, paying scant attention to the items on her list. It was done at last, and glancing at the clock in Bond Street she discovered that she had at least an hour of freedom before her absence would be re-marked as being unduly long. It was a bitter disap-pointment to discover that Perry and Elizabeth were away from home, and that Prudence had been or-dered to rest that day.

'Lord Wentworth will see you, ma'am. At present he is speaking to the doctor, but if you would care to wait...?'

The butler opened the door to the small salon, but Judith shook her head.

'I won't disturb him. Pray give my regards to Lady Wentworth. I will call again at a more convenient time.'

She turned away, and was about to leave when Dan threw open the library door, and hurried towards her.

'I thought I heard your voice. Judith, don't run away. Come and talk to me!'

She hesitated, looking doubtful, but he gave her a reassuring smile.

'Don't worry! I intend to keep my word. I shall say nothing to distress you.'

He had disturbing news, but at Sebastian's insis-tence he knew that he must keep it to himself.

The Bow Street Runner had followed the

Reverend Truscott to his destination in 'The Rookery'. When the preacher left he'd knocked at the same door on the pretext of discovering the whereabouts of a well-known fence, but the man who opened it had sent him on his way.

'Best peddle your wares elsewhere,' he'd snarled. 'There's plenty as will buy your gew-gaws at the drinking shop, and no questions asked.'

The Runner retired to consider his next move. It was soon decided when the man left the hovel with a woman on each arm. He followed them for several yards, and turned in behind them at the drinking shop.

They didn't suspect him, he was sure of it. After all, the man himself had suggested the place as the ideal spot to pursue his supposed nefarious activities.

Smiling pleasantly, he settled himself close by the tattered trio, and received a slight nod of acknowledgement in reply.

He'd been hoping to engage them in conversation, but the older woman was already quarrelling with the owner.

'No more credit, Nellie. If you ain't got blunt you'll get no drink from me—'

'Shut your face!' The woman slammed a coin down on the counter. 'There's plenty more where that came from. Now give me a bottle!'

The man bit the coin, and whistled in surprise.

'Come into money, have you? Where's the body?'

The woman ignored him. Picking up the bottle, she returned to her companions. The three of them soon emptied it, and bought another.

The Runner waited. At the rate they were drinking they would soon begin to talk more freely. He had underestimated their capacity, though the older woman had been far from sober when she'd entered the place. Even so, a third bottle was half-empty before she set it down, wiped her lips, and subsided into helpless giggles.

'It wuz 'is face!' she explained to her companions. 'Proud as Lucifer, 'e is, but we've got 'im now.'

'And not before time!' the man agreed. 'That devil done you wrong, my lass.'

The Runner was puzzled. Had the woman been younger he'd have drawn the obvious conclusion, but this raddled creature must be in her sixties. He eyed her closely. There was something about her features which struck a chord...the nose, perhaps, or the sunken eyes?

From what little he'd seen of the Reverend Truscott's face he couldn't be sure, but his suspicions grew.

'You'll know us next time,' the younger woman snapped. 'Wot you starin at?'

'Just looking about me. I'll move on. Ain't nobody here who's likely to be of use to me...' He scowled and left them.

His report to Sebastian had been succinct, and it roused fresh hope in Dan.

'It does seem that he gave them money,' he said eagerly. 'Why would he do that?'

'There could be a number of reasons...charity among them.'

'But it isn't his parish,' Dan protested. 'Why would he go so far? He seemed to know the place well, or so the Runner said. And how was he able to walk there unmolested? Your man warned me against attempting it.'

'You forget that the Reverend Truscott is a man of the cloth. That alone is sufficient to protect him.'

Dan sniffed. 'He was so heavily muffled that he might have been anyone.'

'Perhaps he's known in the district,' Sebastian said gravely.

'Perhaps he is.' Dan's voice was full of meaning. 'Well, I'm not satisfied, for one. Your own man thought there was something strange. Did he not mention a certain resemblance in the woman?'

'And what of that? Even supposing that it's true, we have no proof. It was merely an impression...'

'It ain't very savoury, though.' Perry had been listening with interest. 'St Giles is the worst sink in London. It wouldn't be the place I'd want to find my relatives...'

'The man can't be blamed for his connections,' Sebastian said firmly.

'But, Seb, only thieves and vagabonds live in "The Rookery". You know its reputation. As for the women...'

'Again, I say we have no proof. The Runner may be mistaken. Truscott's visit may have been no more than a simple act of Christian charity.'

'You sound more like Frederick every day,' Perry told him in disgust. 'Next thing you'll be following our elder brother into Government.'

'Not so!' Sebastian laughed and shook his head. 'And, Perry, he did well enough for you. Without his help you might have lost Elizabeth.'

'I know it. I have much to thank him for. He surprised me then, you know. I thought him a model of rectitude, but he moved fast when there was danger.'

'And I shall do the same.'

Dan's face cleared. 'Then you won't let it go?'

'No! I won't let it go.' Sebastian looked at his adopted son. 'Prudence and Elizabeth are troubled, and I won't have my wife upset at a time like this.'

'Shall you tell them anything?'

'Only that our enquiries are going forward.'

'Then I may not tell Elizabeth of the Runner's findings.'

'Certainly not. We have discovered only that the Reverend Truscott paid a visit to a squalid part of London. All the rest is merely surmise. Would that satisfy Elizabeth?'

Perry smiled at his brother. 'How well you know her! She is afraid of nothing. Not even your famous Runner would stop her if she set her mind upon entering that infamous district.'

'Exactly!' Sebastian looked at his companions. 'This information must go no further than the three of us. I'll let you know when, and if, I have further news.'

With this his listeners had to be content, though Dan had grave misgivings. Of the three of them he alone had seen the preacher's furtive manner, which was not that of a man of God bent upon some charitable enterprise.

Now he led Judith into the library with the air of a man who had no other thought in mind than welcoming an old friend.

She glanced at the sheets of paper which covered a large table.

'But I'm disturbing you,' she protested.

'I'm glad of the interruption.' Dan gave her a mischievous smile. 'Now I shall be able to bore you with some of my ideas…'

'You won't do that.' She glanced down at the drawings. 'Warships, Dan? Surely the war with the French is at an end? Did not the Peace of Amiens come into effect only last month?'

'The Earl of Brandon thinks it but a cessation in hostilities. Perry and Sebastian agree with him.'

'And what do you think?'

'I think we shall be at war quite soon. Napoleon has lost none of his ambition to make himself the master of Europe and beyond. Our Fleet is all that has stopped him until now.'

'But this present Treaty?'

'Will give him time to build up his reserves, and to commission new ships. He has suffered heavy defeats at sea. That is where he must destroy us first.'

'And are the French ships better than ours?'

'They are faster, and lighter too. Our own are built for strength. The first essential role of a warship is to carry armaments into battle, and the gun decks must be able to take the weight of the artillery.'

'I see. It must be difficult to strike the right balance between strength and speed.' Her attention was engaged at once.

'That's it exactly. I knew you'd understand. Too many guns and too much weight reduce the sailing qualities of a vessel. There's so much to consider.'

'Such as?'

'Seaworthiness, maintenance, manoeuvrability, stability, different weather conditions, and accommodation.'

'Such a list!' She began to smile.

'What is it, Judith?'

'Oh, I don't know. I thought you might have

changed in these past years, but I see that you have not.'

He raised an eyebrow in enquiry, but she laughed and shook her head. 'I meant only that you are still intrigued by technical problems. It is the thing I remember most about you.'

'Is it?' His voice was heavy with meaning.

Aware that she was treading on dangerous ground, Judith tried again. 'Of course!' she told him lightly. 'I recall the day we met when you hung upside down on a small craft by the river at Kew. We all thought you were about to dive beneath it to examine the hull.'

He chuckled. 'I remember. Perry gave me a roasting later. You stayed behind when the others moved away. Why did you do that?'

'You didn't worry me!' she murmured. 'You left me to my thoughts. I didn't feel obliged to talk to you.'

Dan grimaced. 'You must have thought me a boor, busy only with my own concerns. Perry informed me that I might, at least, have engaged you in conversation.'

'There was no need,' she told him briefly. 'The silence was so comfortable.' She held out her hand. 'I think I must go now.'

'Not yet!' He took her hand, but he did not release it. 'May I not show you what I'm working on at present?'

Judith was tempted. There was plenty of time before she need return home and when he drew out a chair for her she sat beside him to examine the drawings. There was much she didn't understand, but her questions were both pertinent and sensible. Spurred on by her interest, Dan was soon well launched upon his favourite subject. Apparently absorbed, he was quick to sense her growing ease of manner, and pleased to see that her somewhat strained expression had disappeared.

Then, as the clock struck five, she jumped.

'Great heavens! I have been gone this age,' she cried. 'Will you give my kind regards to Prudence and Elizabeth?' She rose as if to take her leave. Then her heart turned over as he gave her a dazzling smile.

'You have encouraged me to be selfish,' he accused. 'I've spent the last hour speaking of my own affairs, and you have told me nothing of your own.'

Judith returned his smile. 'I couldn't get a word in,' she teased gently.

'But you are still writing? Are they still short pieces?'

Judith hesitated. 'No...'

'Then what?' Dan looked at her averted face, and his eyes began to sparkle. 'Judith, have you started on a book at last? You always meant to write one.'

She blushed. 'I don't know how good it is. It is just that...well...I was trying to make sense of the world, and it helps to put my thoughts on paper.'

'But that is splendid!'

'It is probably quite trivial.'

'No, I won't have that. You haven't got a trivial mind. How much have you done?'

'Just a few chapters,' she murmured. 'Perhaps I'm wasting my time. I'm not the best judge of my own work, I fear.'

'Then I'll indulge in a great impertinence. Will you let me see it?'

She flushed with pleasure. 'I'd be glad of another

opinion,' she confessed. 'You always used to read my things, and I found your comments helpful.'

'Then it's settled. When can you bring the manuscript?'

'I don't know.' Judith's eyes grew shadowed. 'I...I have other commitments...'

'Ah, yes, I understand.' Dan's manner became formal, and for the first time a silence fell between them, though the forbidden subject of her marriage occupied each of their minds.

Judith found the tense atmosphere unbearable. She thrust out her hand and prepared to take her leave.

'Too late!' a merry voice cried. 'We've caught you and we won't let you go.' Elizabeth swept into the room accompanied by a chattering group of children.

Judith smiled in spite of herself as Sebastian's three boys bowed politely to her. They were clearly impatient to reach Dan's side.

Then Perry walked in, holding his elder daughter by the hand, and carrying his younger girl. He was quick to dismiss an anxious tutor, and a hovering nursemaid.

'No, leave them be!' he ordered. 'Here is a lady who will be glad to see them. Judith, shall you object to a nursery invasion?'

'Of course not!' Judith smiled warmly at the children, and took Perry's eldest girl upon her knee.

'We met them as they were coming from the park,' Elizabeth explained. 'As Judith is here we must have a treat. Tea in the salon, do you think?'

This suggestion was greeted with whoops of delight from the boys, and Perry laughed.

'As you wish, my love.' He rang the bell and gave

his orders. 'You spoil them, dearest. Prudence will have your blood! Think of her carpets...'

'We'll be careful, Uncle Perry.' Eleven-year-old Thomas stood upon his dignity, clearly affronted by Peregrine's reference to the nursery. 'Henry doesn't drop things.'

'And I don't drop things either.' The youngest boy glared at his eldest brother.

'Yes, you do, and they always land with the butter side down.' Thomas directed a quelling glance at Crispin.

'He won't do so today.' Judith reached out a hand to Crispin. 'Have you had an exciting day?'

'We went to the Tower to see the wild animals.' The little boy's eyes grew round. 'There were lions, you know...'

'And were they very fierce?'

'I didn't like it when they roared.'

'He put his hands over his ears,' said Thomas in disgust.

'I expect I'd have done the same myself,' Judith announced mildly. 'An unexpected noise can be frightening...' She looked at Henry. 'What did you like best about today?'

Henry was dear to her heart. Less ebullient than his brothers, he had a retiring nature. She and he had struck up a friendship based upon long silences, trust, and occasional conversations when the boy had opened up his innermost feelings to her.

'I liked it all,' he said. 'I made some drawings of the animals. They were all so strange and new. Would you like to see them?'

'I'd love to, Henry, but I must go home. Next time, perhaps?'

'No, Judith, I won't have it.' Elizabeth sprang to her feet. 'We see so little of you nowadays. You must stay and dine with us—'

'But, my dear, I can't. I am expected. In any case, I am not dressed for dinner.'

'Then I won't change. After all, we are dining *en famille*. Dearest Judith, may we not send a message to your home?'

'Oh, please!' The three boys stood in a semi-circle round her. 'We haven't shown you the presents which Dan brought for us.'

'Judith may be expecting her betrothed,' Dan said stiffly.

'No! He is away at present.' Judith spoke without thinking.

'Then there can't be the least objection.'

'Objection to what?' Sebastian had come to join them.

'To Judith dining with us. Sebastian, how is Prudence?' Elizabeth gazed at him with anxious eyes.

'Perfectly well, and all the better for her rest. She will come down for dinner.'

'There, you see!' Elizabeth turned to Judith. 'Now you can't refuse. Prudence will be so glad to see you.'

Judith wavered. The temptation to enjoy the warmth of this happy family circle was almost irresistible, if only for a little longer. Still she hesitated.

'Mrs Aveton dines from home this evening,' she murmured. 'She will require the carriage...'

'Then let us send it back with your message.' Elizabeth clapped her hands. 'We shall see you home, and since Mrs Aveton will be out you won't be missed.'

The circle of pleading faces was too much for Judith.

'Very well,' she agreed. 'I shall be happy to stay.'

Elizabeth beamed at her. 'I'll write the note myself,' she insisted. 'Then there can be no objection.'

'Of course not,' Perry said dryly. 'Who will stand in the way of a *force majeure*?' He turned to Judith. 'Eight years of marriage and two children have not yet reduced my wife to the shrinking violet whom I'd hoped to wed.'

Elizabeth laughed up at him. 'You gave no sign of it when we first met, my love.'

His look of affection was disarming. 'No!' he agreed. 'I like a challenge and I haven't been disappointed. You continue to surprise me.'

Judith looked down as a small hand stole into hers.

'I'm glad you're staying,' Henry told her. 'Now we can show you the things which Dan brought back for us.'

Thomas came to join his brother. 'Mine is a dagger from India. It has a jewelled hilt. I can't carry it yet, of course, but when I'm older I shall do so.'

'And yours?' Judith turned to Henry.

'It is a wooden mask. Dan says that it will ward off evil spirits.'

'A useful item.' Perry twinkled at his nephew. 'And certainly a thing which no gentleman's household is complete without.'

'Perry, I believe you're jealous!' Judith began to smile.

'Of course I am. I was tempted to send Dan away again to fetch a similar thing for me.'

Two small fat hands reached up to touch his face. 'Papa, you won't do that, will you? I love Dan. I don't want him to go away...'

Perry hugged his daughter. 'I'm teasing, Puss. Dan won't go away again.'

'I should think not, after such an unsolicited testimonial.' Sebastian looked amused. 'Now, boys, off you go. Judith will call in upon you later, but your mother wishes to see you.'

Sebastian settled himself in the great wing-chair and Judith lost her charge as the little girl struggled from her lap and ran to climb upon her uncle's knee.

'A daughter next, Sebastian?' Perry asked with a grin.

'Only if she is as pretty as our little Kate here.' His brother dropped a kiss upon the child's head. Then his face grew grave. 'I shall not mind, as long as Prudence and the babe are well.'

Judith was quick to sense his concern. 'Are you worried about her? The doctor gave you a good report, I hope?'

'Prudence is well enough at present, though I can't persuade her to rest. Judith, I'd be grateful if you'd have a word with her. She is accustomed to be so active, but you are always a calming influence.'

'I'll do my best,' she promised.

'Then come and see her now.' Elizabeth jumped to her feet. 'Oh, I had forgot. We've ordered tea in the salon. The boys will be starving...' She held out her hands to her daughter, and led the way across the hall.

Under their father's watchful eye, the boys were on their best behaviour, and to Elizabeth's evident relief, the carpets suffered no disaster. Her own girls ate little, and were clearly flagging after their walk in the park.

'Time for bed, I think,' their mother said firmly. 'Come, Judith, shall you care to see them bathed?'

Her pride in her children was evident, and Perry smiled as the little party left the room.

'Judith is such a dear,' he said warmly. 'She's looking better today, I think, don't you?'

'She's at her best with children,' Sebastian agreed. 'I was surprised to see her here this afternoon. When did she arrive?'

'It must have been a couple of hours ago.' Dan's attempt at a casual reply was unconvincing.

'Why, you sly dog, you've been keeping her to yourself. What will the dreaded Truscott say to that, I wonder?'

'She tells me that he's gone away…'

'For good, I hope?'

'No such luck.' Dan's glance at his companions was filled with meaning. 'He is attending to some family business, so I hear.'

'I wonder if we've flushed him out?' Perry's eyes began to sparkle. 'Odd behaviour…I mean, to leave so suddenly. Don't you agree, Sebastian?'

His brother frowned. 'There may be a good reason. Why must you insist on jumping to the worst conclusions?'

'Don't like the look of the chap.'

'I didn't know you'd seen him. You don't accompany Elizabeth to his sermons, do you?'

'Just thought I'd take a look at him on the night we heard the news.'

'Perry, you are the outside of enough! Did I not warn you not to make enquiries in his parish?'

'I didn't.' Perry looked injured. 'I stood at the back of the church and watched him ranting from the pulpit.'

'Then you'll oblige me by leaving it at that.'

'You've heard nothing more?' Dan intervened.

'No, but he is being followed.' Sebastian gazed at the ceiling. 'I agree that his disappearance is a little strange, especially at this time, but we must take great care not to alarm him.'

'Why so?' Dan was unconvinced.

'Must I explain to you young hot-heads? If the man's dealings are above-board we shall be guilty of unwarranted interference in his affairs.'

'And if not?'

Sebastian hesitated, considering his words with care. 'Our quarry may take fright and disappear.'

'Good riddance!' Dan insisted warmly. 'So much the better for Judith!'

'No, Dan, think! If he is the villain you believe him to be, will he give up the chance to get his hands upon a fortune?'

Dan paled. 'You mean…you mean that we may be putting Judith in great danger?'

'That is possible. Girls have been seized before and forced into marriage with unscrupulous men. Once wed, and with the money in his hands, he would leave no trace behind him.'

Perry sprang from his seat and began to pace the room. 'We can't have that!'

'Agreed!' His brother's face was calm. 'You both see now that we must proceed with caution?' Sebastian leaned back in his chair, satisfied that he had made his point.

Still doubtful, he'd have been concerned to learn that he had hit upon the truth.

The threat of blackmail had caused the Reverend Truscott to spend a sleepless night. Then, as his initial panic subsided he began to pull himself together. Still unaware that he was being followed, he paid a second visit to 'The Rockery', carrying with him the contents of the collection box. This was irritating. Such funds had previously found their way into his private account, but no matter. He had begun to lay his plans.

As he had expected, the money was regarded simply as a down payment. His mother and her friends intended to bleed him white. He permitted himself a grim smile. They did not know him.

With a promise of a further payment before the week was out he explained that he was called away on parish work for the next day or two. He didn't intend to waste this brief respite. Judith must be satisfied with a note explaining his absence. He had other matters to attend.

His next journey took him into the pauper colony of Seven Dials. His destination was a brick-built dwelling, apparently no better than any of the others. He let himself in with his own key, and looked about him with a grunt of satisfaction. This was one in the eye for his high-principled parishioners. He'd lavished money on the place, delighted to be putting it to better use than throwing it away on a bunch of ragged urchins.

The place was empty, and his face grew dark with rage. Where the devil was the wench? She was supposed to be here when he wanted her.

When he heard her footstep on the stair he waited

behind the door, seizing her from behind as she entered the room. Twisting his fingers in her hair he dragged her round to face him, smiling as she whimpered with pain.

'You're hurting me!' she cried.

'I'll hurt you even more, you slut, if you don't obey my orders. Didn't I say that you weren't to leave the house? Been playing me false, have you?' He tightened his grip, forcing her to her knees.

'I wunna do that.' Her eyes were watering with agony. 'I went out for bread...' She pointed to her basket. 'I weren't expecting you. You didn't let me know.'

'I'm not likely to do that,' he said softly. 'Will I give you the chance to get up to some trick?' He dragged her to her feet.

The sight of her pain had roused him. With one swift movement he ripped her gown from neck to hem, flung her on the bed, and threw himself upon her like an animal.

It was growing dark before he was fully satiated. With a growl he kicked her away from him.

'Fetch your brothers!' he ordered. 'I have work for them.'

Chapter Four

Next morning, in a part of London far from the slums of Seven Dials, Judith was summoned to an interview with her stepmother.

'At this hour?' she asked Bessie in surprise. Mrs Aveton was not normally an early riser.

'She said at once, Miss Judith. She's in her bed-chamber.'

Judith entered the room to find Mrs Aveton sitting up in bed, sipping at her chocolate.

'Well, miss, did you enjoy your evening with your friends?'

The enquiry startled Judith. Her own enjoyment had not previously been a subject of any interest to her stepmother.

'Why, yes, ma'am, I thank you. I hoped you would not mind, since you were dining out yourself. The carriage was returned in plenty of time, I believe.'

A short laugh greeted her words. 'Most certainly, together with a most insulting note from Mrs Peregrine Wentworth.' She tossed a letter towards Judith.

'Insulting, ma'am?' Judith scanned the note. 'This

merely explains the invitation, with a promise to see me safely home.'

'You see nothing strange in the fact that Mrs Peregrine sends no compliments to me, or enquiries about my health?'

'She was not aware that you were sick, and nor was I. I'm sorry. Were you unable to visit your friends?'

'I dined with them, and I thank heavens that I did so. I learned more disturbing news.'

'Ma'am?'

'Come, don't play the innocent with me! You were always a sly, secretive creature, but now I know the truth...'

'I don't understand.'

'Don't you? Perhaps you will explain why you didn't tell me that the pauper, Ashburn, is returned to the Wentworth household?'

Judith went cold, but her voice was calm when she replied, 'I did not think that it would interest you.'

'If I'm not mistaken, it interests you, my girl. Such deceit! You knew quite well that had I known I should have forbidden you to go there.'

Judith's hands were shaking. She hid them in the pockets of her gown. 'Must I remind you, ma'am, that I am betrothed to Mr Truscott?'

'I wonder that you remember it. To cheapen yourself in the company of that creature is the outside of enough. Have you not learned your lesson yet?'

Judith's anger threatened to consume her. 'I have learned much in these past few years,' she said quietly. 'I think you have forgotten that Mr Ashburn is Lord Wentworth's adopted son.'

A sniff greeted her reply. 'And that is enough to transform a slum child into a member of the *ton*? What a fool you are! The aristocracy may be allowed their eccentricities. Must you try to ape them?'

'I had no thought of doing so. Mr Ashburn is an old friend. I intend to be civil to him.' Judith was surprised at her own temerity. In the usual way she did not argue with her formidable stepmother.

Mrs Aveton's head went up, and her small black eyes began to glitter.

'Impudence! You are grown mighty high in the instep in these last few weeks. Your husband will knock that nonsense out of you...' She caught herself in time. Judith must not be allowed to guess at the darker side of the Reverend Truscott's nature.

This quiet-looking girl had a streak of iron in her character. Mrs Aveton had seen it only seldom, but her attempts to crush that stubborn will had failed. If Judith should change her mind and put an end to her engagement, she herself might say goodbye to the sum of money soon to be in her hands.

Her malevolent expression vanished. 'I mean, of course, that the Reverend Truscott has a position to uphold. His wife must not be seen to gather about her friends who are...er...unsuitable.'

'He seems happy enough to think that I am friendly with the Wentworth family. He tells me that they will always be welcome in our home.'

'That is quite another matter. Judith, you are placing yourself in a most invidious position. You may have forgotten that unfortunate nonsense of six years ago. The same may not be true of Ashburn. You are an heiress now, and a fine catch for him. Has he made further advances to you?'

'He has not!' Judith ground her teeth. The temptation to strike her questioner was strong.

'Doubtless he will do so. You must not see him again before your marriage.'

Judith drew herself to her full height. 'I have promised to return,' she said stiffly. 'Do you think me so ill-behaved that I won't conduct myself with propriety?'

'You are headstrong, miss. I have never been deceived by your milk-and-water ways. In this you will obey me. You may not leave this house again before I speak to Mr Truscott.'

Dismissed without ceremony, Judith returned to her room. She was seething with rage. If she'd ever had any doubts of the need to escape from Mrs Aveton's clutches, they vanished now. She'd thought long and hard before she had accepted the preacher's offer for her hand, fearing that she was cheating both herself and him. She didn't love him, but in the materialistic circles in which she moved, love seldom played a part in settling a marriage contract.

And she was no longer the timid nineteen-year-old who had given up her love in the face of calumnies and opposition. The years had changed her. Unless she was to wither away in the Aveton household, she could see no alternative to marriage. What else could she do? She might have taught in some small dame school, or become a governess, had she not inherited her fortune. Now it was out of the question.

And she would not cheat Charles Truscott. In her heart she had vowed to make him a good wife. She could help him in his parish work, run his household, and bear his children.

She buried her face in her hands, knowing now that it would never be enough.

Why had Dan come back at just this time? In another month she would be safely wed, and could put him out of her mind for ever. She would not think of him. She mustn't. She pulled down the central flap of her writing desk, and pressed a small knob just behind the hinges. A hidden drawer slid out, revealing a pile of manuscript. Listlessly, she scanned the pages, noting an expression here and there which might possibly be improved to make her meaning more exact. With pen in hand she scored out several lines, and began to write.

When the Reverend Truscott was announced, Judith was not informed immediately. Mrs Aveton received him in her salon.

As always, he was quick to sense trouble.

'What is it, ma'am?' he murmured.

'You may well ask, sir. Your bride-to-be is behaving ill, I fear.'

'How so, dear lady?'

She was quick to put him in possession of the facts.

'Judith was besotted with the creature, and he with her. Now he is returned, and I fear that she may change her mind.'

It was only with the greatest difficulty that he forced a smile. He had drunk deep the night before at the house in Seven Dials, and his head was pounding. A day of debauchery had done nothing for his temper, but a man had to have some relief. The strain of leading an apparently blameless life could be borne for just so long, and the intervals between his visits to his trollop were growing shorter.

It was unfortunate that he'd had to go away, but on this occasion he'd had a purpose other than bedding the wench. His mission had been successful, though her brothers were not, at first, as easily persuaded as he'd hoped.

'Not murder?' the younger one had pleaded. 'Won't a beating serve?'

'No! That won't make an end of it!' He'd indicated the pile of gold upon the table.

'It might make an end of us. I've no wish to dance on air at Newgate...' The elder of the two had shaken his head.

'You aren't thinking straight,' the preacher snarled. 'I'm speaking of an accident.'

'To three people?'

'Three drunken sots. They might be run down by a cart or, better still, fall into the river.'

'What do they want you for, Josh?'

'Mr Ferris to you, my lad. And my quarrel with them is none of your concern. Haven't I always paid you well?'

'Aye, Mr Ferris, if that's your name, which I take leave to doubt. But it were for smaller jobs. This gelt ain't enough for what you're asking us to do.'

'Of course not! There will be more.'

'How much more?'

The preacher named a figure which brought an avaricious sparkle to both pairs of eyes. Then he leaned back, smiling easily, prepared to discuss the details of his plan. He was safe enough. He was known to them only under an assumed name, and they could not trace him.

Now his look was bland as he confronted Mrs Aveton. They'd understood each other from the first, but even she had no idea of the lengths to which he was prepared to go to gain his objective. Inwardly, he was cursing his own ill luck. The fates themselves seemed determined to thwart him, but Judith should not escape. He'd have her and her fortune one way or another.

'I must hope that you haven't distressed our little Judith, ma'am,' he said mildly. 'Nothing could be more fatal to our plans than to set up opposition.'

'She'll do as she is bidden,' came the sharp reply. 'Now, as you may guess, she is sulking in her room. I have forbidden her to go out.'

'Utter folly!' His voice was harsher than he had intended. 'You have no notion of how to handle her.'

'You think you will do better?' A snort of disbelief accompanied Mrs Aveton's words.

'Pray allow me to try. Won't you send for her?'

His glance followed his companion as she rose to ring the bell. He detested her. Aside from anything else, the woman was a fool. His lips twisted in amusement. Did she really believe that she would get her share of Judith's fortune?

An unpleasant surprise awaited her. She might storm and rage to her heart's content, but she would have no redress. She could not force him to pay. Would she sue him in the courts? He thought not.

He turned as Judith came to join them; walking across the room, he took her hand.

'I hope I find you well, my love?' he murmured. 'Are you, perhaps, a little low in spirits? You seem to have no smile for me...'

She looked at him uncertainly.

'Now let us sit down together,' he suggested. 'Your mama has been telling me of her worries about your peace of mind. I have assured her that she is mistaken.'

'Thank you!' she said briefly.

'Come, you shall not be so stiff and formal. Mrs Aveton thinks only of your happiness and my own, my dear. I hope I have convinced her that nothing in your conduct could ever fail to please me.'

Judith gave him a grateful look. 'Then I may visit my friends?'

'Of course! I would not have you consider me an ogre. Why should I object when these visits give you so much pleasure? There can be no possible harm in your going about just as you would wish.'

Judith smiled at him then, feeling that she had never liked him quite so much before.

'You are very good,' she whispered.

'Nonsense! A woman of honour must be the best judge of her own actions. Now, dearest, I have some boring details to discuss with your mama. Will you excuse us? I am somewhat pressed for time today, but I'll call on you tomorrow.'

'I shall look forward to your visit.' With another charming smile Judith left them. Once again he had smoothed over an ugly quarrel. She sighed, wondering why she found so little pleasure in his company. It must be a fault in her own character.

'Well, ma'am?' The Reverend Truscott glanced at his companion. 'Was I right?'

'I suppose so.' The admission was made with some reluctance. 'You are mighty clever, sir, but the girl puts me out of all patience. She will bear watching. I wonder that you allow her so much freedom. Pray heaven that you won't regret it.'

'It won't be for long,' he promised. 'Meantime, Mrs Aveton, you will oblige me by avoiding these unpleasant confrontations. Where shall we be if Judith takes against me? Very much out of pocket, I believe.'

'She needs ruling with an iron hand.'

'Agreed! But not just yet. This is the time to walk more softly. I know these stubborn natures…fight them and you won't succeed. Now, a gentle appeal to honour and a sense of duty, and the game is yours.'

Mrs Aveton felt a first twinge of misgiving. This man was too clever by half. She must keep on the right side of him if she hoped to keep him to their agreement.

She nodded. 'You may be right. I hope so.'

'I am sure of it.' With an ironic bow he took his leave of her.

As promised, Mrs Aveton followed his instructions, and when Judith announced her intention to go out that afternoon she made no objection, though she eyed her stepdaughter with some misgiving.

Judith, who normally took so little interest in her own appearance, had chosen on this occasion to wear a new toilette, chosen as part of her trousseau. The soft blue of her woollen redingote became her well, as did her matching bonnet with its pleated ribbon trim.

The sparkle in her huge grey eyes filled Mrs Aveton with foreboding. She had never before seen the girl so animated. With a faint flush of colour in her cheeks she looked almost pretty.

She herself was in no doubt of the reason for this sudden change in Judith, and all her fears returned. Truscott might believe that his bride-to-be was tied handfast to him, but he was an arrogant creature, too sure of himself to think that he might fail in his objective. She lost no time in sending him a note.

Judith alone rejoiced in her good fortune. Free for once to come and go as she wished, she'd crammed the pages of her manuscript into her largest reticule. Dan would give his honest opinion on her work, giving praise where it was due, but quick to detect any weakness in her story.

Mrs Aveton's surprising change of heart had not extended to the offer of the carriage, but Judith didn't care. The day was fine, with a slight breeze blowing, but she wouldn't have cared if the rain had pelted down. She hurried along, oblivious of the other pedestrians, and deaf to Bessie's chatter.

'Why, miss, I don't believe you've heard a word I said! You'll have me out of breath if you go at this pace!'

Judith slowed, but clearly she was impatient to reach her destination, and Bessie said no more. Her young mistress was in the best of spirits, and it was a pleasure to see her looking so happy.

That Mr Dan should never have gone away. If only he'd returned a year ago the young couple might have made a match of it. She chuckled to herself. They might still do so. With a fine disregard for the conventions she dismissed the Reverend Truscott's offer out of hand. She'd always distrusted him, for all his smarmy ways. If she had the chance she'd see him off, and good riddance.

Judith heard the chuckle. 'What is it, Bess?'

'Nothing, miss.' The girl was too wise to voice her thoughts. 'It's my belief I'm getting fat. I'm out of puff already.'

'We're almost there.' Judith turned the corner of Mount Street and ran up the steps of the Wentworth mansion. Then, as she lifted the knocker, doubts assailed her.

Dan might be out. She hadn't promised to come today; in fact, she hadn't given him any idea of when she might return. She'd scarcely hoped that it would be so soon. Then the door opened and Dan came hurrying towards her, both hands outstretched in welcome. She placed her own in his and he grasped them warmly.

'What luck!' he told her. 'I've been waiting for you since this morning. Truscott is still away?'

'No, he is returned, but he has given permission for me to call upon my friends.'

'Good of him!' Dan's tone was sardonic.

'Indeed it was! Without his intervention I should not have been allowed to leave the house. Mrs Aveton has learned of your return.'

'Then should you be here?' he asked stiffly. 'You won't tell me that my old enemy has lost any of her loathing for me?'

'Oh, Dan, may we not forget about her just for once?' Judith pleaded. 'I've brought my manuscript. I hoped that you would read it…'

'Forgive me!' he said quickly. 'I should know better than to remind you of that harridan. Come into the library. Then we may be comfortable.'

He settled her into a chair, handing her the book he'd been reading. 'Tell me what you think of this. Scott is all the rage, I hear. Have you read his poems?'

She shook her head. Then she opened her reticule and handed him a sheaf of closely written pages.

Dan took the opposite chair, and began to read with total concentration. He was soon absorbed in the book, and as she looked at the red-gold head, bent over work which was hers alone, a surge of affection filled her heart. She longed to throw her arms about him, and to hear again those words of love which had meant so much to her all those years ago.

Now her own decision to send him away filled her with bitter regret. She and Dan should have faced the storm which broke about their heads. He would have done so, and gladly. She had been the weaker partner. She hadn't thought so at the time, believing that she must protect him from Mrs Aveton's insinuations. She'd been a fool, but she and Dan had been so young. Even so, she should have listened to his pleadings.

Better by far to have faced the world beside him than to find herself in her present situation, loving Dan as she did, and promised in marriage to another. She could cry off, even at this late stage, but it would avail her nothing.

Dan had changed. She'd tried to deny it both to herself and to him, but it was true. He was no longer the eager lad who'd believed the world well lost for love. It was only to be expected. Their parting had been bitter, and even now she could not bear to think of his reproaches. The look of agony on his face had cut her to the heart, but she had held to her decision, believing it in his best interests.

Perhaps it was. She glanced at him again. She would have known him anywhere, but there was a certain maturity about his manner which was new to her. Not by a word or a gesture had he indicated that he now thought of her as anyone other than an old friend. Indeed, on occasion his formality had startled her.

What did she expect? She was promised to another man. If Dan had loved her still, his own sense of honour would have prevented him from telling her so. He didn't, and for that she must be grateful. He, at least, had found peace of mind in these last few years. She could only wish him happiness. Then she heard a chuckle, and raised an eyebrow in enquiry.

'Judith, this is very good! I can't put it down. You haven't lost your sense of fun, I see. How cleverly you seize upon the foibles of our world.'

'Perhaps I haven't been very kind…'

'At least you have been honest. Your insight frightens me. I shall have to watch my p's and q's.'

Judith laughed. 'Not you!' she protested. 'I don't intend to ridicule my friends—'

'No, no, I didn't meant that! Your characters are not recognisable, but I'm much amused by your comments on some of our present follies. You are a dangerous woman!' His smile robbed his words of all offence.

'Then you must keep my secret. No one else has seen the book.'

'But, Judith, you must publish it! It would be a great success.'

'No, I can't do that. Think of the scandal!'

'What scandal? Other women have been successful authors. It's more than a hundred years since Mrs Aphra Behn published her plays and novels, and what of Fanny Burney?'

'Madame d'Arblay? That was different. Her father was an author and he encouraged her. Besides, did she not publish anonymously at first?'

'You might do the same.'

Judith shook her head. 'Suppose the truth came out? You forget, I think, that I am to marry a parson. It would be considered unsuitable.'

'I have not forgotten,' he told her savagely. 'That is but one more reason why you should not wed him.'

'Oh, Dan, you promised that we should not speak of it. Give me the manuscript. I wrote it for my own pleasure, but I'm glad you think it entertaining.'

'It's more than that, my dear. May I not keep it for a day or two?' Dan was anxious to chase away the frown which had appeared between her brows. 'I want to know what happens next.'

'Very well, but it must be our secret. Now tell me, how does your own work go on?'

'I keep busy.' He gave her a rueful look. 'Sometimes I wonder if my plans will ever get a hearing.'

'They will,' she comforted him. 'You are still determined that you won't use your connections?'

'I don't want charity.'

'But it wouldn't be that. If your ideas are sound, and I'm sure they are, they should be put to use. After all, even the most willing of acquaintance would not support a scheme to build an unseaworthy vessel.'

'Doubtless my Lords of the Admiralty have no plans to build at all. After all, we are at peace...'

'But not for long, or so you believe. Dan, there must be other men who think as you do. Perry and Sebastian are of the same mind,' Judith paused for a moment. 'Shall you think me interfering if I suggest another scheme?'

'I'll try anything.'

'Then why not write direct to Admiral Nelson? Perry met him but the once, yet he is Nelson's man for life.'

'Another connection?'

'Not at all. The Admiral is unlikely to remember a lowly first lieutenant. In any case, you need not mention it. Why not send him your drawings, and leave them to his judgment?'

The look of affection in Dan's eyes made her heart turn over.

'How like you to think of others rather than yourself,' he murmured. 'When did you decide on this idea?'

'It just came into my head,' she told him hurriedly. She could not explain that he had been constantly in her thoughts since the day he had returned.

Dan rose to his feet and held out his hands to her, drawing her up to face him. His eyes were sparkling.

'Clever Judith!' he said tenderly. 'Why could I not have thought of that myself?'

'Then you will do it?' Her words were almost inaudible. He was much too close, and she found that she was trembling. How well she remembered the touch of those loving hands, and the way the small pulse beat in his throat. She swayed, and he slipped an arm about her waist.

'Judith?' Whatever he had been about to say was lost when the door flew open and Elizabeth hurried into the room.

After a first quick glance she gave no indication of her surprise at finding Judith in Dan's arms.

'Why, there you are, my love!' she cried. 'This is an unexpected pleasure. We hadn't hoped that you would be able to escape again so soon.'

Judith grew scarlet with embarrassment, but Elizabeth was apparently blind to her discomfiture.

'Won't you join us in the salon?' she coaxed. 'We are but this instant back from driving in the Park. Prudence is not so tired today. She will be glad to see you.'

In silence Dan and Judith followed her. Whatever lingering confusion remained in Judith's breast was soon dispelled as she was greeted with delight.

Prudence, she thought, was looking better, and she said so.

'I am obeying orders,' came the dry reply. 'Between Sebastian and Dr Wilton, I find myself wrapped in swansdown. As for you, my dear, I think you have no need of any doctor. How well that shade of blue becomes you!'

Judith blushed at the compliment, and her colour deepened when she found Dan's eyes upon her. He seemed to be in full agreement.

Elizabeth was quick to break the silence which followed. She tugged sharply at the bell-rope.

'Judith, you shall not go away without a visit from your godchild. Kate has learned a poem...'

Perry groaned in mock dismay. 'Again? Judith, would you care to hear my version? I can repeat it word for word.'

'What nonsense!' Elizabeth beamed upon her husband. 'Don't allow Perry to deceive you, my dear. He is so proud of her.'

'And don't forget our little Caroline,' Perry teased. 'I'm sure her chatter must mean something.'

'Of course it does. Did she not say "Papa" this week?'

Sebastian looked at Prudence. 'In a little while we shall be in competition with these proud parents,' he joked.

'And high time too.' Prudence returned his smile. 'They are getting above themselves.'

Elizabeth ignored this gibe as her elder daughter stood upon the hearth rug and entertained the assembled company.

As the burst of clapping died away, Judith held out her arms and the little girl ran to her.

'What a lovely poem,' she said. 'Do you know any more?'

'Don't encourage her,' Perry groaned. 'Kate's latest pleasure lies in jokes. Some of them are more ancient than my own.'

'Serves you right!' his wife announced. 'Who taught them to her in the first place?'

This brought a ripple of amusement from the assembled company.

'Do they not call it "hoist with your own petard"?' his brother enquired unsympathetically. 'Be sure your sins will find you out!'

'Not so!' Perry sat down upon the rug. 'Come, Kate. Let us play at spillikins. Judith will like that.'

'Not in her new gown,' Prudence protested faintly. 'Judith, you must not allow Perry to persuade you—'

'I don't mind at all.' Judith tossed aside her bonnet, and slipped out of her redingote. 'There, I am quite ready, but I think we need another player.'

Dan was more than ready to oblige. He took his place by Judith. 'Watch out!' he warned. 'I shan't care to be beaten.'

At the height of the game, none of them noticed when the door to the salon opened. Then a hush descended at the butler's words.

'The Reverend Charles Truscott,' he announced.

Chapter Five

Judith sprang to her feet at once, scattering the spillikins in all directions.

Beside her Dan rose to his full height, as the Reverend Charles advanced towards them. With punctilious courtesy he bowed first to Prudence, and then to Elizabeth, not forgetting a proprietorial smile for Judith.

'Lord Wentworth, will you forgive me for intruding upon such a happy family scene? I am come to escort my little Judith to her home.'

'I...I thought you were much occupied today,' Judith muttered wildly.

'But never too occupied to consider my beloved.'

Beside her, Judith felt Dan stir. Unconsciously, she drew a little closer to him.

Sebastian rose to greet his visitor. 'Why, sir, you are welcome,' he said smoothly. 'We have been wishing for some time to make your better acquaintance. You are already known, I think, to Lady Wentworth and to my brother's wife, Mrs Peregrine Wentworth?'

The preacher bowed his acknowledgment.

'Pray allow me to present her husband. And this, my dear sir, is my adopted son, Daniel Ashburn.'

'And this pretty little miss?' Truscott bent a benevolent eye on Kate, but the child darted behind her mother's skirts.

'My niece. She is somewhat shy with strangers.'

This assurance was belied when a childish voice piped up. 'I don't like that man. He looks like a black stick.'

Perry made a choking sound, attempting unsuccessfully to turn it into a cough, but Elizabeth was equal to the occasion.

'Forgive my daughter, Mr Truscott. She is but a babe as yet.' Her expression indicated that she was uninterested in his forgiveness.

Truscott gave a hearty laugh. 'Pray don't apologise, ma'am. We hear the truth from the mouths of babes and sucklings. In my clerical garb I must appear formidable to a little one.'

Elizabeth gave him a perfunctory smile. She was undeceived. Left to his own devices the child would have received a beating. She rang quickly for the nurse.

'Such forbearance!' Sebastian said lightly. 'My dear sir, pray sit down. You must allow me to offer you refreshment. A glass of wine, perhaps?'

Any thought of protesting that liquor never touched his lips died away as the preacher saw Sebastian's bland expression. He understood at once. These people hoped to trap him in some way. He smiled inwardly. It would not be with a simple lie.

'Thank you, my lord,' he said. 'A glass of wine would be most welcome. Then, I fear, that we must trespass no longer on your hospitality.'

It was a test of sorts and it succeeded. Perry drew forward a chair.

'Nonsense!' he uttered in jovial tones. 'Now that you are here, we shall not allow you to escape.'

A glance from his brother silenced him, but the Reverend Charles appeared to have read no sinister meaning into his words. He glanced about him at the assembled company.

From the moment he'd entered the room he'd been aware that this aristocratic family had closed ranks against him. A quick assessment of any situation had always been essential to his survival. He wondered if they had the least idea how much he despised them and their kind. How he resented that inborn air of self-assurance, and their calm assumption of authority.

What gave them the right to think themselves superior? In his experience most members of the *ton* led lives which were notable only for folly and extravagance, protected by their wealth and their positions.

Could *any* of them have matched his own achievements? He'd dragged himself from the depths of squalor to the point where he was at least on speaking terms with the leaders of Polite Society. Given one half of their advantages it would not have taken him so long.

And even now, what was he, after all? A preacher, however fashionable, would not receive the invitations for which he craved. Not for him was membership of White's, or any of the other gentlemen's clubs which lined St James's Street. He would receive no cards for routs and balls, nor be asked to make up a party for the Vauxhall Gardens.

Envy welled up in his heart as he looked at the Wentworth brothers, noting the perfect fit of their attire, and the fashionable haircuts. They seemed unconscious of the splendour of their surroundings.

Truscott himself was not. He'd never entered a more magnificent room, with its pastel-coloured walls, fine pictures and elegant furniture. The house in Seven Dials, of which he'd been so proud, now seemed to him to be furnished in tawdry fashion. All that would change, he vowed, once he was in possession of Judith's fortune.

Now he leaned back, apparently at ease, and sipped at a glass of wine which was most certainly of excellent vintage.

Sebastian took a seat beside him. 'We are most anxious to get to know you better, Mr Truscott,' he said pleasantly. 'Your reputation has preceded you. You have blazed like a comet across the London scene.'

'And so unexpectedly,' Perry intervened. 'With your gifts I wonder that we had not heard of you until a year ago.'

The preacher bowed his thanks for the compliment, but he was tempted to laugh aloud. So that was to be their game? Did they not realise that they were fencing with a master of deception?

'My early years were spent among the heathen,' he replied. 'Alas, it was poor health alone which caused me to return to England.'

'How interesting! You must tell us more about your travels...' Prudence was moved to engage their unexpected visitor in conversation. She'd sensed that Judith was struggling to regain some semblance of composure after the shock of Truscott's sudden appearance. Now the girl was on pins, knowing the family's opinion of him.

Truscott himself was equal to the occasion. A fluent command of language was part of his stock in trade, and he'd taken good care to verse himself to perfection in every detail of his story.

Elizabeth could only marvel as his tales of distant lands poured out. She didn't believe a word of them, but she kept her opinion to herself.

Dan was of the same mind. Aware of Judith's pleading look, his bow to the preacher had been courteous, but he had taken no part in the conversation, and nor had she.

Truscott glanced at his betrothed. He favoured her with a loving smile, though briefly. Then he turned back to Lady Wentworth. He'd taken great care not to stare at the man who stood so close to Judith. There was little need. He'd taken in every aspect of the fellow's appearance at first sight.

His inward amusement grew. How like the stupid girl to give her heart to this nonentity! And given it she had. He'd known it from the moment that he'd seen her sitting on the rug, her face alight with pleasure. No childish game had caused the change in her.

The fellow was a blockhead. He hadn't uttered a word for the past hour. Handsome, perhaps, in a fresh-faced guileless way, but that flaming head was an offence to any man of taste. So Mrs Aveton had been right in her suspicions. He'd determined to find out for himself, and when her note arrived he'd made it his business to pay a visit to Mount Street.

Well, they were certainly well-matched, those two, with not an ounce of character between them. If he'd needed any further confirmation of their feelings for each other, he saw it now in Judith's face. She looked as guilty as if she had spent the afternoon locked in her lover's arms.

Upon reflection, he thought it unlikely. Judith was far too much the lady to allow the fellow any liberties. In any case, he doubted if she had any notion of the passions which were his own besetting sin. Cold as ice, he thought gleefully, but he would melt her.

For just a second his expression was unguarded, and he felt Dan's gaze upon him. Looking up, he felt the full glare of those bright blue eyes, and was shaken out of his composure. He rose to his feet.

'My lord, you have been most kind.' He bowed to Sebastian. 'Will you forgive me if I take my little Judith back to her mama? At this present time Mrs Aveton is much in need of her assistance.' He couldn't resist a parting shot. 'Wedding preparations, you understand?' He sensed Dan stiffen, and was satisfied.

With one of the Wentworth carriages placed at their disposal he handed Judith up, and waved a farewell greeting to his host.

'Such condescension!' he murmured as they drove way. 'My love, I don't know when I've spent a happier afternoon. Your friends are charming.'

'Sir, I hope that you were not offended by my goddaughter—'

'The little Kate? Great heavens, no! I confess I was surprised to find her allowed so much latitude.'

He was quick to notice the frown on Judith's face.

'Mr Truscott, she is just a child…'

'Of course, my dear. I meant only that it is not usual to find the young in adult company at that time of day. Perhaps these are the latest ideas. Do you approve of them?'

'Perry and Elizabeth love their children, as do Prudence and Sebastian—'

'Naturally, Judith. That is not in dispute. I understand, however, that it is more usual to have one's offspring brought down by their nurse at a certain time each day, both for correction and chastisement.'

Judith was silent as a strong sense of rebellion seized her.

Truscott knew that he had said too much. Incautiously, he had exposed the iron hand beneath the velvet glove. Immediately, he sought to reassure her.

'Those were the bad old days,' he said cheerfully. 'Now we must move with the times. I cannot fault your friends as parents. What a happy family they are!'

Back in Mount Street, the Wentworth family was looking far from happy.

'What a creature!' Perry said with feeling. 'He's much worse than we thought. Sebastian, you must agree?'

'I found his conversation interesting,' Sebastian said slowly.

Elizabeth looked ready to explode. 'You won't say that you believed him?'

'I used the word interesting, rather than believable, my dear. Some of his stories were familiar. He seemed to be quoting word for word from some of the travel books I've read.'

'The man is a villain,' Dan said savagely. 'My God! Did you see the way he looked at Judith?'

'I did. It confirms my belief that we must go carefully.' Sebastian looked across at his wife. 'My dear, you should rest before we dine tonight. Then we shall spend a quiet evening on our own.'

'Shall you mind?' Elizabeth asked anxiously. 'Darling Prudence, we seem to be having all the fun, whilst you are tied indoors.'

'I am content, my love. A Government reception would not be my chosen entertainment at the present time.' Prudence stretched out her hand towards her husband and he kissed it tenderly.

Elizabeth nodded. She had decided upon a certain plan of her own.

Later that evening she left Perry's side to go in search of his formidable eldest brother.

The Earl of Brandon greeted her with a show of affection which he reserved for her alone. Elizabeth held a special place within his heart, and had done so since the time when she had so nearly been lost to them.

'Well, Puss?' he said kindly. 'I hadn't thought it possible that you could grow more lovely, but you succeed in doing so.'

Elizabeth brushed aside the compliment. She wasn't vain, regarding her startling beauty as an accident of birth, for which she could take no credit.

'Frederick, will you spare me a few moments for a private conversation?' she murmured.

'Certainly, my dear.' He led the way into a small anteroom. 'How may I serve you?'

'It isn't for me,' she told him quickly. 'You remember Judith Aveton?'

'Indeed I do. A quiet girl, with a beautiful speaking voice, as I recall… So different from that Aveton creature who is never out of my home.'

'Quite! Frederick, we fear she is in trouble. You have heard of her betrothal?'

'It has been brought to my attention,' he said drily. 'Why are you so concerned?'

'It is this man, this so-called Reverend Truscott.'

'The preacher? I know of nothing against him.'

'You would not,' she told him bitterly. 'He has all the cunning of the devil which I believe him to be.'

'Strong words, my dear! Have you any proof?'

Elizabeth hesitated. The Earl had always stood her friend. Now she must trust him. 'I can't tell Perry,' she murmured in a low voice. 'But the loathsome creature has made advances to me…'

The Earl's face changed. 'A man of the cloth?' he said in disbelief.

'It's hard to credit,' she agreed. 'But if you don't believe me you should speak to Prudence. She caught him out in his own church.'

Frederick laid a hand upon her arm. 'I do believe you,' he said quietly. 'Have you told Judith?'

'Not in so many words. She knows, of course, that we dislike the man, but we cannot sway her. It is hardly to be wondered at. Marriage must seem to her to be the only alternative to a life of misery with Mrs Aveton.'

'Scarce a fate which one would wish upon one's worst enemy. Judith may be right, my dear. Men have strong passions. Marriage may prove to be the cure for those.'

Frederick was a man of the world. He was well aware of the adulation which a fervent orator could arouse in the female breast. Possibly this Truscott had allowed his admiration for the ladies to go too far upon occasion, but doubtless it was no more than a foolish attempt to cling to a hand for longer than propriety allowed, or to indulge in a few glowing words.

'Frederick, you disappoint me!' his tiny sister-in-law said sharply. 'Truscott did not pay me idle compliments. He was importunate. Perry would have killed him had he known of it.'

'And who, my dear one, is to be the object of my retribution?' Perry strolled towards them. 'What mischief are you planning now?'

Elizabeth coloured and looked confused, wondering how much of the conversation he had heard. Perry was not the mildest of men, and any insult to his wife would not be overlooked.

'We were speaking of Charles Truscott,' Frederick replied easily. 'Not one of Elizabeth's favourites, I hear.'

'Nor mine. He is a shabby fellow, with an unknown background. Do *you* know anything about him?'

'No more than is common knowledge. He has enjoyed a sudden rise to fame, I believe.'

'Too sudden!' Perry stepped upon the hem of his wife's gown, and then looked down in horror. 'Damme! Now I've torn your dress. I'm so sorry, dearest. Shall you be able to pin it up? Blest if I ain't grown clumsier than ever!'

Elizabeth looked at him in mock reproach, and then she gave him a rueful grin. Gathering up her skirt, she departed in search of a maid.

'Clumsy indeed, my dear chap! Sometimes I wonder that your wife does not see through you.'

'Most of the time she does...'

'Well, then, since you wish to speak to me alone, you'd best tell me what is on your mind.'

'It's this Truscott creature. I tell you, Frederick, there is something smoky there. Sebastian had him followed into the stews, and again to Seven Dials. We haven't told Prudence and Elizabeth.'

'I should hope not, Perry. Knowing your wife, I believe she is more than likely to tackle him direct when he might simply be abroad on errands of mercy.'

'Mercy? You don't know him,' Perry said darkly. 'I, for one, trust Elizabeth's judgment.'

'Quite right!' The Earl gave his youngest brother a slight smile. 'It was always better than your own.'

Perry ignored the gibe. 'Call it feminine intuition if you like, but the girls were appalled when they heard of the betrothal. We...I mean Sebastian...thought they were being fanciful at first, but now even he is worried.'

The Earl of Brandon made a steeple of his finger-tips.

'You both believe you are right to interfere?'

'Frederick, you know old Seb. He ain't one to tilt at windmills.'

'Unlike yourself?' came the mocking answer. 'Well, what would you have me do?'

'You have sources which aren't available to the rest of us. Will you not ask around? Discretion will be necessary, of course.'

The Earl was not often heard to laugh aloud, but now he did so. 'I think I can promise you that,' he said. His discretion was a byword in Government circles.

'Yes, I know it,' Perry said earnestly. 'I wouldn't ask except that Judith is a friend of ours. We can't have her made into a human sacrifice.'

'Dear me! You are growing quite poetic. Now tell me, is the lady herself happy with her choice?'

'She is, but, you see, she is an innocent. This clever scoundrel has deceived her.'

'You seem very sure of that. Let us hope that you are mistaken. Leave it with me, Perry. You will forgive me, but I must rejoin my guests.'

Perry was not entirely satisfied, but was forced to be content with his brother's promise of discretion. He decided to add a last clincher to his argument.

'We ain't mistaken,' he muttered. 'Never think that Truscott visits the stews for charitable work. He spent the night at Seven Dials.'

The Earl raised a quizzical eyebrow. 'As a well-known parson, would you expect him to visit the more fashionable ladies of the town?'

He moved away, leaving Perry feeling like a foolish schoolboy. His brother might be right. It was possible that Truscott visited the slums simply to slake his lusts. In a man of the cloth it was not admirable, but it was understandable.

Perry himself had had high-flyers in his keeping before his marriage. Since then, he hadn't even been tempted. Compared with his ravishing Elizabeth, all other women were pale shadows.

Now she returned to join him with a smile upon her lips.

'Need you have sacrificed my gown?' she teased.

'Is it ruined? I'm sorry, love—'

'Sorry about the gown, or sorry for attempting to deceive me?'

He gave a reluctant laugh as he tucked her arm through his. 'Shall I ever be able to do that?'

'I doubt it. You need only have asked me to go away if you wished to speak to Frederick alone.'

'And would you have gone?'

'Only with the greatest reluctance.' The lovely flower-face smiled up at him. 'I wanted to hear your secrets.'

'Secrets, my darling?'

'Yes, my darling. You have been big with news for at least two days. I think it time you shared it.'

'Trust me! You'll hear the whole quite soon, I hope.' Taking her arm, he led her back into the ball-room to take part in a quadrille.

From across the room Elizabeth was soon aware that she was under scrutiny. She nodded pleasantly to her sister-in-law, who was sitting with Mrs Aveton.

Elizabeth looked for Judith, but the girl was no-where to be seen. As the dance ended, she drew Perry towards the two ladies. Perry was surprised. Neither he nor his wife were favourites with these malicious gossips, although it was clear that they had both been under discussion.

Even as he bowed to the Countess and her friend, he found himself wondering at Elizabeth's object. She was more than capable of issuing a crushing set-down, but to his astonishment she favoured Mrs Aveton with a dazzling smile.

'Are we not to have the pleasure of Judith's company this evening?' she asked sweetly.

'Madam, you saw her earlier today, I believe. Did she not explain that she isn't well?'

'On the contrary, we thought her looking better than in recent months.'

'Quite possibly. Her forthcoming marriage must be a source of joy to her. However, the dear child has been overtaxing her strength with all her visiting, which I consider quite unnecessary. Tonight she has the headache...'

Elizabeth murmured a brief expression of sympathy to which Mrs Aveton paid no attention. Instead, she turned to the Countess.

'It is no bad thing that Judith was unable to be here this evening, your ladyship. Her way of life will be very different after she is wed.'

Perry was quick to remove his wife before she could speak the words which he guessed were already upon her lips.

'Let's find Dan,' he suggested as they moved away. 'He knows few people here. He must be feeling out of things...'

As he expected, Dan was looking disconsolate.

'I thought she'd be here tonight,' he murmured. 'Did that creature forbid her to attend?'

'Nothing of the kind,' Elizabeth said briskly. 'Judith has the headache, that is all.'

'Is it serious?' His voice quickened with alarm. 'Could it be a fever, or worse?'

'Great heavens, Dan, you saw Judith yourself today. Was she not looking positively blooming?'

'She was...at least until Truscott arrived. Perhaps he has upset her.' Dan's face grew dark with anger.

'Unlikely! He'll take good care to keep on good terms with her.'

Perry's prediction wasn't much consolation, and

for the rest of the evening Dan's thoughts were with his stricken love.

Judith herself was feeling wretched. The Reverend Truscott's visit to her friends had not been a success in spite of his assurance otherwise.

Always sensitive to tension, she was well aware that the atmosphere at the house in Mount Street had changed with his arrival. Until then it had been the happiest of gatherings, and in playing that childish game she had forgotten all her present worries.

The next hour had been an agony, and she'd been on pins in case the volatile Elizabeth should be tempted to speak her mind. Beside her, Dan too had been bristling with antagonism. Only a promise not to distress her had ensured their civility.

She would not put them in that position again. Her visits to Mount Street must stop. They were naught but self-indulgence, although to be in Dan's company again was rather an exquisite torture.

In accepting Charles Truscott's offer she had sealed her own fate, believing that her decision was for the best. Now she felt ashamed, suspecting that she herself was playing with fire. Was she guilty of deceit and double-dealing? He did not deserve such treatment.

Tomorrow she would go to him, and ask to be given some useful work.

The decision cost her a sleepless night and many bitter tears. She couldn't even be sure of the purity of her own motives. Had she made it simply because she knew beyond all doubt that Dan was lost to her for ever?

How cold he'd looked when he'd spoken of refusing charity, even when that charity might consist only of a recommendation from his highly placed connections to the unapproachable Lords of the Admiralty.

Judith had known then that even had he loved her, her fortune would have proved a far more insurmountable barrier to his pride than any previous opposition. He was lost to her, and she must face the truth.

With a heavy heart she rose next day and announced her intention to visit her betrothed.

'Well, miss, I'm glad to see that you are come to your senses at the last,' Mrs Aveton snapped. 'As I told your precious friends last night, it is high time that you gave up all this gadding about. Most unsuitable for the wife of a man in holy orders—'

'Which friends were those, ma'am?'

'Have you so many? I refer to the Honourable Peregrine Wentworth and his wife…pert baggage that she is! I declare that I was ashamed to see the exhibition which they make of themselves. Why, the man never takes his eyes off her. He must be always holding her hand, or dancing with her…'

'She is very lovely. She is also his wife,' Judith observed quietly.

'One might hope that they would observe the proprieties. Amelia has no patience with them. She thinks it affectation.'

Judith was silent. There was little point in arguing.

'I must hope that you will not follow their example. I should not care to see you always hanging about your husband's neck. Mr Truscott will not care for that, or to see you gazing at him like a moon-calf.'

'There is little danger of that,' Judith replied more sharply than she had intended.

Mrs Aveton stared at her. The girl was not improving. In these last few days there had been more than a hint of rebellion in her tone. She recalled Charles Truscott's words, and did not pursue the matter, though she longed to do so.

Judith would soon be taught a lesson, if she was any judge of men. Her days of balls, reviews and picnics were now over. She could hardly restrain her glee. Now Judith's pride would take a tumble, and that cool reserve which she had always found so trying would be shattered for ever by the worthy Truscott.

Worthy? Her lip curled. He was little better than a common thief. She despised him, having taken his measure from their first meeting. What other man would have agreed to pay for her own good offices in helping to win his bride? She knew that her antagonism was returned, but it did not worry her. The preacher was useful. She would keep him to his part of their bargain.

Unaware that he was the object of her thoughts, Charles Truscott had awakened in a better frame of mind. His plans were going well. No strangers to violence, his henchmen at Seven Dials would serve him as they had done before. After all, there was no greater incentive than the sight of gold.

As for Judith? Let her torture herself and her young lover for these next few weeks. It would make his conquest all the sweeter when it came. When the time was right, he would pluck her from the circle of her friends as easily as one might seize a ripening fruit.

He spared no more than a passing thought for Dan. The man was a nobody, unworthy of his consideration, and possessed of neither birth nor fortune. He might dream of winning Judith and her wealth, but he should never have her.

As always, his morning service was well attended, and the sermon held his congregation enthralled. Quite one of his best, he considered with satisfaction, combining as it did the threat of hellfire with the promise of salvation.

When the service ended he followed his usual practice, standing in the porch and smiling gravely at his departing parishioners. A word or two to the wealthier among them brought congratulations and fervent promises of help with his good works.

As he re-entered the empty church he rubbed his hands. That tiresome task was over for another day. It was a small price to pay for what must be a handsome sum, in the collection boxes. He was looking forward to counting it.

Then he saw the child behind the pillar. He hurried forward, anxious to hear the news for which he had been waiting.

'Well?' he asked impatiently.

The boy stepped back, keeping a heavy pew between them. 'You're wanted, mester. There's a couple of stiff 'uns as needs getting rid of.'

The preacher froze. His hirelings must have botched the affair. Had he not suggested the river, where the bodies would have been carried downstream? But just two corpses? He had to know.

'Who…who is dead?' His throat was dry.

'Friends of yourn, so Nellie says.' The urchin gave him a knowing smile.

Truscott staggered back. He could hardly breathe. A red mist swam before his eyes as an uncontrollable rage consumed him.

At the sight of his contorted face the child began to run, but the preacher was too quick for him. He twisted the stick-like arm behind the urchin's back.

'I won't go,' he hissed.

Tears of agony rolled down the starveling's face.

'It ain't my fault,' he sobbed. 'If you ain't there by nightfall they'll come to you…'

It was then that his tormentor lost the last vestiges of his self-control. Something inside him snapped. He wanted to strike out…to injure those who were responsible for the ruin of his plans. Someone must suffer. He began to punch the boy about the head, splitting the thin lips and closing one terrified eye.

'Stop!' The horrified surprise in Judith's voice reached him even through that bout of murderous anger.

He looked up to see her standing in the open doorway, but this was a Judith whom he did not recognise. Gone was the timid girl who had so little to say. Now she ran towards him with blazing eyes, and caught at his upraised arm.

'Stop, I say! Don't you see that the child is bleeding?'

Truscott released his victim, but his look was terrible. For a moment Judith thought that he would strike her too. She faced him squarely, fully prepared to stand her ground as she pushed the boy behind her.

Chapter Six

Truscott thought fast. His eyes grew blank as he sank into the nearest pew, covering them with a trembling hand.

Judith ignored him. She looked about her for some means of reviving his battered victim. The boy lay half-unconscious at her feet, and he was still bleeding. Water! She must have water! She took out her handkerchief, thrust aside the cover of the christening font, and soaked it thoroughly. Then she knelt down, supporting the child's head upon her arm, whilst she dabbed gently at his lips.

He gazed at her dully for a moment. Then he began to struggle.

'Let me go!' he shrieked.

'You may go when you can stand,' she soothed. 'Would you like to try?'

His face was a fearful sight, but he twisted like a cat as he sprang upright. Then he pointed at the preacher as he backed away.

'He'll pay for this!' he cried.

Judith pretended to misunderstand him. 'Were you to be paid?' She reached into her reticule and handed him some coins. 'You are so thin,' she said. 'Won't you use it to buy food?'

The money disappeared with astonishing speed, but the cracked lips attempted a weak smile.

'You ain't so bad,' the child offered. 'He won't beat you, will he?'

'Most certainly he will not,' Judith told him firmly. 'Off you go, and don't forget the food.'

She watched as he limped painfully to the open door. Then she turned her attention to his tormentor.

'Well, sir, what have you to say?' she asked in icy tones. 'There can be no possible excuse for such a disgraceful attack upon a child.'

Truscott had been watching her through his fingers. Who did she think she was? She'd flown at him like some avenging angel, ready to strike at him herself if he had not obeyed her. She'd pay for her interference, but not just yet.

He dropped his hands, staring at her with a blank expression.

'Where am I?' he murmured. 'What has happened? I have no recollection of anything since the service ended.'

Judith was unimpressed. She suspected him of lying. Was this some ploy to persuade her to excuse the inexcusable? She had been deeply shocked by his behaviour. That a grown man should use such violence to a child was unbelievable.

'You are in your own church, sir. Hardly the place for the scene which I have just witnessed.'

'The boy?' he whispered vaguely. 'Was there a boy? I seem to recall a child approaching me…'

'How could you forget it? You left him stunned and bleeding—'

'No, no! That can't be true! It is unthinkable!'

'Then look at the blood upon the ground, and on my handkerchief.' Judith pointed to the sodden scrap of fabric.

Truscott gave a cry and clutched his head. 'I am going mad! Why would I attack a child? Oh, Judith, help me! I am beset with horrors...' He buried his face in his hands once more and began to sob as if his heart would break.

Judith was both startled and embarrassed. Men did not cry, if her own experience was anything to go by. She hesitated, looking at the heaving shoulders, and felt a twinge of pity. The Reverend Charles had broken down completely. For that to happen there must be something sadly wrong.

'I'm ready to listen, if you wish to speak of it,' she said more kindly.

'I...I can't! You are an angel. Why should I burden you with my troubles?'

'I thought we had promised to share them.' She sat down beside him.

'My dearest, I'd hoped to spare you all distress.'

'Not all, I hope. Charles, you can't protect me from life itself. Please tell me what is troubling you. I'll try to understand.'

The preacher raised a tearstained face to hers. His capacity for histrionics, which included the ability to weep at will, had often caused him to wonder if he should have followed his mother's example, and sought his fortune on the stage. A precarious profession, he'd decided. His present career was much to be preferred.

'So noble!' he whispered in broken tones. 'It shall be as you wish.' He stopped then as if to gather his thoughts. 'It is my mother, dearest one. I remember now...the boy brought me news of her. Oh, Judith, she is dying! The shock destroyed my reason.'

'We must go to her at once.' Judith took his hand. 'You must be strong, my dear. If we delay we may be too late.'

'I won't allow you to put yourself in danger. She has been suffering from the smallpox. Judith, you knew that I was called away on family business. Now you know the truth of it.'

'But, Charles, she must be cared for. We cannot let her die alone.'

'She is in the best of hands. That was my first consideration. We had hopes of a recovery, but now those hopes are shattered. It is all too much to bear...' Apparently crushed, he bent his head.

'I'm not afraid of sickness,' she protested.

'Sickness?' He managed a ghastly smile. 'This is not sickness as you know it, Judith. You can have no idea...'

With sly relish he began to describe the headaches, the agonising muscle pains, the vomiting and the delirium suffered by the victims of the scourge before the appearance of the pustules which often covered the whole body.

Judith's hand flew to her mouth and she gazed at him in horror. He was watching her closely. Had he frightened her enough?

'The disease is highly contagious,' he continued sadly. 'My dear, would you bring such a fate upon your family, let alone yourself? That would be a wicked thing to do.'

'You are right,' she told him earnestly. 'But, Charles, what of you? You must also be in danger.'

'No, no! I had a slight attack in India some years ago. The experience was unpleasant, but it is considered to be a form of vaccination, so I understand. For me, there is no danger of infection.'

'Then go to your mother. I must not delay you.'

'How good you are!' He was wise enough not to attempt to take her hand. Possibly he had regained some standing in her eyes, but he couldn't be quite sure in spite of her expressions of sympathy.

Judith's reaction to his attack upon the child had astounded him. In his murderous rage he had lost all self-control, but she hadn't flinched. Though she had expressed it in a different way, her anger had matched his own.

Had he convinced her of his reason for the outburst? For the first time he sensed that he was on shifting ground. He'd been so sure of his ability to bend her to his will, but today he'd seen another side to her character. He had misjudged her, that was all too clear. It was an unnerving thought.

The ability to assess the nature of his fellow-creatures was all-important to his survival. Today this quiet girl, with her softly spoken ways, had caused him to doubt it. There was unsuspected strength beneath that modest exterior.

'I may be away for several days,' he murmured, as he gave her a covert glance. Was it his imagination, or did he detect a fleeting look of relief?

He'd never come closer to losing her, and he knew it. He must give her time to recover from the shock she'd suffered that day. His mother's fictitious illness gave him the perfect excuse. In any case, the little matter of Nellie and her friends must be dealt with at once.

They'd keep their word. He was in no doubt of it, and he dared not risk a visit from the unsavoury trio.

Judith refused his offer to escort her to her home, urging him to hurry to his mother's side. He wasn't sorry to leave her. There was something in her expression, beyond her usual reserve, which made him feel uncomfortable.

She herself was deeply troubled, feeling that for the first time in her life she had gazed into the pit. She'd accepted Charles Truscott's explanation for his outburst of fury, and even offered her sympathy, but were his words enough? She could not dismiss the memory of the child's small figure, lying insensible on the ground. Charles must have had some kind of fit…some brainstorm to cause him to act in such a way.

A little worm of doubt stirred in her mind. Suppose that her friends were right about him? It didn't bear thinking about, but she must face it.

Suddenly she longed for Dan. She'd settle for his friendship, if for nothing else, but even that would be lost to her if she married the Reverend Charles.

Yet she'd vowed that she wouldn't return to Mount Street.

Judith's thoughts were churning as she went up to her room. Thank heavens that Bessie had stayed outside the church. She hadn't witnessed the ugly scene, which was a blessing. The sight would have sent her in search of help for her young mistress, and her first thought would have been to summon Dan, or another member of the Wentworth household.

Judith took off her coat and bonnet, and sank down upon the window-seat, resting her forehead against the cool glass. She must think. Had Charles been lying to her? It didn't seem possible. Only a consummate actor would have broken down and wept real tears as he had done. Perhaps she herself was lacking in human charity. If he'd been telling the truth she owed him her support.

And if not? The prospect made her shudder. Life in the Aveton household must be preferable to marriage to a liar and a bully. If only she might discover the truth with certainty. She cast about in her mind for some way of doing so, but she could think of nothing. An appeal to her friends was out of the question. Prudence was in no condition to be worried at this time. In any case, she had no right to place the burden on their shoulders.

She must watch and wait. For the next few days, at least, she would have time to think back and consider, but it was difficult to recall in detail the events of these past few months. She must have been living in some kind of trance.

Now all that must change. Her very survival was at stake. She knew it, and her determination hardened. With a strong sense of purpose, she pulled out her papers and began to write. This was one gift which no one could take away from her.

For the next two days she worked on steadily, thankful to be left to her own devices, and pausing only to take her meals with Mrs Aveton and her daughters.

That lady intended to make full use of the remaining weeks before Judith's marriage to order all the gowns and scarves, bonnets, gloves and underwear which she and her children might require for the coming Season. Judith, she imagined, would not examine the bills too closely, and the forthcoming wedding gave her an excellent excuse.

It was Bessie who noticed Judith's pallor.

'Miss, you'll ruin your eyes with all this scribbling,' she announced. 'I don't know how you see at night with just the one candle.'

'I'm all right, Bessie.' Judith smiled up at her.

'No, you ain't! Why, you ain't been out for days. See, miss, the sun is shining. Won't you walk in the Park today?'

Judith hesitated, but at last she allowed herself to be persuaded.

It was pleasant to stretch her legs again, and to feel the sun upon her back. She was pacing slowly beside the press of carriages and horsemen, listening in amusement to Bessie's pithy comments upon the more outrageous toilettes of certain members of the *ton*, when Dan fell into step beside her.

Bessie moved a few steps to the rear, ignoring Judith's look of reproach.

'I think you have an ally, sir,' she said.

'Don't be cross with Bessie! How else was I to see you? You haven't left the house for days...'

'That was my own choice.'

'It was a mistake. You are looking positively hagged!'

'Thank you!' There was a suspicious sparkle in Judith's eyes. She was close to tears. She was plain enough, heaven knew. It was hard to be told that any claim to looks had quite deserted her.

'Don't be foolish!' Dan took her arm and led her down a side path. 'To me you are always beautiful. What is wrong, my dear?'

The tenderness in his voice was her undoing.

'I don't know,' she said unsteadily. 'I wish I did.'

'Something has happened?' His hands rested lightly on her shoulders, holding her away from him as he gazed into her eyes. 'Can you tell me?'

Judith longed to pour out the full story of that ugly scene in the church, but her own uncertainty held her back. Dan had disliked Charles Truscott from the first. How could he give her an unbiased opinion! What she needed most was facts.

'Dan, what do you know about smallpox?' she asked.

'A little, Judith, but why do you ask?'

'I just wondered. Is there an epidemic in the city at the present time? It is infectious, I believe...'

'Most certainly! Dearest Judith, you have not been exposed to it, I hope?'

She managed a faint smile. 'Of course not, but someone told me that there are cases in the city.'

'I have not heard of it,' he frowned. 'In the usual way, you know, the very mention of the word is enough to cause a general exodus.'

'Even if it happened in some outlying part?' Charles Truscott hadn't mentioned his mother's whereabouts.

'It isn't easy to keep the news of an outbreak quiet,' Dan assured her. 'It spreads so quickly.'

This information did nothing to ease Judith's mind. Her uneasiness increased. On the day of the attack upon the child she'd been too shocked and confused to question her betrothed. He'd given her no opportunity to ask why he'd made no previous mention of his mother. She'd taken it for granted that neither of his parents were alive, otherwise she would have been asked to meet them.

It had to be admitted that she knew very little about him. Upon reflection, she realized that they had had few private conversations. Apart from the moment of his proposal, their meetings had always taken place in the presence of Mrs Aveton.

She hadn't found it strange. Propriety dictated that young ladies did not spend time alone with unmarried men. As a parson, Charles was allowed more latitude, but he'd never sought private interviews with her. She'd put it down to a strict regard for the conventions, and she'd been glad of his forbearance. She could never think of anything to say to him.

Now she began to wonder. Had he been afraid that she might ply him with awkward questions?

'So you are sure that even isolated cases could not be concealed?' she asked.

'One can't be sure. There are parts of the city where sickness is rife, and the first symptoms of smallpox resemble those of a chill, with shivering and a headache. My dear, this isn't a cheerful subject. Why are you so concerned?'

'It was just that Charles mentioned—' Her words stuck in her throat. She could not explain her suspicions to Dan.

He was on the alert at once. This was the opening for which he had been waiting.

'He would, of course, be the first aware of it…that is, if he ever ventures into the slums…?' He glanced sideways at her face, but noticed no reaction. It was clear that Truscott had mentioned neither his visit to 'The Rookery', nor to the house in Seven Dials.

'His duties bring him into contact with the poor,'

she admitted. 'But he says that he is in no danger, as he had a mild attack of the disease some years ago. I wanted to go with him, but he wouldn't hear of it.'

Dan stopped, appalled. 'You must not consider entering those places!' he ordered roughly. 'It isn't just the smallpox, Judith. They are the closest thing to hell that anyone might see.'

She looked at him then, and the huge grey eyes were sad. 'I know about the poverty and the over-crowding. Prudence and Sebastian take an interest in these matters.'

'And do you know about the filth, the stench, the drunken beggars, the ragged children, the thieves, and the murderers?'

Judith's face grew pale. 'Then Charles must be in danger every day of his life?'

'Not he! You speak of accompanying him. Did he say where he was going?'

'Not into the slums, my dear.' Her anxiety could no longer be contained. 'He is gone to visit his mama. He fears she has the smallpox.'

Suddenly everything fell into place for Dan. He knew now why Truscott had mentioned the disease.

'Have you met her?' he asked quietly. 'I have not heard her spoken of before.'

'Nor I.' Judith was aware of his startled expression. 'You will think me foolish, but I had not thought to ask.'

'Nor he to tell you?' All the old antagonism was back in his tone, and she laid a gentle hand upon his arm.

'Don't let us quarrel,' she pleaded. 'We have little

time, and I am so very glad to see you.' She looked up at him with an expression of perfect trust.

Dan's heart turned over. He longed to take her in his arms and to swear that he would care for her forever, but he restrained himself.

What could he offer her? He had neither fortune nor position. The idea of living on her money sickened him, though the winning of an heiress was the stated aim of most of the young bachelors of his acquaintance. Let them do so if they could.

He believed that a man should be able to provide for his own family. His face grew dark. Would he ever reach the point where he could do so?

'Dan? What is it?' Judith slipped her hand in his, but he drew it away as if he could not bear her touch.

'Don't!' he said savagely.

'I'm sorry!' Her lips were trembling. 'I didn't mean to offend you.'

'Offend me? Don't you know that I...?' He bit back the words he'd been about to say. 'Excuse me!' he continued. 'I have no wish to quarrel with you.'

They had wandered further from Rotten Row, and the pathway between the bushes was almost deserted.

'We should go back,' she murmured. If any of their acquaintance should see them together in this place it would be construed as an assignation.

'Why?' he demanded. 'Shall we be accused of skulking through the undergrowth?'

Judith smiled at that. 'Skulking is not your style, I think, or mine, but to be found here must give rise to comment.'

He slipped his arm through hers. 'There is no danger of that. It's too early for the beaux. Brummell, you know, is said to spend a full five hours at his toilette each morning…'

'Is that true? I've met him, and I liked him. There's nothing dandified in his appearance, and he is not forever worrying about the set of his coat, or the fall of his cravat.'

'Once dressed, he doesn't give his clothing another thought. One cannot improve on perfection, Judith.'

Dan's blue eyes were twinkling, and Judith felt relieved. This hour with him was a precious time which must not be wasted.

'Have you taken my advice?' she asked eagerly.

'About the drawings? Yes, I did. Lord Nelson is returned to England, as you know. He is staying at Merton with…er…with the Hamiltons. It isn't far from London…'

'And you have written to him?'

'I heard that at the Battle of the Nile, and again at Copenhagen, he was short of frigates. I sent him my designs for a fast vessel, which is easy to manoeuvre.'

Judith clapped her hands. Her eyes were shining.

'Then if you can supply his needs, you must hear something…?'

'I don't wish to raise your hopes. He may not find the time to study my ideas…'

'He will, I know it! Oh, Dan, he is a wonderful man…a genius! Nothing escapes his attention.'

Dan smiled at her enthusiasm. 'You, too, are an admirer of the hero of the hour?'

'Isn't everyone? This present Peace is due to him. Had he not defeated the French and their allies the war would not have ended.'

'Agreed! But enough of my affairs. I've finished

reading the chapters which you left with me. Bessie has them in her pocket. She tells me that you have continued with the book.'

Judith nodded.

'Then may I see the next part? It is so entertaining. I love the way it flows. You have a way with words, my dear.'

'Only on paper,' she protested shyly.

'Nonsense! With us there was never time enough to finish our discussions. Am I not right?'

Blushing with pleasure at his praise, Judith failed to notice the approach of a gentleman who strolled towards them from the opposite direction.

It was only when Dan bowed and uttered a word of greeting that she was aware of him.

Significantly, the man did not stop, but looking up, she saw his surprised expression, and wished that the ground might open up and swallow her.

'Take me back to Rotten Row!' she said quickly.

Dan gave her arm a little shake. 'I know what you are thinking, but there is no need for alarm. Chessington isn't a rattle.'

'That isn't the point. We shouldn't be here alone. I feel like a criminal.'

'A sweet criminal,' he murmured tenderly. 'Must we go back? It is too early for the Grand Strut...'

His teasing served to remove her troubled frown. He knew as well as she that Judith had no interest in admiring the exquisites who strolled among the rank and fashion, quizzing the ladies, indulging in gossip, and speculating upon the likely cost of the newest and most dashing turn-outs of both carriages and horses. This daily event took place between the hours of five o'clock and six.

She gave him a reluctant smile. 'Don't make game of me! You know that I am right.'

'Very well, if you will have it so.' He turned and began to retrace his steps along the path which they had taken from the Row. 'But promise me one thing? You will go on...you will finish the book?'

'I don't think I can stop,' she assured him. 'The words seem to be coming of their own accord.'

'That's good! When may I read the rest?'

Judith looked at his eager face. That open countenance was so very dear to her. She longed to tell him that she'd come to Mount Street that very afternoon, but she hesitated, knowing that it would be unwise.

They were slipping back so easily into their old friendship. The thought was bittersweet. It would make it so much harder when she had to part from him for ever.

Why must she continue to torture herself? He'd been kind, but his love for her was dead. Now he could not even bear to touch her hand. She'd been deeply wounded when he'd dragged his own away so swiftly.

'Why don't you answer me?' he asked. 'Is it Truscott? Did you not tell me that he is away?'

'He is,' she admitted. 'But I feel that I'm deceiving him.'

'Why so? He had not forbidden you to visit your friends, so I understand.'

'No, but it seems wrong of me to go about without a care when he may be in such trouble.'

'Judith, he refused your help, possibly for the worthiest of reasons, but it will do no good to shut yourself away.'

'I'd forgotten how persuasive you can be,' she murmured.

'Have you? I can't agree with you. My efforts in that direction were not always successful...'

This reference to the past made her change the subject hastily. Six years ago they had each said all that there was to say. There was no point in recriminations.

'I'll try,' she promised. 'If it isn't possible I will send Bessie with the manuscript.'

'Prudence will be disappointed. You have not seen her in these past few days.' He paused and a shadow crossed his face.'

'What is it, Dan? She is not sick, I hope?'

'She is not herself. Sebastian is worried, in spite of what the doctor says...'

'Oh, my dear! She will not lose the child?'

'There are no symptoms, but she is so restless, and the tears come easily. It is unlike her.'

'She must be in some discomfort. I am told that these last few months can be a trial. Will Sebastian take her down to Hallwood? The change might do her good.'

'I doubt if he would risk the journey now, but Pru is so bored and crochety that he fears it will affect her health.'

'She is used to being active. For someone of her lively temperament the enforced rest must be a strain, but it will soon be over. Then she will have her babe, and all will be well again.'

Dan gave her a grateful look. 'Always a stalwart, Judith! I hope you may be right. This is an anxious time for all of us.'

Judith understood him perfectly. So many of the

girls she knew had enjoyed but one brief year of marriage before succumbing to the dreaded childbed fever. It was a threat which loomed in many a woman's mind.

'Try not to worry,' she murmured. 'Sebastian has obtained the services of the best physician in London.'

'I know it, but I can't be easy in my mind.'

Judith gave him an anxious look. She knew just how much Prudence meant to him. As a girl of seventeen she'd helped him to escape with her from a life of slavery in the cotton mills of the industrial north. She and Dan were bound by more than the common ties of friendship.

'I think you have forgotten the redoubtable Miss Grantham,' she told him with a chuckle. 'Does she not interview your family physicians as to their views on cleanliness and a sensible diet?'

'She does! And she is forthright in expressing her opinions. The lady may be well into her eighties but she can still reduce the medical profession to a jelly.' The idea cheered him, and he managed a smile. 'Elizabeth did us a great service when she and her aunt became members of the family.'

'I haven't seen Miss Grantham for some time,' Judith told him. 'I always enjoy her company. She is an original...'

'True! But if you wish to see her soon you had best make haste. This present Peace of Amiens has inspired her to consider yet another trip to Turkey.'

'At eighty-three?'

'Certainly! No one has yet been able to dissuade her, though Perry and Elizabeth have tried.'

'I feel like a feeble creature beside such enterprise.'

'Not you, my dear. I know your strength of character.' Dan was unable to say more as they were now within sight of Rotten Row.

'You must leave us now,' Judith murmured. 'We must not be seen together.'

'But when shall we meet again?'

'I don't know,' she said uncertainly. 'Tomorrow I may visit Hatchard's to buy some books...'

'I'll be there,' he promised.

He left her a prey to the most severe misgivings. Dan had complimented her upon her strength of character, whereas in reality she was weak-willed. Had she not vowed to forget him, and to prepare herself with fortitude for the life which lay ahead of her? Now she was behaving in a way which must be considered reprehensible.

The mention of a visit to Hatchard's in Piccadilly was not exactly the offer of a secret meeting. Or was it? Honesty compelled her to admit the truth. She could deceive herself no longer. When her choice lay between her obvious duty to the Reverend Charles, and the opportunity of a meeting with the man she loved, she knew that she would follow the dictates of her heart.

Poor Charles! He might at this very moment be sitting beside a sickbed. She was behaving in a wicked way, and it was only right that the happiness for which she longed should be denied her.

Chapter Seven

That gentleman was suffering in a different way.

On the day of his attack upon the child he'd left Judith in great haste to hurry back to the parish of St Giles. He'd no idea what he would find there, but he took the precaution of arming himself with a serviceable pistol in addition to the knife which he always carried.

A hackney took him as far as the entrance to 'The Rookery', and there he dismissed the jarvey with an acid comment upon the reeking straw which covered the floor of the conveyance.

'Beg pardon, your honour!' the jehu sneered. 'We ain't up to the standards of your own fine carriage.' He backed away from the expression on his passenger's face.

This piece of impertinence did nothing to improve the preacher's temper. By the time he reached his destination he was in murderous mood. Someone should pay for the ruin of his plans.

When he reached his mother's door he didn't knock. Hopefully, he'd take her by surprise. Intent upon his purpose, he didn't hear the sound behind him until it was too late. Then a violent blow between his shoulder-blades sent him sprawling into the room. As a booted foot pinned him to the ground he heard an unfamiliar voice.

'Tie him up!' it ordered.

His wrists were seized and dragged together behind his back. Then they were bound together with a cord so thin and strong that it cut into his flesh.

'Up with him!'

He was lifted to his feet and thrust roughly into the single wicker chair. For the first time he was able to get a good look at his attackers.

The younger man he recognised at once. He'd been present at each of his previous visits to Nellie. His middle-aged companion was a stranger, though there was something about him which Truscott found it difficult to place. He searched his memory without success.

The only other occupant of the room was the child he'd used so cruelly. One of the boy's eyes was closed, but the other regarded him with such malevolence, combined with an unholy glee, that the preacher looked away.

'Where's Nellie?' he demanded.

'She's still alive! No thanks to you!' The younger of his two assailants bunched his fist, and delivered such a crushing blow to Truscott's jaw that both the chair and its occupant flew over backwards.

'Now, Sam, that ain't no way to treat our visitor! Remember, he's our ticket to a life of ease…'

'He's a murdering devil! You won't stop me from giving him a taste of his own medicine…'

'Later, Sam! However, I feel you have a point.

Perhaps we should convince him that we are not to be trifled with. Fetch him through!'

'Best search him first,' the child suggested.

'Certainly! An excellent plan! I promised you that pleasure, Jemmy, if your sharp eyes saw him first. Go ahead, my boy…!'

As the child approached him, Truscott was tempted to kick him away, but something in the older man's expression stopped him. Even so, Jemmy was careful to stand behind the chair, reaching forward to delve into pockets with all the skills of an experienced thief.

The preacher's watch and chain had caught his eye so he removed that first, laying it on the floor beside him. His next discovery was the pistol.

'Well, well! Were you expecting trouble, my dear sir? I think we shall be able to accommodate you.' The smiles on the faces of both his captors were not encouraging.

Jemmy continued with his search, and the pile beside him grew as he added a leather bag of coin, two silk handkerchiefs and a bunch of keys. He stretched out a claw-like hand to open the purse, but this brought him a sharp reproof.

'Not yet, Jemmy! The share-out will come later.' The man's eyes were on his captive's face. The preacher was too calm. He hadn't uttered a word of protest at the loss of his possessions. Perhaps there were still some to be found.

Then Truscott made a mistake. Stretching out his legs, apparently in an effort to ease his cramped position, he slid one booted foot behind the other.

His tormentor gave a grunt of triumph.

'Jemmy, the boots! You have forgot to search the

boots!' He picked up the pistol and examined it. 'Loaded, I see! Now, sir, you will oblige me by not attempting to struggle. I have not the least objection to rendering you unconscious with a blow from the butt of this useful weapon.'

Truscott ground his teeth in fury as Jemmy pounced. When the child rose to his feet again he was holding the knife, which he then proceeded to brandish close to the preacher's eyes.

'No, no, my dear! The reverend gentleman will pay for your injuries in good measure, but you must not be too hasty. Now, Sam, bear a hand!'

Together the two men dragged Truscott to his feet and manhandled him out of the door, across the passage and into the room which faced them. There even Truscott, hardened though he was to villainy, could not repress a shudder. The place was a shambles. Ominous patches of some dark substance stained the floorboards, and the walls were bespattered to above head height with what he knew was blood. Some fearful struggle had taken place here.

'Sam, our visitor will wish to see his friends...'

Sam nodded. He walked over to a closet in the corner, and opened it in silence.

Truscott froze, his eyes starting from his head in horror as he looked at the two corpses. His two accomplices had been murdered with extreme brutality. The shirt of the nearest man was a mass of stab wounds whilst the other man was unrecognisable. His head had been beaten to a pulp.

The preacher swayed as the sweet and unmistakable stench of death assailed his nostrils.

'Dear me! Sam, our friend is not feeling well. We must persuade him to sit down...'

Sam closed the door to the closet and helped his companion to drag the preacher away.

This time his legs were bound. Trussed as he was, he felt completely helpless, and it took all his self-control to crush a rising sense of panic. He swallowed, wishing that his throat were not so dry. It was difficult to speak.

'What has all this to do with me?' he croaked. 'I've never seen those men before...'

'Strange! Before they died they were... er...persuaded to give us a full description of the man who had employed them...though naturally they weren't aware of his true identity.'

'Then why should you think that it was me? They did not know me as—' Truscott stopped. He had almost given himself away.

'As the Reverend Charles Truscott? Of course not! But, sir, you shall not take me for a fool. I had been expecting something of this kind...'

The preacher stared at him. Who was this man? His speech was educated and his manner smooth. Perhaps an unfrocked parson, or a disgraced lawyer?

'I see that you don't remember me. I find that curious since we shared His Majesty's hospitality together. Well, well, my appearance has changed somewhat since then.' The speaker patted his paunch. 'The toll of the years, my friend! When we shared a cell in Newgate I was not as stout, and my hair was as dark as your own.'

'Newgate?' As memory flooded back his captive paled. 'Then you are...?'

'Margrave the forger.' The man's face changed, and his eyes bored into Truscott's own. 'I ain't forgotten you. You served me an ill turn when you stole from me to bribe the turnkey. That money was to buy my own way out...'

'You are mistaken. It wasn't me...'

'I'm not mistaken, though you weren't a reverend then. Some talk of murder, wasn't there? Can't say that I blame you in one way. You were no keener to get your neck stretched than I was myself, but it was a dirty trick...a dirty trick...'

'You must be mad,' Truscott told him coldly.

'Oh, I ain't mad, though it turned my brain a bit at first. I searched for you for years, but you covered your tracks well. It was quite by chance that I fell in with Nellie. It was the name that brought you back to mind. Now you owe me, and you'll pay.'

'I've said I'll pay. I told Nellie so...' Truscott gave up all pretence of ignorance.

He was desperate to escape. They wouldn't kill him, but they knew the errand upon which his accomplices had been sent. He might be in for a beating so severe that it would cripple him. He swallowed convulsively and his captor was quick to see it.

'Don't care for a taste of your own medicine, Reverend? You won't be harmed, much as I'd like to thrash you till you squeal. We have a little task for you.'

'What's that?'

'There is the small matter of your friends next door. They must be disposed of. I believe a funeral is in order. Who better to conduct it than yourself?'

Truscott was silent.

'Nellie has it in hand. She is at this moment ordering two coffins... This evening will be best, I think. Less chance of your being recognised.'

'Even if I were it would not be remarked,' came the haughty reply. The preacher was recovering his confidence.

'Possibly not. You chose the right profession, but even here you aren't so anxious to be seen. Are you being followed?'

'Of course not!' Truscott snapped. 'Why should I be followed? No one suspects—'

'Aye! You were always glib, but this time you overreached yourself.'

'I don't know what you mean…'

'Don't you? Remember the old saying, that if you want a job done well, you must do it yourself?'

Truscott stared at him.

'Didn't want to soil your hands? Even so, you might have thought of a better plan. Your friends from Seven Dials were known here. I spotted them at once. Why would men like that ply Nellie and her friends with drink, and then suggest a gin shop near the river? Too obvious, my dear sir.'

Truscott ground his teeth. So that was how they had been caught. He felt no pity for them. His henchmen had behaved like fools, and richly deserved their fate.

Then he heard the clatter of feet upon the stairs. The door burst open to reveal his mother, with Sam's doxy by her side. Nellie paused for only a moment. Then, with a scream of fury, she rushed towards him, scratching at his face with nails grown as long as talons.

Margrave pulled her away.

'Nellie, my dear, you must control yourself! Would you destroy the good looks of our hopeful bridegroom even further? You won't wish to delay his wedding.' Margrave pushed a bottle towards her. 'Bring that along! We're all in need of refreshment after our exertions.' He smiled pleasantly at his captive. 'I fear that we must leave you now, but we shall return this evening. May I suggest that you spend the time in composing a eulogy for the dead?'

Once alone, the preacher began to struggle with his bonds, but the strong cord would not give. It was cutting into his flesh, he was cold and thirsty, his mouth was swollen from the blow he had received, and the scratches on his face were bleeding freely.

He forced himself to ignore the discomfort. He must think. He was in no immediate danger. If his captors wished to gain their objective they must release him. The loss of his possessions had angered him, but he would recover them and more besides.

This scum would not defeat him. He'd go through with tonight's charade, and then let them take care.

That evening he walked through the streets ahead of the macabre procession, ignoring an occasional chuckle from Margrave. Once the coffins had been consigned to paupers' graves he turned.

'My keys!' he demanded. 'I can't get into the vestry without them.'

Margrave handed them over. 'You won't forget us, my friend? Today's contribution won't go far. Perhaps another visit next week?'

Truscott nodded his assent. Let them believe that he was in their power. He walked away without a backward glance and made his way to the house in Seven Dials. Judith would not wonder at his absence for a day or two. It would take that time for his face to heal. It must be an appalling sight. His mistress

confirmed his suspicions. She backed away from him
in horror.

'What has happened?' she cried.

'What does it look like? I was set upon and
robbed. Is there any money in the house?'

'Only a few coppers. You never leave much here.'

'Brandy?'

'You finished it last time. There's gin…'

'Fetch it, and some food.' He pushed past her, and
pouring some water into a bowl he began to bathe
his battered face. The deep scratches stung, but the
consumption of more than a pint of gin served to
deaden the pain. He no longer felt hungry. Ignoring
the offer of a platter of bread and cheese, he threw
himself upon the bed and slept till morning.

By the end of the following day he had consumed
most of the food in the house and all the liquor. His
demand for more brought a terrified response.

'Sir, they won't serve me without money…'

'Pledge your credit then.'

'What with? Must I take this?' She picked up a
handsome vase.

He took it from her with great care. Then he
slapped her sharply across the face.

'Don't be a fool! You'd be set upon before you'd
gone five yards. There are other ways of getting
money.'

She understood him perfectly, and she coloured.

'I…I don't know how to go about it. What must
I do?'

'If you don't know, then I can't tell you. My God!
Why must I be cursed with idiots?' He threw his

boots at her. 'Take these! Tomorrow you'll be able to retrieve them.'

A plan was forming in his mind. Judith Aveton was the softest touch he knew. The girl must go to her and beg for charity. She would not be refused. He'd be in no danger. His mistress did not know him as Charles Truscott.

Next day he sent her off with strict instructions. She was not to approach the other ladies of the Aveton household. She must ask for Judith and no one else.

The girl came back empty-handed.

'They turned me away from the door,' she explained. 'Don't hit me! I did my best.'

'Fool! You must try again tomorrow.' Truscott realised that he had put himself in an impossible position. Without his boots he was trapped within the house. 'Approach the lady in the street. You can't mistake her. A tall creature, somewhat dowdy-looking, but a gentlewoman, for all that...'

'She didn't walk out today. I waited—'

'She must walk out some time. I'm losing patience with you, my girl. No more excuses, or you'll get a taste of my belt.'

He used her cruelly that night, and sent her out in an exhausted state. Waiting by the railings of the Aveton home she saw Judith almost at once, but hesitated to approach her. The lady was accompanied by her maid. Perhaps in the Park? But no! A gentleman had come to join her. The girl was in despair. She durst not return to Seven Dials to confess her failure yet again. It was only when Judith left the park that desperation forced her into action. She hurried along behind her quarry.

'Miss!' she cried. 'Miss, of your charity, won't you help me?'

Judith didn't hear her. She'd been reliving the precious hour she'd spent with Dan. Then the girl caught at her sleeve.

'Be off with you!' Bessie attempted to shoulder her away, but Judith turned.

'What is it?' she asked quietly. 'No, Bessie, please don't interfere! You may go indoors...'

Bessie ignored the mistress's request, choosing to remain on guard.

'Miss Judith, watch your reticule! I don't like the look of this one!'

A glance from Judith reduced her to silence. Her gentle employer did not often show displeasure, but when she did so Bessie felt it keenly. She subsided.

'Oh, please! I don't mean to rob you, but I must have money. We have no food, and Josh's boots are pledged... Miss, he can't go out until I get them back.'

Bessie snorted in amusement, but Judith did not smile. There was fear in the girl's eyes, and she seemed to be close to collapse.

'I have very little money with me.' Judith pressed all the coins she had into the girl's hand. 'Come indoors, and I will give you more.'

The girl backed away. 'They won't let me in. When I asked for you they threatened to give me over to the magistrate.'

'I see!' Judith tried to contain her rising anger. 'Then we must meet again. Tomorrow I shall be in Piccadilly. Will you come there, to the bookshop?'

'Thank 'ee, miss. What time?'

'Shall we say at noon?' Judith gazed at the pale exhausted face, and suddenly she was puzzled. 'You say you asked for me? How did you know my name?'

'Josh knows the Reverend Truscott, ma'am. He speaks well of you. Josh was sure that you would help us…'

'Until tomorrow, then?' Judith smiled at the girl. 'Pray buy some food, my dear. I fear the boots must wait.'

As the girl hurried away Judith went indoors. She was tempted to take the porter to task for his lack of charity towards their unfortunate caller. It was strange, she mused, how some servants, however lowly their position, showed little kindness to those who were less fortunate than themselves.

She held her tongue. This was Mrs Aveton's house, and here she had no rights.

She felt no such constraints when Bessie brought the subject up again.

'Boots, forsooth! A likely story! These beggars will tell you anything, Miss Judith, and bless me if you don't believe them!'

'You surprise me, Bessie!' Judith's look was stern. 'I thought the girl was telling the truth, but even if not, you must have seen how weak and tired she looked.'

Bessie flushed at the reproach. 'You'd give your last penny, miss, and well you know it!'

'How foolish you must think me!' The words, spoken in Judith's usual quiet tones, were enough to persuade Bessie that she had gone too far. She raised her handkerchief to her eyes.

'No, don't weep! You may leave me now. I shan't need you again today.'

This calm dismissal was too much for Bessie. 'Oh, Miss Judith, don't send me away! I didn't mean—'

'Bessie, don't be such a goose!' Judith's smile returned. 'You thought you were taking care of me. As for sending you away? I meant only that I shan't go out again today.'

The explanation was enough to satisfy her maid, but when she left the room Judith took herself to task. Perhaps she'd been too harsh with this old friend who loved her so, but unkindness was the one thing which never failed to rouse her to anger.

And something else was troubling her. How odd it seemed that Charles had mentioned her name to one of his parishioners as a likely source of charity when he himself had access to the Fund for Paupers. Then she remembered. Charles was at a sickbed. The girl's case must be urgent, or he would have dealt with it on his return. Doubtless he had no idea when that might be.

Having satisfied herself on that point, she opened the drawer in her desk and examined her remaining funds. Her allowance for the quarter was largely untouched. She set aside a small sum for necessities, and put the rest into her reticule.

Hopefully, it would save the girl from immediate want for the next few weeks at least. The pale, stricken face could not be banished from her mind. How young she was, barely out of her teens, if Judith herself was any judge. And she'd looked so frail and weak, thin to the point of emaciation. Possibly it was due to hunger, but the pallid skin and the sunken eyes suggested something more. It seemed to her that the girl was ill.

Her anger rose. Who was this Josh...this man she'd mentioned? Not her husband, certainly. Judith had seen no wedding ring. But whether he was a relative or a casual protector, he might have taken better care of the poor soul.

When Charles returned she would speak to him about the case. There might be something he could do to help.

She was still preoccupied with the problem when she walked to Piccadilly on the following day. Dan was waiting for her by the door of Hatchard's, and he came towards her, his blue eyes sparkling with pleasure.

She was about to greet him when she saw the girl.

'Dan, will you excuse me for a moment?' she murmured. She thrust her purse into the girl's hand. 'This will help,' she said with her sweetest smile. 'If you come to me next week, I may be able to do more for you.'

To her surprise, the girl produced a folded paper and thrust it into her hand.

'Why, what is this?' she asked.

'It's a message, miss.'

'From whom?'

The girl looked terrified. 'I wasn't to answer any questions,' she muttered. Then she disappeared into the crowd.

'A mystery?' Dan teased. 'Who was that girl? Does she bring you a message from a secret admirer?'

'I doubt it!' Judith opened the note. It was brief,

ill-spelt, and written in an illiterate hand on a torn
scrap of paper. 'I don't understand,' she murmured
as she handed it to Dan. 'Can you make sense of it?'

'Parson sez as you ain't to worrit. Girl knows
nothing, so save your breath. Rev. comes back ter-
morrer.' Dan read the words aloud. 'My dear, this is
a mystery indeed. The parson, I take it, is the
Reverend Charles. Why could he not write to you
himself?'

'I don't know. Perhaps he feared to spread the infection…?'

'Did he not tell you that he was immune?'

'He did.' Judith searched the crowd in vain for
some trace of the girl. 'Oh, dear! I should have read
it before I let her go. She might have been able to
tell me what is happening…and given me some word
of Charles and his mother.'

Dan's eyes rested on her face. 'I fear she would
tell you nothing. You do not recognise the writing?'
He was beginning to have his own suspicions as to
the author of the note, but wisely he did not voice
them.

'No. It seems to be from a man…perhaps this Josh
that the girl has mentioned. Charles is acquainted
with him. That was how she knew my name and
where to find me.'

'For what purpose?'

Judith coloured. 'She was in need of help.'

'So that was why you handed her your purse? My
dear Judith, Mr Truscott should have taken care of it
from the Parish Funds.'

'But, Dan, he isn't there, and you could see from
her appearance that the case is urgent.'

Dan wasn't satisfied, but he sensed that Judith felt

distressed. 'Doubtless Mr Truscott will explain when next you see him,' he comforted her. He would not betray his feelings to her, but his suspicions grew. It was only with an effort that he forced a smile.

'Shall we go in?' He took her arm to lead her into the bookshop.

Judith shook her head. 'You will think me a pea-goose, but shall you mind if we do not? I...I am not in the mood to choose a book today.'

Dan guessed at once that she had parted with all the money in her possession.

'Not even one?' he urged. 'I was hoping to make you a present of something that would please you.'

'Oh, please...you must not!'

'Why not? It would be just a token of appreciation from an old friend.'

'Appreciation? For what?' Judith was blushing. She looked so adorable in her confusion that he longed to take her in his arms and smother her face with kisses. If only he might do so...

'Why, for all the pleasure which your own book has given me,' he said lightly. 'I can't wait for the day when we see it displayed in Hatchard's window.'

'You are dreaming!' Judith chuckled. 'Take care, or you will give me a swollen head!'

'I hope not! I like your head exactly the way it is, and that bonnet is a triumph!'

'Dan! You never used to speak so foolishly,' she reproached him, although she flushed with pleasure. She'd been doubtful about the full poke-front of the satin straw, but the puffs of ribbon trimming matched her new spencer so exactly that Bessie had coaxed her into buying it.

'Then I must have been a prosy bore...or blind,'

Dan joked. 'Perhaps I saw the jewel, rather than the setting.' He saw that this reference to the past had disturbed her. He had said too much, and he was quick to change the subject.

'I too have a message for you, Judith. Prudence would like to see you. She begged me to invite you to join us for a late nuncheon.'

'I had supposed that visitors would tire her.' The half-truth was excusable, but it was not Judith's main reason for ending her visits to Mount Street.

'She is alone today. Perry and Elizabeth are gone to visit Miss Grantham, and Sebastian has a meeting with his man of business.'

'Oh, Dan, you should not have left her!'

'When I said that I might see you, she insisted. My dear, do come! As I told you yesterday, she is low in spirits at this present time, and much in need of a change of conversation.'

Judith thought for a moment. Nothing would give her greater pleasure than to accompany him to Mount Street.

'You have other commitments?' he asked anxiously. 'Must you return to Mrs Aveton?'

Judith made a quick decision. 'I shan't be missed,' she said with a half smile. 'When I come to Hatchard's I forget the time. Mrs Aveton will not look for me for hours.'

Dan's face brightened, and he gave her a dazzling smile as he took her arm. 'Then I shall steal you away,' he said. 'Shall we walk, or must I summon a hackney?'

'I prefer to walk in this fine spring weather.' It was not the wisest of decisions in this crowded part of London, as Judith realised too late. They might be seen by some of their acquaintance. She comforted herself with the thought that at this hour most members of the ton were still abed. Polite society did not stir abroad much before five in the afternoon.

Even so, she turned to the left when they crossed Piccadilly.

'You don't wish to see the shops in Bond Street?' Dan teased.

'May we not take a quieter way? It will be quicker.'

Dan made no objection. He fell into step beside her, and slipped her arm through his as they turned into Berkeley Street.

'Is speed essential, Judith?' He was glancing down at her with an expression which made her heart turn over. 'I welcome the chance to have you to myself.'

Judith looked away, and was surprised to see that one or two of the passers-by were smiling at them in fond amusement. She crimsoned. She and Dan must look like lovers. She pulled away from him.

'What is it?' he asked.

'We should have taken a hackney. Oh, Dan, this is all wrong. I shouldn't be here with you.'

'Why not?' Dan continued to walk on beside her.

'Because…because I am betrothed, and you know it is not proper for us to walk alone.'

'Bessie is but a yard or two behind us,' he told her calmly. 'Besides, we are almost there…'

'No!' she said. 'I've changed my mind. I must go home.'

He stopped then, looking at her gravely. 'Judith, we have not spoken of the past. I believe it is time we did so.' Without waiting for her reply he turned into Mount Street, but she did not follow him.

Dan retraced his steps and held out a hand to her. 'My dear, you know that I am right. We cannot go on like this.'

Chapter Eight

Judith found herself at a loss for words. Even then she might have fled, but she stood transfixed as she tried to resolve the chaos in her mind.

Dan stood in silence as he awaited her decision, and at last she gave him a look which was painful in its intensity.

'Perhaps you are right,' she whispered. 'Then we shall lay old ghosts to rest...'

It had been an agonising choice. She had no wish to discuss the past, to have old wounds reopened, or to relive the pain of parting all those years ago, but she couldn't pretend that it hadn't happened.

Above all, she didn't want to hear what Dan was so clearly about to tell her. He no longer loved her. She'd been deceiving herself to imagine that there was sometimes more than friendly affection in his manner. Now she was making him uncomfortable, behaving in such a missish way, blushing like a schoolgirl at his compliments, and babbling on about the proprieties like some dowager.

She must pull herself together. There was such a thing as civilised behaviour. Engagements were bro-

ken every day, but hearts did not break so easily.
The world went on, and old lovers met again, but
surely they could not suffer as she was suffering
now.

And she had brought this suffering on herself. It
would have been easier, so much easier, not to have
agreed to meet him. She must have been mad. In two
short weeks she would be married to another man.
Now she was being fair to neither Dan nor her betrothed. Her behaviour was unworthy of any woman
of character, and it must change.

Pale but resolute, she allowed Dan to lead her
through the hall of the Wentworth mansion, and into
the library.

He offered her a chair, and then he began to pace
the room. She guessed that he was wondering how
to begin.

'What did you wish to say to me?' she asked at
last. The silence had become unbearable.

'So much that it would take a lifetime! Oh, my
dear, I have no wish to distress you, but—'

'We haven't got a lifetime,' she said dully. 'In two
weeks' time I shall be wed.'

He came to her then and knelt beside her, taking
her hands in his. 'Look at me!' he begged. 'I know
that you aren't happy. I haven't seen you look like
this since the day we parted all those years ago...'

Judith disengaged her hands and turned her head
away.

'I'm tired, that is all. Brides have these attacks of
nerves, or so I hear. It is the strain of all the preparations—' Dan silenced her with a finger on her lips.

'Dearest, this is Dan,' he reminded her. 'I know

your every look…your every gesture. Were we not once as close as a man and a woman could be?'

Judith took her courage in both hands. She must not allow him to suspect that the memory of their love had never faded. He must not know how much all remembrance of the past distressed her, or he would blame himself for her pain.

'We were very young,' she whispered. 'When I look back it seems to me that we were little more than children.'

'You didn't think so then.'

'I know, but it was all so long ago. In extreme youth one's emotions are at their most intense. It wasn't the time to make decisions for the future.'

'You made yours,' he said simply. 'And it broke my heart. Oh, Judith, for years there was not a single day when I didn't feel your hand in mine, or sense your presence near me, even at the far ends of the earth.'

'You knew my reasons…'

'I couldn't accept them then.' Dan rose to his feet and resumed his pacing. 'I tried to hate you for the way you sacrificed our love because of Mrs Aveton's slanders. I thought we might have faced them.'

Judith was silent.

'Later I realised that I was wrong,' he continued. 'I must have been mad to think that I could win you. What could I have offered you? A lad without breeding or fortune?'

'You would have made your way,' she whispered.

'Through patronage, or as one of Sebastian's dependents? I would not have had it so, and neither would you.'

Judith did not argue, though she longed to do so.

She cared nothing about his birth or lack of fortune, but at nineteen she could not see his life destroyed by the actions of an evil woman.

'Then perhaps it was for the best,' she told him in a neutral tone. 'Won't you take me to Prudence?'

'Not yet. Bear with me for another moment. For the sake of our old friendship, I'll ask you once again. Are you happy?'

Judith would not meet his eyes. 'I am content,' she murmured.

He slipped a finger beneath her chin and raised her face to his. 'Tell me the truth! Do you love this man as we once loved? If you do, I shall not say another word.'

Driven beyond endurance, Judith struck his hand away. 'You have no right to ask!' she cried wildly.

'That's true, but you have given me my answer. Oh, my dear, won't you reconsider this betrothal before it is too late?'

'Stop!' She raised a hand to silence him. 'You promised not to interfere. Why should I listen to you? What do you want of me?'

'Only your happiness, believe me. Give yourself time…'

'I can't.' Judith rose to her feet. 'I won't cry off now.'

All hope had left her. She had given Dan his opportunity to tell her that he loved her still. He had not done so.

He'd changed more than she had at first suspected. The boy who once considered the world well lost for love had matured into a man who understood the values of the society in which he lived. Yet they were not his own. Dan would never seek the prize of a rich wife. He'd made it clear that he would make his way through his own efforts, or not at all.

She too had changed. At nineteen she would have scorned the notion of contentment as a basis for marriage. In those days love was all. She and Dan had shared something precious, something beyond a meeting of minds. In that halcyon time their passion had consumed them, giving their lives a radiance which she would never know again. In his every look and touch her world had been born anew.

'Oh, Dan!' It was a cry of despair. Unconsciously, she stretched out her hands to him.

If he'd taken her in his arms she would have offered him herself, her fortune and her love. Pride was a luxury which a woman in love could not afford.

He did not touch her. She did not know it, but he dared not or his resolve would have crumbled.

'Perhaps you are right,' he told her stiffly. 'I shall not speak of it again.'

His situation was unchanged. All he could offer her was his love. He knew her tender heart. She might accept him out of pity, and that he could not bear. All he could do now was to protect her as best he could, putting her own happiness before his own.

'Prudence will be waiting,' he said quietly.

Judith's hands fell to her sides. It had been a mistake to come here. Dan had asked only that she give herself time. Time for what? If she entered into another relationship, it would not bring her the happiness for which she longed. First love was an illusion, so she'd heard. It wasn't so in her case. Dan was all she wanted. She would love him, and him alone, for the rest of her days.

The look on her face destroyed his hard-won composure.

'Forgive me!' he murmured. 'I have upset you. You were right. It was a mistake to speak of the past. We can't change it now...'

Judith was perilously close to tears. Perhaps they could not change the past, but they could change the future. She was about to tell him so, but his face was set, and she knew it would be useless to attempt to sway him.

Now she longed to be alone with her misery. To be so close to him was simply to prolong her torture, but there was Prudence to consider. She made a valiant effort to speak of something else.

'Have...have you heard from Admiral Nelson?' she asked.

'No!' he told her shortly. 'I have long ceased to hope for miracles.'

'Or even ceased to hope?' Judith lost her temper then as frustration and unhappiness overwhelmed her. 'You disappoint me, Dan! Why won't you fight for what you want? Go to Merton! See the Admiral! What have you got to lose?' She rounded on him with eyes ablaze, only to find that he was smiling down at her.

'That's better!' he said gently. 'I see that you haven't lost your spirit.'

'Have you?'

'Judith, as I told you, I've tried for years to promote my own designs—'

'Well, try again! Oh, if I were a man I should not be so easily discouraged... Promise me that you will visit Lord Nelson!' In her eagerness to persuade him Judith had come alive again.

'Peace!' he begged as he backed away in mock terror. 'I promise to obey you. Indeed, as I value my life I can do no other.'

He was happy to see her smile, reluctant though it was. The years had dropped away, and now she was much more like the girl he'd known in his youth.

Unknown to Judith, he'd already made up his mind to go to Merton. The Great Man might refuse to see him, or worse, dismiss his ideas as totally impractical, but he had to try. The matter was urgent.

In suggesting that Judith give herself time to reconsider, he'd cherished the faint hope that if success should come his way at last, it might not be too late.

With the certain prospect of a career as a naval architect he would work until his reputation was second to none. Others had done it in different fields, with no better start than his. Sir Christopher Wren had rebuilt much of London, and so many of the churches were the work of Nicholas Hawksmoor. Inigo Jones had started his career apprenticed to a joiner, Dan thought in some amusement. It was a modest start for one whose genius as an architect was now well recognised.

If they could do it, so could he, but he needed time, and time was running out for him. He found himself praying that she would heed his words, and at least postpone her marriage.

Then, if all went well for him, he would woo her once again. Perhaps he was dreaming, but he could hope. There had been something in her manner when she'd flown out at him in fury which suggested that she still cared deeply what became of him.

Yet he must not raise her expectations, or his own.

It would be too cruel. He took Judith's hand and kissed it.

'Friends again?' he asked.

It was at this point that Sebastian entered the room. With his customary good manners he betrayed no surprise at finding Dan and Judith alone.

'Dan has persuaded you to visit us?' he said with a smile. 'My dear, you are our saviour. Prudence will be delighted...'

He led the way across the hall, and up the massive staircase to his wife's room. Prudence was lying on a day-bed, turning the pages of her book in a way which suggested that it did not hold her interest.

Beautifully groomed, as always, her glorious hair was caught high in a bandeau which matched her embroidered negligée of sea-green gauze.

'My dear, you look quite lovely!' Judith exclaimed. 'How do you feel today?'

'Much like a barrel!' Prudence said with feeling. 'I wonder if I shall ever see my toes again.'

'Nothing is more certain.' Sebastian bent and kissed his wife. 'My love, you ladies will have much to say to each other. Shall you mind if I steal Dan away for a few moments?'

'Secrets?' Prudence gave him a quizzical look. 'Are we to hear about them later?'

'All in good time, I promise.' He signalled to Dan, and walked swiftly from the room.

Prudence smiled at Judith. 'I fear that I have a cruel husband. Tales of a mystery would have been a welcome diversion, but now I have your company, so I shan't complain.'

'This is a trying time for you,' Judith said with

sympathy. 'Can I do anything to make you more comfortable?'

'The pillow behind my back has slipped. If you could raise it a little…?' Prudence struggled to sit upright.

Judith slipped an arm around her and pushed the pillow into place. She noticed that Prudence was sweating.

'Would you like me to bathe your head?' she suggested. 'It is so warm today.'

'I should like that,' Prudence murmured. 'Oh dear, I am a dreadful bore at present! I wonder how Sebastian bears with me…'

'He understands.' Judith poured water into a bowl and soaked a cloth. 'You are the light of his life, as you know…'

'But sadly dimmed for the moment…' Prudence hadn't lost her sense of humour. 'Oh, Judith, that feels so good!' She lay back and closed her eyes, enjoying the feel of the cool cloth against her brow. 'Can you stay for a time?'

'Of course, if that is what you wish…' Judith continued with her task.

'I do. You are such a peaceful person. You don't fuss, or worry me with stupid questions. I cannot abide a fidget.'

'Of course not!' Judith soothed her. 'There is nothing worse than a busy person when one is feeling not quite up to the mark.'

'I am not sick, you know.' Prudence managed a weary smile. 'But I have a million things to do. It is so galling to be forced to lie here thinking about them.'

'Then don't.' Judith had an inspiration. 'You can

help me if you will...just by listening as you lie there.'

Prudence sighed. 'My dear, I should not dream of offering you advice. Did we not promise not to speak of your betrothal?'

'It isn't that. Pru, how could you think that I should worry you about it? This is something else...'

'More secrets?'

'Well, yes, in a way.' Judith looked a little conscious. 'I'd like your opinion on...on my book.'

'Your book?' Prudence opened her eyes and sat up suddenly. 'You are actually writing a book? My dear, how wonderful! We said always that you should do so. Do you have it with you?'

Judith chuckled, though her colour rose. 'It is not so wonderful that I must carry it about with me, but Dan has asked to see it, so I brought the manuscript today. Of course, I have not spoken of it to...to...'

'To anyone else? Never fear! Your secret is safe with me. I confess that I'm flattered to be asked for my opinion.'

'I could be wasting my time,' Judith told her gravely. 'I am not the best judge of my own work. Dan liked the first few chapters, but it may be that he is simply offering me encouragement.'

Prudence considered for a moment. 'No, you are mistaken! I'm sure he would be honest, even if you did not enjoy his criticism. You are much too sensible to ask for an opinion if you did not wish to hear the truth.'

'I'm glad you think as I do. Flattery is valueless. I prefer to have my weaknesses pointed out. It can be helpful to a novice.'

'Hardly a novice, Judith! Have you not been writing since you could first put pen to paper?'

'That's true, but they were childish efforts—'

'And what of your essays which made us laugh so much? Is the book in the same amusing vein?'

'Perhaps you'd like to judge for yourself? That is, if it won't tire you to hear me read aloud?'

'My dear, it will be a godsend! I quite fancy myself a literary critic. How foolish I have been to trouble my mind with lesser matters! You have quite restored me. Read on, I beg of you.'

'Now you are funning,' Judith said severely. 'I believe you to be the most complete hand…and quite as bad as Perry.'

'Never doubt it! Sebastian despairs of me… I rely on the patience of my friends.' Prudence leaned back against her pillows, but her expression was so comical that Judith began to laugh.

'No, Madame Author, pray be serious! This will not do, you know. We are to have a serious discussion…'

Judith gave up. She took the manuscript from her reticule, leafing over several pages until she reached the chapter which had pleased her most. Then, in her clear and beautiful tones, she launched into her story.

Prudence said nothing for a time. Then Judith heard a chuckle. Encouraged, she continued until the chuckle became an outright shout of laughter.

'Judith, I shall never ask you to another party, you sly creature! You sit there, looking as if butter wouldn't melt, whilst you look into our hearts as if we were made of glass.'

'Not yours, Prudence, nor those of any of my friends. Have I been too cruel? I did not mean to

pillory any one particular person. It is just that sometimes I feel that we…Polite Society, I mean…are
like the froth upon a seething cauldron. Skimmed off,
and thrown away, we should be no great loss.'

'Never say so, Judith!' Prudence grew serious.
'Excellence may appear in the most unlikely circumstances. Take the Prince Regent, for example. He is
extravagant, self-indulgent, almost certainly a biga-
mist, and an uncertain friend. Yet consider his
achievements! The first member of the Royal Family
for centuries with a true regard for culture.'

'Yes, but…'

'But his influence is felt throughout society. Look
about you, not only in this house, but in others. Have
you seen such craftsmanship in furniture, in decora-
tion, in clothing, and…oh, I don't know…I suppose
I must describe it as a way of life… You won't deny
that it is civilised?'

'Of course not, but is it enough?'

'It isn't!' Prudence gave her a straight look. 'Why
do you think I am fretting so? Pregnancy? Not so! I
am used to this condition, and happy to give
Sebastian our children. Yet I can't forget the evils
which surround us. I'd made a start in changing the
conditions in the northern mills, especially for the
children, but now I feel so helpless.'

'You will continue with the work. I wish that I
might say the same.'

'Then that was why…? Forgive me, as I am being
indiscreet, but we all wondered at your decision to
marry a parson.'

'I hope I can be useful,' Judith told her warmly.
'Oh, Pru, I know that you don't like Charles Truscott,

but you don't know him. He means to devote his life to helping others.'

This sanguine belief was not echoed in the library below.

'You have news?' Dan had scarcely been able to contain himself until he was out of earshot of the servants.

'Yes! There have been developments. I thought it best to meet our Runner in a coffee house.' Sebastian gave the younger man a hard look. 'You will keep this to yourself, of course?'

'Of course! But tell me what has happened…'

'Truscott returned to the parish of St Giles. He spent the day in a certain house. When he emerged it was to conduct a funeral.'

'Outside his own parish?'

'Unusual, perhaps, but nothing out of the way, except that one of the mourners was well known to our man. His name is Margrave.'

Dan looked mystified. 'You've heard of him?'

'So has half the world. Dick Margrave is a well-known forger. There were ugly rumours. He escaped the noose by a whisker. He was due for transportation when he disappeared.'

'Our quarry keeps strange company,' Dan observed.

'There is more. Truscott was well muffled, but at the graveside he was forced to reveal his face. He appeared to have been beaten…'

'A quarrel among thieves? I'm only sorry that they didn't kill him.'

'You are jumping to conclusions, Dan.'

'Am I? If he'd been attacked by strangers, why did he stay in "the Rookery"? The obvious course would have been to lay a complaint before the magistrates. Instead, he conducts a *burial*?'

'One must wonder, of course. My man attempted to discover the identity of the two corpses, but he was unsuccessful. Paupers' graves are unmarked.'

'He might have questioned the other mourners.'

'Impossible! Margrave keeps his eye upon the three of them. He is suspicious of all strangers, and would probably have recognised our man.'

'Well, why do we wait? If this Margrave is a felon he must be given up to the law.'

'And lose our best chance of success? No, we must wait longer for certain proof of our belief that there is something wrong here.' Sebastian paused. 'When Truscott left them he went on to the house in Seven Dials.'

Dan's eyes scanned his face. 'You do suspect him, don't you?' he said earnestly. 'Let me tell you what I learned today.'

He went on to describe the strange girl who had accosted Judith in Piccadilly, and given her the cryptic message.

'Now, Seb, you'll agree there's something smoky here? Why should Truscott mention Judith to these beggars in the first place? The relief of poverty should be his affair. And to send a message to her in this way...? Why could he not write to her himself? I may tell you I don't like it!'

Sebastian liked it even less, but he decided to keep the rest of his information to himself. The Bow Street Runner had kept track of him for some time, and a full description of Margrave's previous activities had been disquieting.

Sebastian had heard of him, but only as a forger.

The revelation of a long history of extortion, violence, and possibly murder made his blood run cold.

What was Truscott's connection with this man? And who was the girl who had spoken to Judith in the street, bearing a message to her from an intermediary?

'Nor do I!' he said slowly, as his gaze rested for a long moment on the younger man's face. Dan was already seriously alarmed, and he must do nothing to increase it.

'Of course there may be a simple explanation,' he continued. 'If Truscott has been injured, he may not wish to frighten Judith by appearing in his present state.'

'Begging your pardon, Seb, but that won't wear with me! It's my belief that he's quarrelled with his cronies, and now he's gone to ground. I think he wrote the note himself!'

'You may be right,' Sebastian told him mildly. 'But if it's true, it's scarcely a hanging matter. Shall we join the ladies?'

'You mean you will do nothing?' Dan sprang to his feet. 'I can't believe it! Judith may be in the greatest danger—'

'Not for the moment, I believe. If our suspicions are correct, Truscott will do nothing to delay his marriage. Judith will be in danger only if she decides to break her engagement. Do you understand me?'

Dan flushed. 'You mean that I must not continue to persuade her?'

'I mean exactly that,' Sebastian said in level tones. 'I have no wish to alarm you further, but if we are right, Truscott won't allow his prize to slip away.

You have seen how easy it is for anyone to approach her.'

The colour left Dan's face, and he swallowed. 'You can't think it possible that he would abduct her?'

'I don't know, but we must take no chances.'

'Then I must warn her to be careful.'

'You will say nothing!' Sebastian told him sharply. 'She is still firm in her decision to wed him?'

Dan nodded, his face a picture of desolation.

'That's good! For the present it is her safeguard. Once let him doubt her willingness, and I won't answer for the consequences.'

It was stern advice, but he felt obliged to give it. He knew Dan's heart. The years apart had not changed his passionate devotion for his first love.

He hadn't been so sure of Judith's constancy, though Prudence had assured him of it.

'You must be mistaken, my love,' he'd argued gently. 'Have you asked her?'

'Of course not!' His wife had taken his hand and held it against her cheek. 'One needs only to see them together.'

'You are a romantic!' He'd dropped a kiss upon her hair. 'If it is true, then Dan must offer for her. Judith is not wed yet—'

'He won't do that!'

'Why not?' Sebastian was mystified.

'Need you ask? It is the fortune, my dearest. You know him. Would he ever take anything from you?'

Sebastian frowned. 'No! That stubborn refusal of my help has been the cause of what few differences we have had, but this is another matter. The happiness of two people is at stake.'

'I can't persuade him.' Her eyes were sad.

It was this sadness more than anything which had persuaded him to take such a close interest in Judith's affairs, though at first it had been much against his better judgment. Now he could only marvel at feminine intuition. Prudence and Elizabeth had been right to distrust the Reverend Charles Truscott. His determination to worst the creature hardened, but his expression was apparently untroubled as he re-entered his wife's boudoir.

There he was delighted to find that his wife had been enjoying herself. She gave him a brilliant smile, and her eyes were sparkling with mischief.

'Feeling better?' he teased. 'What have you been up to?'

'Not I, my love, but Judith! Now who would believe that beneath that air of calm reserve lies the wickedest sense of the ridiculous?'

'I would, for one, and so would Dan.' Sebastian glanced at the scattered sheets of manuscript, and pretended to shudder. 'Dan, I fear that we have been pinned to the board once more as interesting specimens.'

Judith gathered up the pages. 'How can you say so?' she reproached. 'You know it is not true.'

'Not even interesting?' Sebastian glanced at Dan and pulled a face. 'I'm crushed, aren't you?'

'Now, my darling, I won't have Judith teased. You may not care to know it, but I've been working hard. I am now a literary critic...'

'But you always were...' Dan joined in the teasing '...the harshest one I've known, and always against the popular opinion. I had thought you must be sunk

beneath reproach when you gave your view on
Alexander Pope at Lady Denton's soirée.'

'Turgid stuff! Besides, I was asked for my opinion.
Would you have had me lie?'

'Perish the thought!' Sebastian sat beside her on
the day-bed. 'Shall you come down for nuncheon,
dearest?'

'Great heavens! You must all be starving! Give
me ten minutes and I'll join you. Dearest, will you
ring the bell for Dutton?'

Sebastian did as he was bidden, and led their guest
from the room. In the corridor he took her arm.

'Judith, how can I thank you? Pru is quite herself
again today. Dan, don't you agree?'

Judith looked at her love, and caught her breath as
she saw the warmth of his expression.

'How could it be otherwise?' he murmured slowly.
'Judith has a certain quality which it is not easy to
explain…' He caught Sebastian's eye and looked
away.

Their nuncheon was a gay affair, and Sebastian's
chef, who had tried for weeks to tempt the flagging
appetite of his mistress, was clearly on his mettle.
Well aware that a lady in an interesting condition
was likely to feel queasy at the sight of food, he had
produced the lightest, freshest dishes imaginable.

Imaginative salads flanked the glazed ham and the
platters of smoked duck. The épigrammes of chicken
with a celery puree were tempting, and even lighter
were the quenelles, tiny fish balls done *à la
Flamande*. They were followed by a featherlight or-
ange soufflé, and a selection of fruit jellies.

Sebastian smiled to himself. His more usual nuncheon, if he took one, consisted of a selection of cold

meats and fruit. On this occasion, he announced that he was very hungry. Prudence beamed at him. Animated for the first time in days, she allowed herself to be helped to an excellent meal, almost without noticing.

Later he took Judith to one side. A plan was forming in his mind. It was a long shot, but it might succeed.

'What a difference you have made to Prudence!' he murmured. 'Today, my dear, she is a different person. To see her so much more herself is a great joy to me.'

Judith smiled. 'I think you have no need to worry. She has enjoyed her nuncheon…'

'For the first time in weeks. I've tried not to let her see it, but I have been concerned about her.'

Judith scanned his face with anxious eyes. 'She tells me that she is not sick.'

'No, Judith, she is bored to death. What she needs is stimulation. You have given it to her.'

'You can't quarrel with her temperament. In the usual way she is so full of projects… These last few weeks are hard for her.'

'My dear, I know it. How I wish that you might come to us, if only for a day or two! I have no right to ask. Your own marriage is so close, but is there the least chance that it might be possible?'

'I should like nothing more,' she told him wistfully. 'But Charles is to return tomorrow. I must be at home to greet him.'

'Of course! It is selfish of me to put my own concerns before your own…'

Sebastian did not press her further. He knew that

her affection for Prudence would lead her to stay at
Mount Street if she could. That would be the answer
for a time. Events were moving fast, and he trusted
neither the preacher nor his friends.

Chapter Nine

The subject of his thoughts was still abed at the house in Seven Dials. Truscott was nursing an aching head.

He'd awakened in the worst of moods after a restless night. Sleep had proved elusive, and he'd tossed for hours, seeking in vain for some solution to his problems. This had required the consumption of the best part of a bottle of brandy, but it had served only to send him into a stupor.

Now he regretted his indulgence. He needed all his wits about him if he were to deal with Margrave. Damn the man! He'd seen the chance of easy pickings and he'd taken it. But he'd chosen the wrong victim.

He raised his throbbing head and glanced about the room to find that he was alone.

'Nan?' he yelled. Then he picked up one of his boots and threw it at the door.

'What is it, Josh?' The girl came hurrying to his side.

'Fetch me some ale, and be quick about it!' He

caught sight of her face. 'What happened to you? God, but you're a sight this morning!'

'You beat me, Josh.' She touched her swollen face and winced.

'You must have deserved it!' He grunted and turned over. He had no recollection of striking her, but it was no matter. Women needed to be kept in line.

'I...I did everything you asked...and the lady gave me money...' At the look on his face she fled.

As Truscott sipped at his ale, the mists cleared from his mind. His decision to send the girl to seek out Judith had been a good one. He now had money enough for his immediate expenses, but better still, the meeting had provided him with useful information which might prove vital at some future date.

How easy it had been for Nan, a stranger, to approach Judith in the street, and even to arrange a further meeting. Not for the first time he blessed the stupidity of her stepmother. How many young women were allowed to walk the London thoroughfares with only a maid for company, and unattended by either a footman or a groom for protection? It was Mrs Aveton's selfishness and spite which allowed Judith such infrequent use of the family carriage, and then only when she was to be conveyed to the homes of such members of the aristocracy as Mrs Aveton hoped to cultivate.

He'd wondered at it since the early days of their acquaintance, but he'd made no protest. His heiress must not be too closely guarded. If ever his original plan should go awry, he might turn that fact to his advantage.

He'd run no risk in sending Nan to Judith. The girl

knew him only as Josh Ferris, and he'd warned her not to answer questions. All in all, it had been a successful operation. The note had been an extra flourish. He'd thought long and hard before putting pen to paper, and then it was not from a desire to reassure her as to his health.

He'd promised to call upon her on the following day. That should put a stop to any awkward enquiries from that long-nosed stepmother of hers.

'Fetch me a mirror!' he demanded. Close examination of his features showed that most of the scratches were healing, though one, across his cheek, was so deep that he would probably bear the scar for life. The purple bruising around his mouth and nose was fading. By the following day there should be little injury apparent.

If Judith mentioned it he would think of some explanation. Nothing, he vowed fiercely, would lose him his prize at his late stage. She'd hold to her bargain, as long as she continued to believe in him.

That was the danger now. His mother and Margrave had him firm within their grasp, with their threats of blackmail. He doubted if they would carry them out unless they wished to cast to the four winds all hope of sharing in his fortune.

The preacher's worries rested more upon his future. He'd never be allowed to enjoy the money in peace. And there was his reputation. His rise to fame had been meteoric, but he was not quite at the top of his profession. That would come when he was invited to preach at the Chapel Royal, in St James's Palace.

What a sermon he would give them! Let the fat old Royal Dukes comment upon it in stentorian tones, even as he spoke. He wouldn't care. It would be enough that they were there, and that he would be preaching before Royalty.

He could almost taste the feeling of power...the sensation of holding his audience in the palm of his hand. He smiled to himself. More properly it should be called a congregation, but for him, standing at the pulpit, the entire setting was pure theatre.

Then a vision of Margrave sprang unbidden to his mind. The man would be constantly at his back, smiling, reminding him always that success must be bought at a price. The preacher's eyes narrowed. He'd no intention of spending the rest of his life in looking over his shoulder. Margrave must be removed, together with his cronies, but how? The man was as fast and dangerous as a striking snake.

He was still considering the problem when Nan came over to the bed and stood beside him, pulling nervously at her kerchief.

'What is it now?' he asked impatiently.

'I need some money, Josh.'

'I gave you enough for food and drink. What else can there be?'

'It's the baby, Josh. I ain't been able to pay the woman for her keep—'

'That's none of my affair. I told you to get rid of it.'

'I know you did, but it was too late when I found out. Old Mother Gisburn wouldn't touch me—'

'I'm not surprised! She must have thought that you'd have croaked on her.'

'I wish I had!' The tears poured down Nan's face.

'Stop your caterwauling!' Truscott flung a coin at her. As he did so he eyed her with distaste. When her brothers had brought her from the country she'd been a plump and rosy wench, and a comfortable armful for any man.

They'd been aware of it, and hoped to earn good money from her charms, but Truscott had seen her first. Now he considered that he'd had the worst of the bargain. Since the birth of her child Nan had grown scrawny and pale. Life seemed to have drained from her, leaving her dull and listless. Time for a change, he thought to himself. It wouldn't be difficult to replace her.

He was confirmed in this belief when she began to plead.

'Josh, let me have the baby here. I don't trust that woman down in Lambeth, and it would cost you nothing. She's but a few weeks old, and I want to care for her myself. I'll keep her quiet, I promise you!'

'Bring her here, and I'll keep her quiet for you...'

Nan could not mistake his meaning, and she backed away from him. 'Your own flesh and blood? You can't be so heartless. I thought she would be company for me. It's lonely here without you. I ain't even seen my brothers for a day or two.'

'They must be off on business of their own,' he told her carelessly.

'I thought you asked them to do a job for you?'

'Didn't work out!' he said. 'Get off, then, if you intend to go to Lambeth.'

He waited until she'd left the house. Then he examined his outer clothing. She'd done her best to sponge away the traces of his enforced stay in that stinking attic, and, as always, he'd removed his collar and clerical bands before he entered the house in Seven Dials.

When he left here he would bathe and change before presenting himself to Judith, though he doubted if she'd notice anything amiss whatever his appearance. He could never guess what she was thinking. She seemed always to be out of reach, as if she lived in a world of her own. That would change, he vowed. He'd bring her down to earth.

He dismissed her from his mind. Judith was not his immediate problem. What mattered now was to find some way of foiling Margrave. He'd need all his guile. Truscott considered several possibilities.

He could lay evidence of the fellow's whereabouts before the magistrates. He guessed that the forger was still wanted by the authorities. It would not serve. If Margrave went down, he would take his former cellmate with him in revenge.

As for paying him off? The idea was laughable. The forger and his friends would not be satisfied until their victim had no more to give. There was never an end to blackmail.

There was but one solution, and the preacher had known it from the first. His enemies must be silenced, and permanently. Next time he would not make the mistake of employing idiots. He would do the job himself, but how?

He was still considering the matter when Nan returned. Her eyes were red with weeping.

'Stop your blubbing!' he ordered. 'I want some food.'

For once she didn't hurry to obey him.

'Josh, please listen to me! The baby isn't well. I'm

sure she isn't being fed…and I don't trust Mrs Daggett.'

'She found you a wet-nurse, didn't she?'

'The woman is feeding several children. She hasn't enough milk for all, and two of those I saw last week have disappeared.'

'Daggett don't keep them for ever…only till they are collected by whoever owns them.'

'I…I can't be sure of that. Her neighbour says she is a baby farmer.'

'What of it? If she sells them it's probably for the best. It saves a lot of trouble all round.'

'*If* she sells them…' Nan burst into a storm of weeping. 'Last week there were two bodies found in the river!'

'Brats die from natural causes,' Truscott said impatiently. 'Daggett can't afford to pay for burials.' Her news didn't surprise him. If payment for a child's keep was not forthcoming, Mrs Daggett would solve the problem in the simplest way. It had been in his mind when he sent Nan to her with the child.

Now he gazed angrily at the weeping girl. 'I said I wanted food,' he growled. 'Set about it, or you'll find yourself in the street…'

He was tempted to carry out his threat at once, but it would wait. He didn't want her running about the neighbourhood asking for her brothers. He doubted if they had discussed his orders with any of their friends, but it was best to take no chances.

Next day he left her with the unspoken resolve to throw her out as soon as it was practicable. After his marriage he would keep the house at Seven Dials, but he would have a change of mistress. Nan's connection with the murdered men would, in time, become a problem. He didn't fancy constant questioning. Besides, she was little more than skin and bone. His taste ran to a plumper armful.

With this decision made, he began to feel more cheerful. No solution as to the question of Margrave had, as yet, come to mind, but he would think of something. Meantime, he must not allow his enemies to suspect that he intended to outwit them. Robbed of his prey, Margrave would make every effort to destroy him, even to the extent of approaching Judith with his story.

He arrived at the Aveton household to find it in an uproar. The strident tones of Judith's stepmother were audible beyond the closed door of the salon.

When he was announced, Mrs Aveton looked up and paused for breath. Judith stood before her, flushed and silent.

Truscott raised an eyebrow in enquiry, but before he could speak he heard a gasp from Judith.

'Charles, your face! What has happened to your face?'

Involuntarily, he lifted a hand to touch the healing scratches. 'A sad business, my dear! In her delirium my mother did not know me. She imagined that I was come to take her to the madhouse. It was difficult to restrain her.'

'How dreadful for you! Is there no change in her condition?'

'Alas, she grows weaker by the day…' Truscott bent his head and covered his eyes.

'Oh, Charles, I am so sorry!' Judith came towards him. 'There is still no hope of a recovery?'

'None! I fear I must return to her without delay.' He was aware that Mrs Aveton had not uttered a word of sympathy and, looking up, he met her hard, suspicious eyes.

'Judith, you may leave us!' she snapped. 'I wish to have a private word with Mr Truscott.'

She waited until the door had closed before she rounded on him.

'Now, sir, what are you about?' she demanded. 'Don't try to gammon me with your stories. Where have you been for these past few days?'

'Judith must have told you,' he replied smoothly.

'Stuff! I don't believe a word of it. Smallpox, forsooth! Even if it were true, I don't credit you with sufficient Christian charity to spend your time beside a sickbed.'

'Would you care to tell me what concern it is of yours?'

'It *is* my concern, and it should be yours. Sir, you are a fool! Here is Judith, constantly with her friends, the Wentworths, and in the company of that penniless creature who still dangles after her. Do you wish to lose her?'

'I won't lose her!' The preacher towered over Mrs Aveton, and there was something in his face which made her back away.

'You are the fool!' he told her softly. 'Won't you ever learn? Must you always be at odds with her? What was it this time? The Wentworths?'

'Not exactly!' An angry flush stained his companion's cheeks. 'That wicked, ungrateful girl had the impertinence to inform me that I...that we were spending beyond reason on her wedding.'

'Really?' Truscott jeered. 'She cannot be referring

to her trousseau, since you tell me that her own purchases have been frugal. I take it that she's been
alarmed by the accounts from your modiste?'

'There are three of us to dress,' Mrs Aveton said
defensively. 'It is expensive.'

'Especially when one provides for the whole of
the coming season? No, don't bother to deny it. I
fully understand.'

She gave him an uncertain look.

'But there is something you must understand,' he
continued. 'These bills will not be settled from
Judith's estate. You will pay them from the share
which I have promised you.'

He almost laughed aloud when he saw her stunned
expression. For a moment she was robbed of speech.
Then she broke into a violent diatribe against him.

'And *I* shall not pay them,' she said finally.

'Then they will remain unpaid...your credit will
suffer with the London mantua-makers.'

'You don't know Judith,' she sneered. 'She won't
allow it. She has a positive abhorrence of debt—'

'Judith will have nothing to say in the matter,' he
said significantly. 'Come, madam, I am well up to
your tricks. You thought to milk the estate of as
much as possible in advance. I won't have it!'

Mrs Aveton was silent, but the look she gave him
spoke volumes. From now on she would be his enemy, but until her share of Judith's fortune was in
her hands she must hide her feelings.

Truscott was undeceived, and again he wanted to
laugh. She wouldn't receive a penny, and her bills
would most certainly remain unpaid, but he'd
thought it wise to frighten her a little. Their quarrel
had drawn her attention from the questions she'd

been about to ask. Sharp as a fox, he thought idly, but he was a match for her.

'Do you tell me that Judith spends much time with the Wentworths?' he enquired.

'Too much, in my opinion! You should forbid it, sir. Socialising as she does! Most unsuitable for a parson's wife… Of course, she is not yet your wife, is she?' It was a sly dig, and he was about to answer when Wentworth himself was announced.

Mrs Aveton's manner underwent a sea-change. No member of the Wentworth family had ever graced her home before.

Conscious of the fact that a carriage bearing a well-known coat-of-arms must at this moment be standing at her door, she was wreathed in smiles as she advanced towards her noble visitor.

'My lord, what a pleasure!' She sank into a curtsy.

Sebastian bowed both to her and then to Truscott, favouring them with one of his most charming smiles.

'I am so glad to find you both together,' he said. 'I am come on my wife's behalf to ask for your indulgence towards her.'

Mrs Aveton begged him to be seated. Then she rang for refreshment.

'How is your good lady wife?' she asked in saccharine tones. 'Believe me, my lord, if there is anything we can do to help…?'

'Well, ma'am, there is.' Sebastian accepted a glass of wine. 'Perhaps I should explain. My brother and his wife are gone to visit Mrs Peregrine's aunt, and the only other member of my household, my adopted son, is also called away from London at this time.' He shot a covert look at the faces of his companions, guessing correctly that this final piece of information would aid his cause.

'The thing is that Prudence is sadly low in spirits,' he continued. 'She cannot go about in society at this time…'

'Of course not…so trying for dear Lady Wentworth.' Mrs Aveton was flattered beyond measure to be taken into the confidence of this august personage whom she had previously considered somewhat distant.

'Ah, I knew you'd understand!' Sebastian leaned towards her. 'You encourage me to ask if Judith might be spared for just a day or two. My wife is fond of her, and is much in need of someone to bear her company.'

Mrs Aveton looked uncertain. 'Lord Wentworth, if it had been at any other time…but Judith's marriage is now so close. I fear that it will be impossible…' She glanced at Truscott and subsided.

The preacher had been thinking fast. He'd sensed the purpose of Wentworth's errand from his lordship's opening words, and had given the matter his consideration.

Within these next few days he must settle with Margrave and his cronies once and for all. With Judith safe in the hands of the Wentworth family, Margrave and Nellie might threaten him to their heart's content. They would never find her.

Truscott smiled at Mrs Aveton. 'Surely not impossible, ma'am?' he coaxed. 'Consider! Is it not an excellent suggestion? Our little Judith has been looking tired. She too would be happy to spend time with her friends. We should thank Lord Wentworth for his kindness.'

'The pleasure is mine. I must thank you for your understanding and forbearance, sir.' Sebastian was puzzled. What was the fellow up to? He seemed positively thankful for the opportunity to remove Judith from the Aveton household.

'Shall we ask our little bride-to-be for her opinion of this invitation?' Truscott said archly. 'I dare swear that she will be delighted to accept. Ma'am, will you send for her?'

Mrs Aveton raised no further objections, which also surprised Sebastian. He'd been expecting a much more difficult task. Perhaps it was the fact that Dan had gone away which had prevented a refusal.

Judith herself grew radiant when his proposal was explained to her.

'Of course I'll come—that is, if there is no objection…?' She looked at both Truscott and her stepmother, to find them nodding their agreement. 'When will it be convenient?'

'I have my carriage waiting, and there is no time like the present,' Sebastian chuckled. 'I am rushing you, my dear, but perhaps your maid might be allowed to fetch your things this afternoon?'

'There now, his lordship has thought of everything. Off you go, my dearest one. You will give my duty to her ladyship?' Truscott was all smiles.

'Of course!' Judith thought that she had never liked him better. In the midst of all his troubles he was thinking only of her pleasure. 'You will let me know how your mama goes on? Charles, I would come with you if you'd let me…'

'My love, it is out of the question, as I have explained. There is all the danger of carrying infection. Now you shall not keep his lordship waiting. I'm happy to know that you'll be with your friends whilst I am away.' He took her hand and kissed it reverently, and was rewarded with a dazzling smile.

'Such a dear child!' he said when she had gone to put on her pelisse. 'I am unworthy of her!'

Privately, Sebastian considered that a truer word was never spoken, but he contented himself with polite enquiries as to the health of Truscott's mother.

The man was glib, he thought to himself. He had all the symptoms of smallpox at his fingertips, but other than that Sebastian learned nothing of the whereabouts of the sick woman, or why she had not previously been introduced to Judith. He hadn't expected to, and no trace of his suspicions appeared in his expression.

Judith herself was smiling as he handed her into the carriage. The news that Dan was away had been bittersweet, but she prayed that he had gone to Merton to see Lord Nelson.

And if he had still been at Mount Street? Would she have agreed to visit Prudence? It was difficult to decide. She knew the danger. Her treacherous heart still longed for him. She should have been thankful that he had given her no encouragement, but the thought of her lost love still left her desolate. He was away, and she was safe from temptation. The knowledge should have comforted her, but it didn't.

Sebastian saw that she was looking pensive.

'Forgive me?' he asked.

'For what?'

'I stole you away without a by-your-leave. My dear, are you happy to come to us for a few days?'

'I am!' she told him simply. 'Sebastian, you must

now think better of Charles. You saw how much he wished for me to spend some time with Prudence. It was kind of him, when he might have raised objections—'

'Indeed! Judith, you must never think that we wish for anything other than your happiness. I suspect that Prudence and Elizabeth have no wish to lose you, even to your worthy preacher.' He gave her a cheerful grin, hoping that she would believe this excuse for their objections.

His own suspicions had increased, and Truscott's ready agreement to Judith's visit to Mount Street had done nothing to allay them. The fellow was up to something, but what? To date the Bow Street Runner had brought no further news.

Sebastian glanced down at his companion. Once away from the Aveton household she was a different person. All her grave reserve had disappeared, and those large, expressive eyes were shining with pleasure as she questioned him about his boys.

'Inexhaustible!' he said ruefully. 'They intend to make the most of this visit to London. Our next expedition is to be to Madame Tussaud's. The blood-thirsty little creatures have a taste for horrors.'

'It will be educational,' she answered primly, but her face was alive with amusement. 'You must be delighted that they are anxious to improve their minds.'

They were still laughing when the carriage stopped and he helped her to alight. His plan had worked so far, and he was further rewarded by a cry of delight from Prudence.

'Oh, my dear, you've brought her! I had not dared

to hope. Judith, am I very greedy to wish to have you here?'

It was the warmest of welcomes, and Judith flushed with pleasure as she shook her head. 'I was happy to come to you,' she said.

Sebastian left them chattering gaily. He was content, at least for the moment, to have removed Judith from possible danger, but he was deeply concerned for her future safety.

He strolled down to the library and sifted through his morning post. It consisted mainly of invitations to one function or another. There was no message from the Runner.

For some time he was lost in thought. During his visit to Mrs Aveton he had watched Truscott closely. A shifty fellow, he decided, with something on his mind. Had he discovered that he was being watched? Sebastian thought not. This was something else, something which had caused a fleeting look of relief at his own suggestion that Judith came to Mount Street.

It was a riddle for which, at present, he had no answer.

Perhaps he imagined that the less he was in Judith's company the less likely it might be that she would change her mind and refuse to wed him.

Truscott appeared to be a consummate actor, but even he must find it a strain to keep up a front of benevolent respectability. There was always the chance that he would make a slip and say or do something to give her a distaste of him.

That was the danger now. Judith still thought kindly of her betrothed, or did she? Sebastian wondered if, at times, she were not a little too insistent as to his virtues.

He hoped that he was wrong. With Judith's fortune almost within his grasp, the preacher would not let his prize escape him. Should Judith break off her engagement, the man would stop at nothing.

Prudence, he knew, would say nothing further against the Reverend Truscott. She had too much regard for Judith's peace of mind. Elizabeth was more outspoken, but she and Perry were away.

And what of Dan, who loved her? He was the fiercest opponent of this marriage, yet he could put Judith into deadly danger if he betrayed his feelings for her.

Sebastian resolved that he would speak to Dan again, but it was not until late that evening that his adopted son returned.

Sebastian heard the bustle in the hall and strolled through from the salon in time to hear the butler announce that her ladyship had come downstairs and was at present with her husband and Miss Aveton.

'She's here?' Dan's face lit up. 'I must go to them!'

'Dan, a word with you, if you please!' Sebastian threw open the door to the library.

'Isn't this great?' Dan threw aside his riding coat, and laid his crop beside it. 'How did you manage to rescue Judith? At this hour she must be staying—'

'She is, but only for a day or two. Nothing has changed, Dan, and I must ask you once again to do nothing to persuade Judith to end her betrothal.'

Dan's dismay was evident. 'She is still to wed that

creature? Then what is she doing here? The marriage is so close…'

'I am well aware of that.' Sebastian paused, considering his words with care. 'We must be patient for just a little longer. I saw Truscott today. The man is worried. I believe that something is afoot.'

'He knows that he is being watched?'

'I don't think so, but I've heard nothing from the Bow Street man.'

'Then what?'

'Who can say? He seemed relieved that Judith was to come to us.'

'That's strange! He is as fond of me as I am of him.'

'He believes you to be away…' A faint smile touched Sebastian's lips.

Dan frowned at him. 'Why is Judith here? It can't have been easy to persuade the old harpy to let her go.'

'Prudence longed to see her.'

'And that was enough to send you off to visit that harridan?'

'As you know, my wife's wishes are of paramount importance to me,' Sebastian told him smoothly.

'I know that, but it ain't enough for me.' Dan's eyes were filled with suspicion. 'There's something else…something you aren't telling me.'

'Dear me! How sceptical you are grown! You are right, of course. Shall we say that I am hoping that matters will resolve themselves within these next few days. Judith will be safe with us.'

'Then you think her still in danger?' Dan grew so pale that the freckles stood out sharply against his skin.

'I was somewhat concerned to find that she is allowed to walk abroad without protection. It was much too easy for someone to approach her in the street.'

'Beggars and thieves, you mean?'

'No, I don't mean that!' Sebastian decided to lay his cards upon the table. 'I am come round to your way of thinking. There is something very smoky going on. It is best to take no chances... For the moment, Judith's safety lies in the fact that she is still betrothed to Truscott. You must do nothing to put her in danger.'

'I'd like to wring his neck!' Dan said savagely.

'Agreed! In time I feel that someone may perform that desirable task for you, given the opportunity. Meantime, you will heed my wishes?'

'I will, but it won't be easy!' Dan rose to his feet. 'May I see her now?'

'Of course!' Sebastian clapped him on the shoulder. 'I know it won't be easy, but you would do more than that for her, I think.'

'Anything!' Dan turned his face away, unwilling to say more.

'Well, then, let us join the ladies. They must be longing to hear your news.'

'It isn't good!' Dan fell into step beside him as they strolled across the hall.

'Nevertheless, they will wish to hear it.' Sebastian entered the salon and was greeted happily by his wife.

Judith said nothing. She looked up at Dan and her heart was in her eyes.

Chapter Ten

Prudence appeared to notice nothing. She patted her sofa invitingly.

'Come and sit down,' she said. 'Sebastian has been keeping you from us. Was it to build up the suspense? How did you go on at Merton?'

Judith had recovered her composure, and now she smiled her encouragement for him to begin. She was both proud and pleased that he'd taken her advice, even to the point of telling Prudence and Sebastian of his plans.

Dan looked at the circle of eager faces, and then he grimaced. 'Foiled again!' he joked. 'The Admiral was away from home.'

'Oh, my dear, what a disappointment! To go all that way for nothing!' Prudence was dismayed.

'Not for nothing, Pru. Now that I've found my way to his door he'll find it difficult to be rid of me. I left my card, and I shall go again next week, when he is returned from Portsmouth.' Dan grinned at her. He *had* been disappointed, but he wouldn't let her see it.

'That's the spirit! I'm glad to see that you don't plan to give up.' Sebastian nodded his approval.

'Oh, I shan't give up!' Dan caught Sebastian's eye and then he looked away. His meaning had been clear, but he would heed the warning.

Prudence looked her relief. She'd been afraid that yet another blow to his hopes would depress his spirits, but the bright blue eyes were smiling fondly at her, with a tiny spark of mischief in their depths.

'And what have you been up to?' he demanded. 'I mean, apart from abducting Judith with some cock-and-bull story about your failing health. You look positively blooming.'

'Judith does me good,' she confided. 'It's such a pleasure to have an intelligent woman in the house when I'm usually surrounded by great clumping males.' She peeped up at Sebastian from beneath her long lashes, laughing as she did so.

'Witch! Are you trying to put me in my place?' He picked up her hand and kissed it. 'I won't have it! You wheedled permission to stay up until Dan returned, and now it is time you were abed.' He lifted her in his arms, ignoring all her protests, and carried her from the room.

Silence reigned in the salon. Then both Dan and Judith began to speak at once. The confusion broke the ice and they began to laugh.

'You first, if you please!' Judith begged.

'I was about to say that it was a pleasant surprise to find you here. Prudence looks so much better...'

'She does, but she had such hopes for you, as did I. Oh, Dan, you must have been disappointed not to find the Admiral at home, in spite of what you told her.'

'I was, but it is no matter. I won't be put off. Judith, I think I must become a man of business. It is not of the slightest use to spend my time designing if I can't sell my work.'

'Splendid!' Judith clapped her hands. 'Have you a fat portfolio to take about with you? If Lord Nelson does not care for one idea, he may like another.'

As she had expected, Dan was quickly launched upon his favourite topic. The technicalities were lost on her, but she was happy to watch his eager face, under the thatch of red-gold hair, alive with interest as he explained his latest invention.

How very dear he was. She loved everything about him, from the startling blue of his eyes to the dusting of freckles across his nose. And those fine hands were never still as he sought to make her understand.

Even he became aware of it.

'Tie my hands together, and I'm speechless,' he joked.

'Never! That I shan't believe!'

'But you must be tired of listening to me. How do you go on?'

Her face changed at once. When she replied it was with an oddly closed expression.

'Much as usual,' she said in neutral tones.

'But you are happy to be here?' he asked.

Her smile returned at once. 'Of course. This is such a happy household. You had best prepare yourself. I fear you are to accompany Sebastian and the boys to Madame Tussaud's.'

'That place in the Strand?'

'The very spot! I see you've heard of it.'

'The boys mentioned some kind of a waxworks.

It has just been opened, hasn't it? It sounds dull to me.'

'Madame Tussaud had a great success in Paris with her exhibition at the Palais Royal. I believe it was started by her uncle, who taught her the skills of modelling. She is Swiss, you know.'

'So now she has moved to London. Well, I suppose that travelling must be easier since the peace with France, but a waxworks? Shall you care to see it?'

Judith laughed. 'I am not invited. This, I feel, is to be an expedition for gentlemen only.'

She left him then. They had spent a pleasant hour together, and Dan had been friendly, but no more.

With burning cheeks, she went up to her room. What was she expecting? That by some miracle his old love for her had been revived? He'd given her no sign of it. Even if it were so, would he approach her now, when she was betrothed to another man? His own sense of honour would prevent it.

And he hadn't mentioned Charles Truscott. Knowing his feelings on the subject of her marriage to the preacher, she had half expected yet another attempt to persuade her to break off her engagement, but Dan had said nothing more.

At their last meeting she must have convinced him finally of her determination to wed Charles. The knowledge should have pleased her, but it didn't.

What a fool she was. She'd been clutching at straws, hoping that Dan would return from Merton basking in the approval of Admiral Nelson, and with the prospect of a promising career ahead of him. In her heart she'd wondered if it was her fortune which had changed his feelings. With his own future assured that barrier would have been removed, but he'd met with no success at Merton.

She must be wrong. He'd taken the reverse with the greatest of good spirits, and was fully prepared to wait until the Great Man should agree to see him.

It wasn't the behaviour of a man whose only love was to wed another in ten short days. She must accept the fact that Dan no longer cared for her in the old way. It was a bitter pill to swallow. She tried to put him from her mind, but it was impossible. The face she loved so much would not be banished from her thoughts.

She climbed into bed and closed her eyes. Then she fell to dreaming. Things might have been so different, but she was drifting into a world of fantasy. Just for a second she allowed herself to wonder what she would do if Dan should offer for her now.

She knew the answer, and honesty compelled her to admit it. She held Charles in high regard, but Dan was the man she loved. She would fall into his arms in the wildest of raptures, forgetting her betrothal, the coming wedding, Charles Truscott's disappointment, and Mrs Aveton's undoubted fury. It was a small price to pay for a life of happiness.

Knowing that it could never be, it was long before she slept, but in the Wentworth household it was impossible to be miserable for long.

Judith wakened to find the sunlight streaming into her room as Bessie drew back her curtains. Then she was given the unexpected treat of breakfast in bed.

'Miss Judith, what will you wear today?' Bessie held up a gown in either hand. 'I packed some others if these don't please you.'

'Great heavens, Bessie, what were you thinking of? I am to stay for only a day or two. You seem to have brought a large part of my trousseau...'

'I thought you'd like to look your best,' Bessie said slyly. 'There's no telling what you'll be needing...'

Judith gave her a sharp look, but Bessie's face was the picture of innocence.

'You know quite well that I am here to bear Lady Wentworth company. Her ladyship does not go abroad at present.'

'No, miss, but you might do so...'

'Don't be foolish, Bessie.' Judith glanced briefly at the garments. 'I'll wear the blue today.'

Bessie beamed at her.

'And you may take that expression off your face,' Judith scolded. 'Why you wish to turn me out as fine as fivepence I really can't imagine.'

This wasn't strictly true. Bessie's intentions were transparent. Dan was to be so overcome by the charming appearance of her young mistress that he would offer for her without delay.

Her maid could have no idea of the true state of affairs, Judith thought sadly. Even so, when she was dressed she could only be pleased with her new gown.

It became her well. The soft blue was a perfect background for her delicate colouring, and the cut of the garment was excellent. It was of exquisite simplicity, the fine cambric caught with a matching ribbon from immediately below her splendid bosom, and falling in folds to a gathered flounce at the hem.

Judith glanced at her reflection in the pier-glass, pleased that she'd rejected the modiste's attempt to persuade her into buying extreme puffed sleeves. These were much more modest in design, swelling only slightly at the shoulder above the tight fabric which covered her arms as far as the wrist.

She smiled a little. For once she looked positively modish, though the morning-dress was quite suitable for a day at home. She left her room and made her way to the head of the staircase, but before she reached it a small hand slid into her own.

Judith gave a pretended jump of terror. 'Why, Crispin, how you startled me! I thought I had been seized by some terrible monster...'

This brought a peal of laughter from Sebastian's youngest son.

'You didn't!' he accused. 'You knew that it was me.'

'How could I? I didn't see you. You crept up behind me like a redskin, and I didn't hear a thing.'

'Truly?' His face grew serious. 'I have been practicing, you know.'

Judith nodded. 'I can tell.'

'I'd have come to see you earlier,' the little boy continued. 'But Mama said that you were not to be disturbed. We were very quiet this morning. You didn't hear us, did you?'

'Not a sound!' she assured him.

'Well, that's all right then.' Crispin heaved an open sigh of relief. 'I wanted to ask you...shall you come with us to the waxworks?'

'Not today, my dear one. Dan and your papa will go with you, and I shall stay with your mama...'

Crispin sat down on the top stair. 'I hoped you'd come,' he told her wistfully. 'You always know the best stories.'

'Well, suppose you try to remember all the things you see. You might even write them down if you think you will forget. Then you may tell me all about them...'

He brightened at that, and hand in hand they walked down the staircase as Dan came out of the library.

The sight of Judith with the child struck him like a knife thrust into his breast. If they had married all those years ago she would now have sons and daughters of her own. Children adored her, and she was at her best with them, entering into their world without the slightest difficulty.

He was careful not to betray his feelings. He greeted her with a polite enquiry as to whether she was well rested.

'Very well rested, Dan, I thank you!' Her radiant smile brought little response from him. 'Are you ready for your outing?'

'There has been a change of plan,' he told her shortly. 'Prudence is not too well today. Sebastian has sent for the doctor. Naturally, he will wait for the man's opinion...'

'Then are we not to go to the waxworks?' Crispin's lip began to tremble.

'Of course you are, my lad!' Sebastian strode towards them, lifting up his son, and throwing the boy high into the air. 'I'm going to tease Judith into going with you. How shall you like that?'

Crispin squealed with delight. 'Better than anything!' he yelled. Then he scurried off as fast as his fat little legs would carry him to impart the good news to his brothers.

'Spurned by my own flesh and blood!' Sebastian mourned. 'Judith, you have much to answer for!'

As she began to smile he grew more serious. 'Shall you mind accompanying them?' he asked. 'I could send their tutor, or one of the servants to go with Dan, but it would not be the same...more of a lesson than a holiday, I believe.'

'You think it will not be the same with me?' she teased. 'My dear Sebastian, I intend to return one gentleman and three small boys to you with their minds quite over-burdened with useless information.'

'What a dear you are!' Sebastian pressed her hand.

'Tell me about Prudence,' she replied. 'Sebastian, what is wrong?'

'Possibly just exhaustion. As you know, she insisted on waiting up for Dan. I sent for the doctor just as a precaution.' He frowned. 'She feels that this pregnancy is unlike any of the others... Believe me, it will be the last! I couldn't go through all this again, and nor could she.' With that he walked away.

Judith was aware of Dan standing stiff and silent beside her. She could guess at his agony of mind. Prudence had been his first and only friend.

'Don't worry!' she said softly. 'We must make allowances for Sebastian's natural concern. Prudence is strong, both in body and in mind. This may be nothing more than the weariness common in the last few weeks before a birth.'

'You may be right.' It was only with an effort that he forced a smile. 'Forgive me, but I can't help feeling anxious about her.'

'Of course you do!' She was searching her mind for further words of comfort when the boys came hurrying towards them, eager with anticipation.

'Are you ready, ma'am?' Thomas asked politely.

'Give me two minutes. I shan't keep you waiting.'

She was as good as her word, and the little party was soon ensconced in the family carriage, and bowling over the cobblestones towards the Strand.

It was Madam Tussaude herself who greeted all visitors to her exhibition. Judith looked at her with interest.

It was difficult to believe that this dowdy-looking person in her old-fashioned high-crowned bonnet with a snowy pleated frill framing her face was in reality an astute business woman.

In prettily accented English she handed them a programme and left them to wander at will through the rows of models on display.

Judith was impressed. The wax figures were so life-like that it was easy to mistake them for living people, were it not for their splendid costumes of an earlier period. These were correct to the last detail, and Judith could only marvel at the amount of research which must have been involved. Madame must be something of a historian.

The kings and queens of both England and France were well represented, together with heroic figures from both countries, and the boys were soon attracted by the military men.

'See! Here is General Wolfe!' Thomas stood before his hero with shining eyes. 'Papa told me all about him. He defeated the French in Canada, you know, at the Plains of Abraham—'

'But he was killed there,' Henry murmured.

'It was still a famous victory,' his brother insisted. 'Don't be such a milksop! I bet you don't even want to see the Chamber of Horrors...'

This statement could not be allowed to go un-challenged and it was swiftly refuted. 'Oh, yes I do! And Crispin will come too!'

'Well, I most certainly do not!' Judith told them firmly. 'I was hoping that Crispin would stay with me. I've been saving one of my best stories for him.'

She feared that scenes of executions would give the little boy nightmares and was tempted to suggest that Henry too should stay with her, but she was too wise to insist. She was well aware of the natural ri-valry between Henry and his elder brother.

'We could hear it first and then go in,' Thomas said hopefully.

'No, this one is especially for Crispin.' She took the little boy's hand in hers and gave it a friendly squeeze. 'It shall be our secret.'

The promise quelled his likely objections to being left out by the others.

'It may be best,' Thomas told her kindly. 'Ladies don't care for things like death-masks and murderers being hanged.'

'Ghoul!' Dan aimed a playful blow at him. 'I won-der if you'll feel so brave when you get inside.' Without more ado he led the boys towards the dread-ful Chamber.

Judith moved away to seat Crispin beside the fig-ure of King Canute.

'Now you shall tell me what you think,' she said. 'This king was very wise, but his courtiers thought he could do anything. He took them to the seashore to prove that they were wrong.'

'How?'

'He made them bring his throne right down to the water. Then he sat down by the waves.'

'What did he do then?'

'Can't you guess?' Judith sprang to her feet and stretched out an imperious arm. 'He told the sea to go back...'

'But that was silly!' Crispin objected. 'If the tide was coming in he'd get his feet wet.'

'He did, but he knew that it would happen. It showed his courtiers that he had no power over it.'

'Did...did he cut their heads off?'

'Oh, no! He was a kindly man, and he ruled England well. He became known as Canute the Great.'

'I'll tell Papa about him. Do you know any more stories?'

'I know one which will make you laugh.' Judith looked about her until she spied the figure which she sought. 'Do you see this man sitting by a fire? What is he doing, do you suppose?'

'Cooking?'

'Not exactly. He was a king, you see, but at one time he was asked to watch some cakes upon the fire.'

'Kings don't do that!'

'This one was in disguise. King Alfred was hiding from his enemies. He started to think how he might outwit them, and he forgot the cakes. When they burned the old lady in the hut was furious.'

'What did she do?' Crispin was chuckling.

'I believe she beat him soundly.'

'Well, he must have cut off her head, Judith.'

'Good gracious, my love! I believe you to be every bit as bloodthirsty as your brothers. If you were king, would you wish to reign over a race of headless people?'

This nonsensical notion made him shout with glee, and he was still laughing when his brothers returned.

They were strangely silent, and Judith raised an enquiring eyebrow as she looked at Dan. He twinkled back at her.

'I think we've had our fill of horrors,' he announced. 'It's time for a treat. What do you boys say to ices at Gunter's?'

This suggestion met with cries of delight, and together he and Judith shepherded their charges towards the exit. As they gained the street again she saw an elderly couple smiling at the little group.

'What a charming couple!' the woman said audibly. 'And so young to be the parents of those three stout boys.'

Judith coloured, but Dan smiled at her.

'Don't take it so hard!' he whispered. 'She did say that you were rather young to be a staid mama.'

'Yes, I know. It is just that…well, I must suppose that it was easy to make the mistake. I am not in my first youth—'

'Nor in your dotage, Judith. Prudence isn't much older than you are yourself. Would you describe her as being at her last prayers?'

'Of course not!' she told him roundly, thankful that he had imagined that her evident confusion arose from the fact that the woman had supposed her to be older than she was. It had not. She'd been startled because she and Dan had been taken for husband and wife.

She peeped up at him, but there was nothing in his expression to indicate that he felt the same. Smiling blandly, he was handing the boys up into the carriage.

At Gunter's, the ices disappeared with lightning speed, but as Dan was about to order more, Judith nudged him.

'No more!' she pleaded in a whisper. 'The boys have had enough excitement for one day. We shall be in trouble if we take them home with upset stomachs.'

He laughed at that. 'In my experience small boys don't suffer in that way.'

'Don't be too sure! You won't be too pleased if Crispin casts up his accounts over your fine breeches.'

Dan shuddered. 'You are right, as always. Let us return our monsters to their loving parents without delay.'

It was a tired but happy party which turned the corner into Mount Street. Then Dan frowned as he saw the carriage standing at the door.

'Brandon?' he murmured in surprise. 'What in the world brings him to Mount Street at this time of day?' He was out of the carriage in a flash.

Judith realised that his anxiety was for Prudence. Was she worse? If the family had been summoned there must be something wrong. It was with a sinking heart that she allowed him to lead her into the salon.

A glance at Sebastian's face told her that her fears were unfounded. His visitor was not the Earl of Brandon, but Amelia, his brother's wife.

With his customary good manners, Sebastian was engaging her in polite conversation, but as she and Dan entered the room, followed by the boys, she saw the look of relief in his eyes.

'Amelia, I think you know Miss Judith Aveton? And Dan, of course? Boys?'

At a nod from their father, his sons advanced towards their aunt and bowed.

'Growing fast, I see. What great creatures they are! Sebastian, you will soon have a full quiver.'

Sebastian chose to ignore her last remark.

'Amelia is come to enquire about Prudence. I was happy to be able to tell her that the doctor is quite satisfied with her progress.'

'I shall go up to her.' The Countess gathered up her shawl and her reticule. 'Such a mistake for a woman in her condition to be giving way to fads and fancies and to be keeping to her bed. I hope to advise her to think better of it.'

'No, ma'am!' Sebastian's tone held a hint of steel. 'Prudence is forbidden all visitors for the moment. I will give her your regards.'

'Good of you!' The Countess glared at him. 'Then I must wonder what this lady is doing here. I understand from her stepmama that Miss Aveton was invited for the purpose of keeping Lady Wentworth company.'

'That is correct.' Sebastian was unfazed by her angry look. 'Judith did so yesterday, and will do so again tomorrow. On this occasion she has been kind enough to accompany the boys upon their outing. Such a relief to me!'

'You might have sent their tutor, or a servant with them, if this...er...gentleman was unable to control them on his own.'

'I might have done so, but I did not. Is your memory failing, Amelia? This is Dan, my adopted son. You cannot have forgotten him?'

An ugly flush stained Amelia's face. It went much against the grain, but she was forced to acknowledge Dan with a brief nod of her head. His own bow was perfection.

Judith felt dismayed. She was in no doubt as to the reason for Amelia's visit. Since it was clearly impossible for Mrs Aveton to invite herself to Mount Street, she must have begged her friend to pay this visit with the promise of a tasty piece of gossip.

Prudence and Amelia were not favourites with each other. To Judith's knowledge the Countess had not called before with enquiries as to the health of her sister-in-law. Amelia was here to spy, and to carry her tales back to Judith's stepmother.

How gratified she must have been when Judith arrived with Dan. It had been the most innocent of outings, but Judith felt consumed with guilt. The look of triumph in Amelia's eyes did nothing to reassure her.

She murmured some fictitious excuse, and was about to hurry away when the door to the salon opened.

'Miss Grantham!' the footman announced.

That lady swept towards Sebastian with all the dignity of her advancing years. Her authoritarian manner put the Countess of Brandon in the shade.

'Well, my boy, how do you go on?' She gave him her hand to kiss.

'I am well, ma'am, as you see.' Sebastian's smile was dazzling as he led her to a chair. 'As for you, I have no need to ask, I think. Your energy puts us all to shame.'

'It ain't what it was, but I'll do for a year or two

yet...' Miss Grantham settled herself more comfortably and looked about her.

'At your age you should take more care, ma'am,' Amelia murmured spitefully. 'I believe I have been misinformed. I heard some talk of your venturing abroad, to Turkey, of all places. Pray assure me that it isn't true. It would be so unwise—'

'Thank'ee for your advice, Amelia. When I want your opinion, I'll ask for it! You ain't been misinformed. I leave within the week.'

'Oh, Miss Grantham, you are making game of us,' Amelia tittered. 'To joke is all very well, but you must not tease your friends.'

'I never joke, and I wasn't aware that you were any friend of mine.' The old lady eyed the Countess coldly. 'Wouldn't do for you, of course. You'd never stand the journey. You're getting fat, Amelia. Keep on eating as you do, and you'll never get out of your chair.'

Judith heard a choking sound behind her, and cast a reproachful look at Dan. She felt that it was time to intervene in what promised to become an ugly scene.

'Won't you tell Miss Grantham and your aunt about the waxworks?' she said to Thomas in desperation. She'd noticed that the boys had retreated behind their father's chair. It was their usual manoeuvre when in the presence of their formidable aunt.

Miss Grantham would have none of it. She beckoned to Thomas.

'Come here, boy,' she ordered. 'Waxworks, indeed! What have you learned today?' Her tone was sharp, but Thomas was encouraged by the twinkle in her eyes.

'The figures looked like real people, ma'am. We saw the kings and queens of England, and of France.'

'Recite them!'

Thomas made a creditable effort and was rewarded with a nod of approval.

'And what did you like best?'

Thomas looked at Judith and was urged on by her smile.

'We went into the Chamber of Horrors, ma'am. We saw Charlotte Corday murdering Marat in his bath.' His look of relish brought a sharp reproof from the Countess.

'Disgusting!' she snapped. 'Sebastian, I wonder that you allow your children to be exposed to such dreadful sights. It is enough to turn their brains.'

'Crispin didn't see them,' Judith said swiftly.

'Miss Aveton, you too have surprised me, though your stepmama assures me that you puzzle her. What could you have been thinking of to behave in such an irresponsible way? I say nothing of your companion's behaviour. Some gentlemen have not the slightest notion of what is proper.'

Judith saw Sebastian's face grow dark. Under his own roof he would not insult a visitor, but she was in no doubt that he was very angry. He opened his mouth to speak, but before he could do so Miss Grantham intervened.

'Stuff!' she said rudely. 'Amelia, you put me out of patience with your nonsense. The child has had a history lesson. Would you have him learn anything other than the truth? The past was not all sweetness and light, however much you care to stick your own head in the sand...'

This was too much for her adversary. Amelia rose

to her feet and, bidding the company farewell in icy tones, she took her leave of them. Sebastian accompanied her to her carriage.

'I have never been so insulted in my life,' she said in awful tones. 'Brandon shall hear of this. Why you tolerate that rude old woman I can't imagine! Her age leads her to believe that she may go beyond the bounds of what is permissible.'

Sebastian smiled down at her. 'You shouldn't have offered your advice,' he said gently.

Amelia tossed her head. 'It was merely out of some small regard for Miss Grantham's safety,' she replied. 'Believe me, I shall not make the same mistake again. The woman should be in Bedlam.'

With that, she stepped into her carriage and was borne away.

When he returned to his elderly guest, Sebastian found her unrepentant.

'Seen her off?' she cried cheerfully. 'Thank the Lord for that! Her face is enough to turn milk sour.' Miss Grantham glanced slyly at her host. 'I hope you ain't expecting me to apologise?'

'Ma'am, I know you better! The thought never crossed my mind.' With all the ease of an old acquaintance Sebastian took a seat beside her and tapped her wrist. 'I should scold you, you wicked creature. You don't change in the least. I believe you take a positive delight in making mischief.'

Miss Grantham beamed at him. 'I do indeed! It is one of the pleasures of old age.' Her impish grin was that of a five-year-old.

'One day you will meet your match,' he warned.

'My dear boy, whoever it is had best be quick about it. I ain't immortal.'

'Does that mean that you are going to die quite soon?'

Judith was amused to see that all three boys had gravitated towards their visitor, recognising a fellow rebel, however unlikely in appearance. It was Henry who had asked the question, and his elder brother nudged him.

'You shouldn't ask that,' he whispered. 'It isn't polite.'

'Nonsense! It's a perfectly sensible question.' The old face, which resembled nothing so much as an ancient walnut, cracked into a smile. 'I meant only that I can't hope to live forever. A great pity! Life is so interesting. Don't you think so?'

'Yes, I do.' Henry thought for a moment. 'The waxworks were interesting, but I didn't like the blood in Marat's bath.'

'It wasn't blood…it was dye,' his brother told him in disgust. 'I know…I tasted it!'

This brought a ripple of amusement from his listeners, and Miss Grantham was moved to congratulate Sebastian.

'You have bred a scientist, I see. Well done, Thomas! Never accept the obvious without question. Always test if you wish to know the truth.'

A lively discussion seemed likely to ensue until Sebastian intervened. 'I think I must send my scientists off to find their supper, ma'am.' Smiling, he dismissed the boys, and with a murmured promise to return, Judith followed them from the room.

Dan too begged to be excused, and Sebastian was left alone with his visitor. He looked at her and raised an eyebrow in amused enquiry.

'Aye, you may well wonder, sir! I've come to get to the bottom of this mystery which you are all keeping to yourselves.'

Chapter Eleven

Sebastian stared at her. 'You know?'

'I know nothing, but I suspect that something is afoot. To me, your brother's face is like an open book. Dissimulation was never a strong point with Perry, as you well know.'

Sebastian smiled as he was forced to acknowledge the truth of this pithy statement.

'As for Elizabeth…she, too, has looked preoccupied. My dear boy, what is wrong? Is it Prudence? Are you keeping something from us?'

'Prudence is well, ma'am, though she has been trying to do too much. At present she must rest, but the doctor is satisfied with her progress.'

'A sensible fellow! I'm glad you took my advice when you engaged him. At least he doesn't believe in this fashionable notion of starving pregnant women and robbing them of their strength.' She was about to assure him that her protegée also washed his hands before examining a patient, and engaged also in the eccentric habit of boiling his instruments before use, but she thought better of it. This was no time to remind Sebastian of those hideous implements.

'Yes, ma'am. I believe him to be the best in London, and I thank you for bringing him to our attention.' Sebastian began to chuckle. 'What does he say to your plan to travel to Turkey?'

'He don't know of it,' Miss Grantham replied in triumph. 'I ain't consulted a member of the medical profession in years, and I don't plan to do so now.'

Sebastian shook his head in mock reproof. Then he began to laugh. 'In spite of what you told my boys, I believe you are an immortal.'

'Don't change the subject, sir. You haven't answered my question.'

'There is something...' he admitted. 'Both Prudence and Elizabeth are worried about Judith.'

'The girl is to wed quite soon, I'm told, to some fashionable preacher?'

'Yes, ma'am.' Sebastian was reluctant to go further.

'Well, marriage ain't a hanging matter, though some would disagree with me. I shouldn't choose a preacher for myself, of course. They are a sanctimonious lot, always happy to get their feet beneath someone else's table... Is that the trouble? Don't they like the fellow? I ain't seen him myself, or heard his rantings.'

Sebastian hid a smile. Miss Grantham's humanist views were well known to him. It was highly unlikely that she would ever listen to a preacher, however fashionable.

'Something like that,' he agreed.

The old eyes rested on his face. 'You ain't the man

to be swayed by female fancies. There's more to this than you will tell.'

'Yes, ma'am. I wish I could be more open with you, but it would not be wise. I have so little information…'

'Is there anything I can do?'

Sebastian shook his head. 'All we can do is to wait.'

'I don't like it,' she said decisively. 'But I shall not trouble you further by poking my nose into matters which you prefer to keep to yourself.'

He looked up then and saw the anxiety in her face. On an impulse he took her hands in his.

'Don't worry!' he said gently. 'All will be well. You need have no fears about Elizabeth, or any of us.'

He could see that her lips were trembling. Then she straightened her back.

'I should hope not!' she announced with some asperity. 'Now, sir, I must go. Perry and Elizabeth brought me to you, and now they shall take me home. You will give my love to Prudence?'

'Won't you go up to her?' he suggested. 'She is so fond of you, and will be sorry not to see you.'

'Flatterer!' Miss Grantham hesitated. 'It will not tire her if I stay for just a moment?'

'Of course not!' He led her through the hall and up the staircase, a hand outstretched to help her if she found the climb too much.

She had no need of it. Miss Grantham ate sparingly and was a firm believer in the value of walking as an exercise. There was surprising strength in the thin, wiry figure and she marched along beside him without a pause to catch her breath.

She was greeted by a cry of pleasure from Prudence, and was persuaded to sit down for a brief five minutes.

Then Miss Grantham reappeared and joined Sebastian in the hall.

'Nothing to worry about there!' she said with satisfaction. 'Only your precious mystery need concern you now,' She began to draw on her gloves. 'Sebastian, you will take care?'

'Certainly, ma'am.'

'And you might look to Dan. He's changed in these past years.'

Sebastian could only marvel at her shrewdness. Dan had been in her company for so short a time, and they had barely exchanged a word.

'You ain't thinking of playing Cupid, are you?'

Sebastian laughed. 'I'm not the build to be a cherub, ma'am. Look about you! Do you see a bow and arrow?' He bent and kissed the withered cheek.

She pushed him away, but he could see that she was pleased. Then Perry and Elizabeth came towards them.

'There you are, my dears! Come, we must make haste! I have still to pack my books and papers...'

Perry began to tease her. 'And don't forget a sharp knife, Aunt. In a month or two you will be dining on camel and yaks' tails.'

'Yaks? In Turkey? Bless me, the man is totally uneducated. Yaks, my dear Perry, are found only in Tibet.' With this quelling statement Miss Grantham allowed herself to be led away.

Sebastian returned upstairs to find his wife convulsed with laughter.

'Oh, my dear!' she gasped. 'I have been missing

all the fun. Judith tells me that Amelia was well and truly routed.'

'Wicked creature!' he said fondly. 'Where is your spirit of Christian charity?'

'I haven't one where Amelia is concerned. Dear Miss Grantham! Is she not a treasure?'

'She is a wise old woman. What's more, my love, she found you looking well. You must not spoil it. Will you dine up here this evening?'

'Only if you will join me.' Prudence looked up at him, her eyes aglow with love.

'Would you have me ignore my duties as a host?'

'Judith will not mind. She and Dan have always so much to say to one another. They are fast friends, just as we are ourselves.'

Sebastian dropped a kiss upon her hair. Then he looked at Judith. 'Shall you mind, my dear?'

'Not at all!' It wasn't strictly true. Judith had sensed a growing estrangement between herself and Dan. Was it her imagination, or did he seem to be growing ever more distant? She racked her mind to find an answer.

Their outing with the boys had been enjoyable. She could think of nothing that she might have done or said which might account for his strange reserve.

It didn't matter now, she thought sadly. The Countess would lose no time in carrying her tale to Mrs Aveton, and then she would be summoned home.

Whilst she dressed for dinner, she tried to fight off a growing feeling of depression.

In an effort to raise her spirits Bessie had laid out a gown in the softest shade of rose-pink muslin, with appliqué at the hem.

'Bessie, I am not attending a ball,' she protested.

'I should think not, miss. Otherwise, you might have worn the yellow brocade.'

'Great heavens, you did not pack that too?'

'No, I didn't!' her maid said firmly. 'I packed only those which were suitable for wear at home. Now, miss, do give over with your arguments, or you'll be late for dinner.'

Judith submitted to the ministrations of her maid without further protest, though she refused the offer of an attempt to train her fine soft hair into a high knot, with ringlets arranged to frame her face.

'Bessie, you know it is a waste of time,' she laughed. 'My hair will be down about my ears before I reach the dining-room.'

'Very well, miss. At least the bandeau matches your gown, and you do look a picture, if I do say so myself.'

'You'll turn my head with your nonsense,' Judith predicted darkly. 'I shan't be late abed tonight, but you need not wait up for me.'

'As if I wouldn't, Miss Judith.' Bessie hid a secret smile. Nothing would have persuaded her to retire before her young mistress. Besides, she had great hopes of the coming dinner *à deux*. A look at Judith's face would tell her how it had gone.

Judith found Dan waiting for her in the salon. The door was slightly ajar, and her ribbon-tied silk sandals made no sound upon the carpet.

'Dan?'

He turned, caught off guard, and his eyes glowed as he looked at her. That look was quickly banished, but it was enough to make her heart beat faster. Had she imagined it?

He gave her a smile which held no more than a friendly welcome.

'Judith, you are in famous looks tonight. I had thought that our outing might have tired you.'

'No, no!' she protested. 'It was the greatest fun. How much the boys enjoyed it!'

'Perhaps we should do it again. Have you any ideas? There are military reviews in the Park, balloon ascents, firework displays and Astley's Royal Amphitheatre, all guaranteed to delight the heart of any boy…'

'And mine, too, I make no doubt.'

'I was sure of it,' he grinned. 'At Astley's you may see a spectacular piece called *The Flight of the Saracens*, unless you prefer *Make Way for Liberty*. Confess it, they sound irresistible…'

Judith returned his smile. 'The boys are keen to go there. I have had a full description of the sawdust ring in which John Astley and his wife show off their equestrian skills.'

'It could be a mistake,' he teased. 'I foresee broken bones when Thomas and Henry return to Cheshire. Thank heavens they have no ponies here, or we should be treated to similar attempts at acrobatics.'

At the sound of the gong he took her arm and led her into the dining-room. Two of the leaves had been removed from the table to provide a more intimate setting, and the light from a single candelabra shone softly upon fine silver and antique glass.

Judith gave a sigh of pleasure as she looked about her. Tonight this lovely room, with its panelled walls, seemed like a haven of peace. Just for once she would be self-indulgent, revelling in the prospect of a precious evening alone with the man she loved.

Sebastian's chef was a master of his craft, but Judith was in a dreamlike state, unaware of what she was eating. She nibbled at a tiny lobster vol-au-vent and allowed herself to be helped to a serving of broiled fowl, but she waved aside the preserved goose, the dish of ham in madeira sauce, a fine serpent of mutton, and the chef's speciality, neats' tongues dressed to a jealously guarded recipe.

'My dear Judith, you will cause the wizard in the kitchen to pack his bags if you spurn his efforts,' Dan protested. 'You haven't eaten enough to keep a bird alive.'

'I'm sorry, I wasn't thinking.' Judith collected her wandering thoughts. 'The syllabub looks delicious, and so do the fruit jellies.' She took a little of both dishes, hoping to restore herself to favour with the god below stairs.

Dan signalled to the butler to replenish her glass.

'No, thank you!' She laid her hand across the rim.

'Nonsense, it will do you good! Red wine, you know, is said to be the answer to all ills.' He removed her hand, and watched as the ruby liquid flowed.

Judith laughed. 'Not if it results in a dreadful headache,' she protested.

'Two glasses cannot hurt you.'

'But, Dan, I shall be chattering like a monkey.'

'It will be a change. You have been quiet tonight.'

'Have I? I beg your pardon. I didn't mean to be a dull companion.'

'You are never that, my best of friends, but you have not spoken for the past ten minutes.'

'Forgive me! It is just that…well…I was enjoying the peace in this lovely restful room.'

'Is peace so rare with you, my dear?'

'It has been,' she admitted. 'Life at home is not always pleasant.'

He sat back then, his eyes intent upon her face.

'I would describe that as the understatement of the year, Judith. I can't think how you have survived your life with Mrs Aveton. I had thought you must have married long ago. Were you never tempted?'

'No!' she said briefly. 'You will wish to enjoy your port and a cigar. I told Bessie that I should not be late tonight. Will you excuse me if I leave you now?'

'No, I will not! Must you run away? I don't want port and I don't want a cigar. What I do want is to talk to you. Shall we go into the salon?'

Judith glanced at the butler, and at the impassive faces of the footmen. To refuse might lead to an undignified argument before the servants. In silence she preceded him from the room.

'Cross with me?' he asked lightly.

'Of course not!' Judith felt uneasy. She had been foolish to bring up the subject of Mrs Aveton. Her face clouded. By tomorrow that lady would be in full possession of the news that Judith had accompanied Dan to Madame Tussaud's with no other members of the family present except for Sebastian's boys.

Then, unwittingly, Dan added to her worries.

'I'm still waiting for your decision,' he said.

'About what?'

'About your next expedition. Is it to be to Astley's, to the fireworks, or to the balloon ascent?'

A lump came to Judith's throat. 'I doubt if I shall be here,' she whispered in choked tones.

'Why ever not? I thought that the dragon had given you permission to stay for several days.'

'That was before she knew that you were likely to return. Oh, Dan, don't you see? The Countess will tell her. Then I shall be summoned home.'

'I think you haven't reckoned with Sebastian.'

'It won't make any difference. If she insists he can do nothing. Besides, I feel so guilty as it is...' A slow tear trickled down her cheek.

'Ah, don't!'

Neither of them seemed to move, but suddenly she was in his arms, her cheek pressed to his coat. Through the fine fabric she could feel the pounding of his heart, and it seemed as if, at last, her dearest wish was to be granted. Now he would tell her that his affections were unchanged, and he still loved her.

She lifted her face to his, longing for the kiss that would wipe away all memory of those years of loss and desolation. Her heart was in her eyes as she looked at him, but he made no move to seek her mouth.

Gently he placed his hands upon her shoulders, and held her away.

'I can't bear to see you so distressed,' he murmured. 'Trust Sebastian, Judith! He won't allow you to be taken away so soon.'

She couldn't have been more stunned if he had struck her. She'd have preferred it. A blow would have sent her spinning into oblivion, unaware of the agony of mind which now possessed her.

She had thrown herself at him and been rejected. Her passionate embrace had been so warm that he must have known that she was offering her heart. He had refused it. Judith felt that she wanted to die. She grew so pale that he helped her to a chair. She did not notice that he too was trembling.

His anguish matched her own. Nothing in his previous life had caused him so much pain as that bleak refusal to tell her of his love, but he dared not. Her safety must be his sole concern.

In silence he poured out a glass of brandy. 'You are upset!' he murmured. 'You had best drink this.'

She waved it away and stumbled to her feet. Dan reached out a hand to steady her, but she drew back sharply.

'Please...don't touch me!' The despairing cry cut him to the heart, but Judith fled before he could reply.

She wanted to run and to hide herself away, but her limbs were leaden. To climb the staircase felt like wading through a morass which tugged her back with every step, but she reached her room at last.

As the door opened, Bessie sprang to her feet expectantly. Then she saw Judith's face.

'Why, miss, whatever is it? Here, you had best sit down. You look as if you've seen a ghost.'

Judith did not speak. She *had* seen a ghost, but it was a ghost of the past which had vanished, never to return. She sat on the edge of her bed, staring into space. Now she could no longer hope, and only the black void of her future lay before her.

It was all too much for Bessie. She gathered her mistress in her arms, rocking back and forth and crooning gently to Judith as if she'd been a child.

'There, don't take on!' she murmured. 'Things always look bad at night. You'll feel better in the morning.'

The love and sympathy in her voice was Judith's undoing. The tears came then, and she wept as if her heart would break.

'I can't bear it!' she cried in anguish. 'Oh, Bessie, if you only knew…'

Wisely, Bessie did not question her. There was no need. Something had gone wrong between her young mistress and the man she loved, but there was nothing she could do to put matters right. All she could offer now was comfort.

'Let's get you into bed,' she murmured. 'Then you shall have a drink of milk and honey to send you off to sleep.' She drew Judith to her feet, and began to undress her. Then she settled the unresisting figure into a chair, and began to brush her hair.

The long, slow strokes were soothing, and Judith closed her eyes. Then Bessie laid aside the brush and placed a hand on either side of Judith's temples, moving her fingers in circles at each end of her brow. It was Bessie's favourite remedy for a pounding headache.

'Better?' she asked.

Judith nodded.

'Well, then, drink your hot milk, and don't you dare get up for breakfast in the morning. You are living on your nerves, Miss Judith, and it won't do. Next thing we'll have you falling sick, and where will you be then?'

'In bed, I expect.' Judith managed a feeble smile.

'It's no joke!' Bessie insisted. 'You won't wish to worry Lady Wentworth. I thought you'd come to cheer her up. You won't do that if you go about like that there Sarah Siddons…!'

Judith caught her hand and looked at her with fond affection.

'Don't scold!' she begged. 'I won't behave like a tragedy queen.'

Bessie's expression softened. 'I know that, miss. You keep up a brave front. It's only me as knows…well, I won't say more.' She blew out the candles, and crept softly from the room, leaving her mistress to stare into the dark until nature won the day and emotional exhaustion sent her off to sleep.

Below, in the salon, Dan was sitting by the dying embers of the fire. He'd refused the footman's offer to build it up, or to replace the candles which were now guttering in their sockets.

The shadows matched his mood. Judith's unhappiness had shaken him to the very core of his being, and his endurance had reached its limit. Nothing in the world was worth this misery. Beside it, his own stiff-necked pride was meaningless. He cursed himself for a selfish prig. Judith did not care about her fortune, and he knew now that she loved him. Was it right to allow his own principles to stand in the way of their happiness? Suddenly it seemed like nothing more than vanity.

He reached a decision at last. Tomorrow he would ask Sebastian to release him from his promise. If he and Judith were to marry quickly, she would no longer be in danger.

He stubbed out the butt of his cigar. He'd picked up the habit of smoking the rolled tobacco leaves whilst in the West Indies, and he preferred it to the more fashionable custom of taking snuff.

Suddenly, his feelings of depression vanished. He'd been a fool not to think of the obvious solution before. With Judith's fortune out of reach, the avaricious parson would be forced to look elsewhere.

As for himself? Let the world accuse him of marrying for money. It wouldn't even be a nine-day

wonder. The *ton* would see him as no better or no
worse than any other bachelor on the look-out for a
rich wife. Was not matchmaking the main objective
during the coming Season?

It was his own pride which had caused him to
reject the notion. Now it was high time that he considered Judith rather than himself. Neither of them
cared for the opinion of Polite Society, and in time
his own talent would be recognised.

Lost in thought, he strolled across the hall.
Tomorrow he would ask Sebastian how to procure a
special licence. There was still a little worm of doubt
in his mind. Could he persuade Judith to accept him?
And even if she did, would she agree to this hasty
marriage? She might reject all notion of such a hole-
and-corner affair, but he dared not wait. Sebastian
had warned him what might happen if Judith tried to
break off her engagement to Charles Truscott.

Then he noticed a streak of light beneath the library door. Sebastian must be reading late. He tapped
a brief tattoo and entered the room.

Then he paused. Sebastian wasn't alone. Seated
opposite him was the brawny figure of the Bow
Street Runner.

The man gave Dan a brief nod of recognition and
then fell silent.

'It's all right, Babb! You may continue to speak
freely. I have no secrets from my adopted son.'
Sebastian signalled to Dan to take a seat.

'Well, my lord, as I was saying…our quarry is on
the move again. Today he went back to the rookery
in St Giles, and spent the afternoon drinking with
Margrave in a gin shop.'

'So they are friends?' Sebastian frowned.

'It would appear so. I didn't see the other three today.'

'Were you able to get close to him…to hear?'

'No, my lord. Margrave knows me, and he's as wary as a cat. I thought you wouldn't wish him to suspect that there was anything in the wind, so I kept out of sight.'

'But you must have got some impression? Were they quarrelling?'

'Thick as thieves, they were! Laughing and joking for three hours… Then Truscott left. I followed him to Seven Dials. He's there for the night, as usual, I believe, so I came to you.'

'Quite right! You must follow him again tomorrow. Do you need more men?'

'Not for the moment, sir. I'll let you know. Now I'll be off, if I'm to make an early start tomorrow.'

Dan waited until the door had closed behind him.

'What's happening, Sebastian?'

'I don't know, but I don't like it…'

'Nor do I. We are getting nowhere. It's all much too slow. Judith will wed that creature before we know it.'

'My dear boy, I did counsel patience. Let us wait for another day or two…'

'I can't!' Dan told him flatly. 'I've made up my mind. I wonder that I didn't think of it before. If I wed Judith now…tomorrow…she will be safe.'

Sebastian shook his head. 'It isn't the answer, Dan. I warned you of the danger. Suppose that something should go wrong?'

'How could it? We could leave this house in secret, and be wed within the hour. How can I get a special licence?'

'That may prove to be the least of your problems,' Sebastian said deliberately. 'Have you spoken to Judith of this plan?'

Dan coloured. 'No, I haven't, but, well, I don't think she's indifferent to me. I thought so at first, especially as she had agreed to marry Truscott, but now I am certain that her affections have not changed.'

'You may be right, but how will you explain to her the need for this sudden haste?'

'I'll tell her the truth about Truscott.'

'And will she believe you? You have no proof of your suspicions.'

'Does it matter?' Dan cried impatiently. 'If she loves me she'll agree to wed me, whenever and however.'

'I wish you'd reconsider.' Sebastian rose from his chair and began to pace the room. 'Are you quite sure that this is what you want? There is still the matter of Judith's fortune...'

Dan coloured. 'You guessed that it was the stumbling block? We haven't discussed it, you and I.'

'There was no need. I know you well, my boy. Can you stomach the notion of being dependent on your wife?' His words were cruel, but Sebastian was desperate to prevent what he considered to be an act of folly.

Dan's colour deepened. 'That's hitting below the belt,' he said with dignity. 'If you must know, I'm ashamed of my own pride. I've let it stand in the way for much too long. Now Judith's safety must come first.'

'This is not the way to ensure it. Truscott must be taken beforehand.'

'I've almost given up hope of that. Sebastian, I hate to go against your wishes, but I've quite made up my mind.'

'Very well. Bishop Henderson will provide you with a special licence. I'll give you his address.' He scribbled a few lines on a card. 'Now, if you'll excuse me, I must go up to Prudence.'

'You'll say nothing to her?' Dan's face was anxious.

'Certainly not, and nor will you! The only advice I'll give you now is to keep this plan to yourself.' Sebastian looked grave as he walked away.

Chapter Twelve

Dan was up betimes next day, but obtaining the licence was not as easy as he had at first supposed.

The bishop was not receiving visitors before morning service, and later he had a number of appointments. The day was well advanced before Dan was admitted to his presence.

Another hour passed as he was well catechised as to the reasons for his unusual request. The bishop was adamant that he would issue no licence in aid of an elopement.

'No, my lord bishop. It is nothing like that, I assure you. It is just that…well, the matter is urgent.'

Bishop Henderson looked at Dan's troubled face, and sighed. He had long since ceased to marvel at the tangles into which young people fell so readily. At last he reached into a drawer and drew out a form.

'I may tell you, sir, that were it not for the fact that you are connected to Lord Wentworth I should have no hesitation in refusing you. Does his lordship know of this?'

'He does, Your Grace. I spoke to him last night. It was he who suggested that I came to you.'

This succeeded in disposing of any further argument, and when Dan hurried back to Mount Street he had the precious piece of paper safely in his pocket.

To his chagrin he found that for the rest of the day it was impossible to get Judith to himself.

Perry and Elizabeth were to dine at home that evening, and Prudence, much rested, had elected to join the family party for their meal.

Dan glanced at Sebastian in despair, but the bland face told him nothing. Sebastian made no enquiries as to the success of his adopted son's mission, whilst Judith herself seemed determined to avoid all his efforts to speak to her alone.

When the ladies retired to the salon, Dan was impatient to follow them. The licence was burning a hole in his pocket, and he paid only scant attention to his two companions. He had eaten nothing.

Perry passed the port, but Dan waved it away.

'Sickening for something, Dan? Great heavens, man, when *you* lose your appetite it must be serious. You were always a famous trencherman...' Perry grinned at him.

Even Sebastian smiled. 'It's too early in the season for raspberry tart. When I first met Dan I suspected that he had hollow legs. He demolished two full tarts on our first day together. Even after that there was no way of filling him.'

Dan responded to the teasing with a reluctant smile, but he couldn't hide his impatience to be done with the custom of the gentlemen lingering in the dining-room after their evening meal.

'You'll have to watch him, Seb, old chap,' Perry

murmured slyly. 'Our Dan is becoming quite a ladies' man.'

Goaded beyond endurance, Dan was tempted to make a sharp retort, but a look from Sebastian stopped him.

'Dan is right,' his lordship murmured. 'We had best join the ladies. It grows late, and Prudence must not overtax her strength.'

Dan shot him a look of gratitude, but his optimism was short-lived. When Prudence decided to retire, Judith went with her. He was forced to spend another sleepless night wondering how he might manage to approach her and tell her of his plans.

On the following day it seemed that everything conspired against him. It was Henry's birthday, and he had promised the lad a gift of a Pedestrian Curricle. This interesting machine consisted of two wheels with a saddle slung between them. The rider propelled it forward with his feet until he attained sufficient speed. Then he lifted them and coasted for as long as possible.

Prudence had at first protested that Henry was too young to manage this alarming vehicle, but she had been overridden by a chorus of male voices. Now Dan and Perry were to take the boys in search of Henry's birthday gift.

The celebration continued with a visit to the New Mint which boasted gas lighting and a fascinating collection of steam engines. They were even allowed to watch the stamping of the coins, but by the time they returned to Mount Street the day was gone.

Overwhelmed with expressions of youthful thanks, Dan went up to change for dinner.

He would wait no longer. Tonight, he vowed, he would speak to Judith, if it meant asking her for a private interview within hearing of the rest of the family.

He couldn't hope that she would be allowed to remain with Prudence for much longer, although her fears that she would have been summoned home on the previous day had proved unfounded. He wondered at that. The Countess must, by now, have informed Mrs Aveton that he had returned and was squiring Judith about the town. It seemed strange that his old enemy should prove to be so unexpectedly compliant.

This was far from true. Mrs Aveton had been furious, but mindful of Truscott's wishes she had not sent for Judith.

Again Dan struggled through what seemed to him to be an interminable meal. He made a valiant effort to take part in the usual lively conversation, aware that Judith too was doing her best to play her part. Pale but composed, she confined most of her attention to the ladies, refusing to meet his eyes.

Then Sebastian took pity on him. When the ladies had left them he cut short Perry's enjoyment of the port with the laughing excuse that Prudence had taken him to task on the previous evening.

As he left the dining-room he drew Dan aside.

'Are you still of the same mind?' he murmured.

Dan nodded.

'Then best get it over with. You will let me know how you go on?' With that he led his companions into the salon.

Scarcely able to contain his eagerness, Dan made his way to Judith's side.

'I must speak to you alone,' he murmured.

At first she seemed not to have heard him, but Sebastian had drawn the others to the far side of the room, and he was able to repeat his words.

Judith flushed painfully and shook her head. Then, with a muttered excuse, she moved away.

'Judith, my dear, I wonder if you'd mind? Prudence has left her vinaigrette upstairs. I'm sure you will know where to find it.' Ignoring his wife's astonished look, Sebastian smiled at their guest.

As Judith hurried away, he gave Dan an imperceptible signal, and turned back to the others.

Dan needed no second urging. He followed Judith from the room, and caught her at the foot of the stairs.

'Please, I beg of you! Won't you listen to me for a moment?' He took her arm and attempted to lead her back into the dining-room.

Judith tried to pull away. 'No!' she cried in desperation. 'Please leave me alone!'

'Not until you've heard me out.'

'Very well, then.' Judith was aware of the footman standing in the hall. The man's face was wooden, but the story of an undignified struggle would, she knew, be a source of gossip in the servants' hall.

She felt very angry, and when he closed the door behind him, she rounded on Dan with blazing eyes.

'Must you put me in this position?' she asked coldly. 'I thought I had made my wishes clear. I won't listen to you, Dan. I'm tired of being worried and hounded and driven to distraction. Everyone knows what is best for me, with the apparent exception of myself.'

Dan tried to take her hand, but she drew away.

'Please don't presume upon our friendship. Say what you have to say, and let me go.'

'Won't you sit down?' Dan drew a chair towards her, but she turned her back on him, standing very stiff and straight.

'You aren't making this easy,' he murmured. 'I'm asking you to marry me.'

She spun round then, and he thought he had never seen her look so angry.

'How dare you?' she cried. 'Must you offer for me out of pity?'

It was Dan's turn to lose his temper. 'Do you think so little of me? I'm asking you because I love you.'

'You have a curious way of showing it. I don't believe you—'

'But you must.' He drew the licence from his pocket. 'Judith, we could be wed tomorrow, if only you will have me.'

Her eyes fell upon the paper. 'A special licence? You surprise me! Why this sudden haste? Since you returned I've seen no sign that your affections are unchanged.'

Dan stood as if turned to stone. Sebastian's prediction had come true. It would be impossible to explain his actions with any hope of success.

'There were reasons,' he said lamely. 'I mean...there was your fortune to consider.'

'I still have it.'

'And, Judith, I couldn't be sure that you still cared for me. You were betrothed to Truscott.'

'You didn't ask.' Her voice was almost inaudible.

'I'm asking now. Oh, my dear, tell me that you won't marry him!'

'So that's it! You'll have your way, no matter

what. This is unworthy of you, Dan. Who are you to judge Charles Truscott? He, at least, does not pretend to a passion which he does not feel.'

'Then you won't change your mind?' Dan was shaken by her fury. Her face was set, and to go on would only make matters worse. He made a last despairing effort. 'You are mistaken, Judith. I love you more than life itself. Will you condemn yourself to a life of misery with that creature?'

'Stop! I'll hear no more of this! How dare you presume to criticise the man I am to marry? Charles is good, and kind, and I want to marry him. I do! I do!' Bursting into tears, she fled from the room.

Dan sat down suddenly, feeling that the void had opened beneath his feet. He'd played his part too well. Judith didn't believe that he loved her, and now he'd never be able to convince her. She thought him merely mean and spiteful.

If only he'd been able to offer her some proof of Truscott's villainy. He had none, and that was the truth of it.

In an agony of mind he cursed Truscott, himself, the Bow Street Runner, and the cruel fate which had kept him away from England for so long.

Now he had lost his only love for ever. He buried his face in his hands.

He hadn't moved when Sebastian came to find him some time later. Dan felt a sympathetic hand upon his shoulder.

'Well?' Sebastian asked.

'She won't have me. I can't believe it! I was so sure that she still loved me.'

'Don't give up hope, old chap. This may be for the best.'

'Oh, I know you warned me. I've only made matters worse. She said that I'd offered for her out of pity and…and an unreasonable dislike of Truscott. She won't hear a word against him. What could I say to her? Now she's more determined than ever to marry him.'

'Judith isn't married yet. Will you come back to the ladies, Dan? Prudence has been wondering where you are.'

Dan shook his head. 'Will you make my excuses? I can't face Judith just at present.'

'Judith has retired. She claimed to have the headache.' Sebastian rose and led his companion back into the salon.

Judith had not lied. At that moment she was lying on her bed with her hands pressed to her temples in a vain attempt to dull the pain.

The memory of Dan's astonishing behaviour only made it worse. Two days ago he had rejected her, thrusting her away when he must have known how much she loved him. He hadn't even tried to kiss her.

Now it seemed that she was to fall into his arms in simple gratitude for being rescued from a marriage of which he disapproved.

The sight of the special licence had disgusted her. There could be no reason for such unseemly haste unless he had determined to get his hands upon her fortune. His plan to interest Admiral Nelson in his drawings had met with no success. Perhaps he had given up all hope of a promising career.

In her heart she knew that it wasn't true. Dan cared

nothing for her money, and he still believed in his own talent.

If only he'd told her of his love when she'd thrown herself into his arms. She would have believed him then, but the pain of rejection was still with her.

He didn't return her affection, though tonight he'd tried to convince her. She closed her eyes in pain. It had been the coldest of proposals. Dan had made no attempt to crush her to his breast and silence all her objections with his lips against her own.

Instead he'd been at pains to convince her of her own folly, her lack of judgment in accepting Charles Truscott. She'd have no more of it. Reaching out, she rang her bell for Bessie.

'I'd like you to pack my things without delay,' she said.

'Tonight, Miss Judith?' Bessie looked her surprise.

'Tonight, or first thing in the morning. I must leave tomorrow.'

'But, miss, I thought you was to stay? Won't Lady Wentworth think it strange of you to rush away?'

'Don't argue with me, Bessie! Her ladyship won't find it strange at all since the date of my marriage is so close. There must be a thousand things to do.'

Bessie sniffed. 'I'll pack tomorrow, then.' As she undressed her mistress she made her disapproval clear, but Judith ignored her mutterings.

She'd made her decision to leave and she would stand by it. Prudence would be disappointed, but she would understand. After all, this visit was intended to be short. Judith prayed only that she might be allowed to leave the house without the need to bid farewell to Dan. If that could be managed she would be wed before they met again, and safe from further persuasion. She felt that she could take no more.

Her wish was granted. Sebastian had foreseen that she would wish to go, and had sent Dan off on some errand of his own. He had also warned Prudence that she must take Judith's probable departure with good grace.

Prudence obeyed him, though it went much against the grain. She held out her arms to Judith and clasped her friend in a warm embrace.

'My dear, I'm sorry that I shan't be with you on your wedding day,' she murmured. 'I wonder...shall you like Sebastian to give you away? Mrs Aveton hinted at it when he came to fetch you.'

Judith felt a twinge of panic. The suggestion brought the date of her marriage so much closer. Then Sebastian smiled, and she felt reassured.

'That would be kind,' she said. 'It is good of you. I have no male relatives, you see.'

'It will be a pleasure.' Sebastian bowed, though he felt that the lie must choke him. He still hoped that Truscott would be unmasked. If not, Judith must be assured of his support. He couldn't shake off a sense of deep foreboding, but his worries were not apparent as he settled Judith into the family carriage.

Judith swallowed a lump in her throat as she was borne away. Parting with her friends had not been easy. When she saw them again she would be Charles Truscott's wife.

This fact was recalled to her attention by Mrs Aveton. Summoned to that lady's presence, she was left in no doubt of her stepmother's opinion of her conduct.

'Of all the sly, deceitful creatures, you must be the worst!' the older woman shouted. 'Did you imagine that I should not hear of your disgraceful behaviour?'

'Disgraceful, ma'am? I am not aware of it.'

'How else would you describe yourself? Don't play the innocent with me! Will you deny that you spent the day alone with that…that pauper?'

'We weren't alone, ma'am. We had three children with us… Besides, I am not yet wed.'

'Nor likely to be, if Mr Truscott hears of this. What will he say, I wonder, to the idea of you and your old paramour whispering and making sheep's eyes at each other in dark corners?'

'I must hope, ma'am, that his mind is rather more elevated than your own.'

'Why, you impudent baggage! How dare you speak to me like that?' A dark flush stained Mrs Aveton's face, mottling her nose and cheeks with dull red. 'When I think of what you owe to me, bringing you up as one of my own!'

Judith's patience snapped. Tall and straight, she eyed her stepmother with contempt.

'I owe you nothing, ma'am, except for some plain speaking. Since my father died, you've done your best to make my life a misery. I haven't forgotten all I've suffered at your hands. I thank heavens that it is almost at an end. Carry your tales to Mr Truscott if you wish. It will make no difference. Wed to him or not, I fully intend to leave this house.'

Mrs Aveton knew that she had gone too far.

'You…you can't do that,' she said uncertainly.

'Why not? I now have the money to set up an establishment of my own.'

A snort of disbelief greeted this remark.

'Nonsense! Young women do not live alone. It would cause a scandal!'

Judith smiled, but there was no amusement in her eyes. 'Do you suppose that gossip would worry me? I have no fears of your mischief-making in that direction. Scandal harms only those who care for the opinion of Polite Society. I do not.'

Her words struck a chill in Mrs Aveton's heart. Her hopes of a share in Judith's fortune were disappearing fast, and Truscott would be furious. If the truth were known, she was a little afraid of him.

'You misunderstand me,' she said more calmly. 'I was thinking only of your future happiness.'

'Since when?' Judith turned on her heel and left the room.

Her mood had changed completely and she now felt much more cheerful. When confronted, Mrs Aveton had collapsed like a pricked balloon. Perhaps that was true of all such bullies. For the first time, Judith felt in full command of herself. She should have spoken out years ago.

With a fine disregard of all depredations to her trousseau, she decided to wear her most expensive gown that evening, and she made no objection when Bessie offered to dress her hair in the latest and most fashionable style.

It was a subdued Mrs Aveton who was moved to compliment her upon her appearance. Judith nodded an acknowledgment, but she wanted to laugh. No such praise had ever come her way before.

The Aveton girls gazed at their mother in astonishment, but she bid them sharply to get on with their meal. Then she turned to Judith.

'Did you hear from the Reverend Truscott whilst you were at Mount Street?' she enquired.

'No, ma'am. He sent no messages here?'

Mrs Aveton shook her head. Then she forced a smile. 'I think we need have no fears about him, Judith. With sickness it is never possible to predict the course of a disease with any certainty. It is much to his credit that he refuses to leave his mother's bedside. For the present, his thoughts will be for her alone.'

'As they must be, ma'am. I offered to go with him, but he wouldn't hear of it.'

Mrs Aveton was unsurprised by this news. Of a naturally suspicious mind, she'd never trusted her accomplice. What fool would believe his story? Truscott was not the man to waste his sympathy on the sick.

This cock-and-bull tale about his mother's illness was pure fiction. Only a guileless creature like her stepdaughter would be taken in by it. Truscott was up to something, and she would have given much to know the truth of it. Whatever his activities, she was convinced that they would not bear inspection. What a comfort it would be to have some hold over him...some threat which she might use to force him into keeping his part of their bargain.

There was little likelihood of that. The preacher had always evaded her attempts to learn anything of his past life. Now she found herself wondering as to his present dealings.

She wasn't overly concerned. The avarice of the Reverend Charles fully matched her own. He'd surprised her with his willingness to leave his bride-to-be in these few days before their marriage, and with his obvious wish for Judith to remove herself to Mount Street, but he must have good reasons. Charles Truscott took no decisions without giving them careful thought.

She was right. Three days earlier the preacher had returned to the house in Seven Dials to consider all the options open to him. After much deliberation he had hit upon the solution to his problems.

Margrave was the main danger. The forger was the brains behind the plot against him. He must be dealt with first. Cut off the head of a venomous snake and the writhing body of the reptile could do no further harm. Deprived of Margrave's leadership, Nellie and her friends would present no problem. He could deal with them at his own leisure.

And he would handle all these matters himself. His last attempt to dispose of his enemies had convinced him that he could trust no one to follow out his orders.

First, he must get close to Margrave. It wouldn't be easy. The man was as wily as a fox, and as wary.

Truscott lay upon his bed for hours, until the answer came to him. Then a grim smile played about his lips as he remembered the old adage: 'divide and rule' was excellent advice. He would follow it without delay.

He threw back the coverlet and called to Nan to fetch his clothing.

Her reddened eyes told him that she had been weeping. He'd used her cruelly the previous night, but she had given him no pleasure. She might have been a block of wood for all the response she offered.

God, but he was tiring of her constant whining, and the endless questions about her brothers. She'd have to go. He'd see to it before the week was out, but now he had other matters to attend.

Wrapping his cloak about him, and with a slouch hat pulled well down to hide his face, he set off for the parish of St Giles.

His mother's house was empty, but he knew where to find her. Turning into the nearest gin shop, he saw her sitting in the corner with her friends. As he had expected, Margrave was one of the party.

'This is an unexpected pleasure, Charlie.' The forger gave him a sly smile.

'I promised, didn't I?' Truscott pulled out a leather purse and laid it on the table.

Nellie's claw-like hands reached out, and then she gave a little yelp of pain as Margrave rapped her across the knuckles with his cane.

'Don't be greedy, Nellie!' he reproved. 'I'll take charge of that.'

'There's plenty for all, and more where that came from,' Truscott told him carelessly.

'Thought it over, have you?' the forger jeered. 'Very wise! I never thought you a fool.'

'I'm not! I don't waste my time bemoaning anything I can't change.'

'Splendid! Nellie, I must congratulate you upon your son's good sense.' Margrave tipped out the contents of the purse. Then his lips pursed and he shook his head. 'A modest offering, I fear. You must do better than this.'

'I'm not such a fool as to carry gold about me in

this place. If you want more you'll have to come with me to fetch it.'

Margrave laughed in his face. 'To Seven Dials? Charlie, do you take me for a plucked 'un? I'd as soon walk through the gates of hell as go to your house alone.'

'I shouldn't ask it of you. I leave no money there. It's safest at the church. There's always a tidy sum from the collections.'

Margrave leaned back in his chair, and eyed Truscott with great deliberation. Then he shook his head.

'I don't think so. I don't trust you, Charlie. You've been at pains to keep us all away from your precious parish. What is so different now?'

'I don't mean all of you,' the preacher cried impatiently. 'I can't have Nellie about the place, but you would pass for one of the congregation.'

'Thank 'ee! I'm flattered, but not convinced. You'd best come here every day, and bring as much as you can.'

'I can't do that. I'm to be wed next week. My absence is already giving rise to comment with the lady's stepmother. Would you have me lose my bride?'

Margrave looked shocked. 'My dear sir, I hope that you will not do so. The lady is to be the source of all our fortunes, is she not?'

'Then heed my words. I cannot come to you again before my marriage. After that, I cannot say. You claim that this present sum is modest. I agree. For the present the only money at my disposal is locked within the vestry. It will provide for you for several weeks. After that, there will be papers to be signed and perhaps a lengthy wait before I am in possession of my wife's inheritance.'

'So you are offering us your savings? My dear chap, how very generous of you, though sadly out of character, I fear. We must prepare ourselves to wait, I believe.'

'As you please!' Truscott rose to his feet, and prepared to take his leave of them. Then Nellie intervened.

'We can't live on this!' she snarled. With a quick movement of her hand she scattered the coins across the table in disgust. 'Don't trust him, Dick! Once he's wed he won't come back.'

'Oh, I think he will, but you are right. We can't live on air. Very well, sir, I will go with you, but I warn you. I am armed.'

Truscott ignored the implied threat. His plan was going well, and he was in no hurry. He allowed his companion to comment upon the fine spring weather as they strolled along together, and permitted himself a smile at Margrave's pleasantries.

'This is better,' the forger observed as he gave his hat a jaunty tilt. 'Charlie, you ain't short of brains. We ought to be good friends.'

'I agree. It's a pity you have the others hanging on to you. A fortune shared between you won't go far.'

'You express my own thoughts to perfection, but for the moment I have no alternative. There is safety in numbers, as you know.'

'Careful, as always?' Truscott chuckled. 'I was thinking only that we might come to some arrangement, just the two of us. You might be useful to me.

As I say, you would pass for a member of my congregation…'

'A partnership? It's certainly worth of consideration. Shall we step into this hostelry?'

They were now well away from the pauper colony, and he turned through the doors of a nearby inn. Avoiding the noisy taproom, he led the way through to a small parlour with smoke-blackened walls and windows so heavily leaded as to admit only the faintest trace of light.

The two men seated themselves in the far corner of the room, almost concealed by the shadows. Truscott looked about him.

'You know this place?' he asked.

'I've used it on occasion. No questions asked, you understand, and plenty of warning if strangers are about. Can't always tell who's in the taproom, naturally, but it will be quiet enough in here.'

Truscott nodded. He was well satisfied with this quiet spot in which to pursue his objective.

'This plan of yours?' the forger continued. 'What's in it for me?'

Truscott considered his next words carefully. At no time must he alert his quarry to the fate in store for him.

'You have certain skills,' he said at last. 'It may be that at some time in the future there will be a need to alter various documents in my…in our favour.'

'Very true! That should present no problems.'

'Aside from that, you have a smooth address. Why not make use of it? The fools of women who attend my services are begging to be parted from their dibs.'

Deliberately, he used thieves' cant as he grinned at

his companion. 'We might even make a preacher of you!'

'No, no! I'll leave all that to you. You could always talk, and you might have made your fortune on the boards. As for me, my face is too well known in certain quarters. I believe in keeping low.'

'Just as you wish, but my offer holds. Work with me, and I'll make you a rich man. Now, what do you say?'

'I'll think about it.' It was as far as Margrave would go. 'There's only one thing worries me. You were always a selfish devil, Charlie, looking out for number one. Why the sudden change?'

'Oh, I haven't changed, but I don't close my eyes to facts. Let's say I'd rather have you with me than against me. You know the old saying "If you can't beat 'em, join 'em"?'

'You're a marvel, sir...a positive marvel!' The older man gave his companion a look of admiration. 'It's a pleasure to do business with you.' He downed his drink in one. 'Now about this money? Shall we go?'

'Dick, you must give me an hour or two. I shan't be wasting my time. You'll agree that I must keep the lady sweet? I've been neglecting her in recent days. I'd best go to see her.'

Margrave's look was speculative. 'You wouldn't be trying to do me down? I warn you—'

'No, no, it's nothing like that! We are in full agreement, aren't we?' Truscott favoured his companion with an encouraging smile. 'Why not come to my church tonight? If you attend the evening service you'll see what I mean. When you cast your eye over those plump pigeons ready for the plucking, you'll hesitate no longer.'

'Why must it be tonight?' Margrave was immediately suspicious.

'The church will be full. Your presence will go unnoticed, and I'll give you the money after the service. You won't object to adding tonight's collection to your purse, will you?'

Greed fought with suspicion in the forger's mind. Then, as Truscott had expected, he agreed to the plan, albeit with some misgivings.

'No tricks, mind!' He tapped his pocket significantly, comforted by the weight of the pistol which reposed there.

Truscott shook his head in apparent sorrow. 'You must learn to trust me. Would I be likely to attack you in full view of my congregation? Didn't you say something about there being safety in numbers? I thought you'd welcome the idea.'

With that he strode away. He was well pleased with the result of this interview with Margrave, and not all of his story had been false. He *had* been neglecting Judith. By now she must be wondering what had become of him. It was time to pull the strings and draw his puppet back to him.

Now he had no fear that any of his enemies would approach her. Margrave would see to that. She must return home without delay. Mrs Aveton would be happy to send a note to that effect to Lady Wentworth.

He was surprised to learn that Judith had already parted from her friends. Was she anxious for her wedding? He doubted it, but his lips curved in pleasurable anticipation. He banished that smile as he was shown into the salon, but he sensed at once that Mrs Aveton was not her usual bombastic self.

'Thank heavens you are come!' she said with feeling. 'Sir, it was folly to leave us for so long.'

'Is something wrong?'

A bitter laugh greeted his words. 'You may judge for yourself. Judith is much changed...'

'How so?' Truscott was alarmed, but his face was bland as he looked at her.

'Why, she is very much upon her mettle, and is lost to all sense of propriety. Whether it is the influence of her friends, or the thought of her inheritance I cannot say, but she answered me in such a way! I must say, I was shocked by her pert behaviour.'

'Have you been quarrelling with her?' There was something in his eyes which made her back away.

'I had cause to speak to her upon a certain matter,' she said defensively.

'Ma'am, you are a fool! Did I not warn you to keep the peace? When will you learn that you must leave her to me?' Truscott's face was working as he took a step towards her.

'Let me send for her,' she said hurriedly. She retreated to the far end of the room and tugged at the bell-pull.

'I won't tell you again,' he warned. 'You will keep a still tongue in your head. God knows what damage you have done!'

His fears were stilled when Judith entered the room. She came towards him quickly.

'Charles, you have news? How is your mama?'

'Sad news, my love! She is gone, alas, and is at this moment in the presence of her Maker.' He sat

down suddenly, and covered his eyes with a shaking
hand.

'Oh, my dear, I am so sorry. At least you were
with her. That must have been a comfort in her dying
moments...' She rested a gentle hand upon his
bowed shoulders.

He seized it and pressed his lips against her fingers.

'Too good, my angel! Now I have only you. You
are all that is left to me.' Truscott lifted his face to
hers, ignoring a sardonic look from Mrs Aveton. 'I
must be strong,' he murmured. 'There will be much
to do in the days ahead...the funeral, you know.'

'Shall...shall you wish to postpone our wedding?
At a time of mourning, it would be unseemly for the
ceremony to take place.'

'Ah, my dearest, how like you to consider me, but
I made a death-bed promise. It was my mother's
dearest wish that our marriage should go ahead, just
as we had planned. We cannot bring her back to us,
but before she died she urged that nothing must stand
in the way of our future happiness.'

'Then the delirium passed?'

'At the last her mind was clear, and I thank God
for it. She knew me, Judith, and gave us both her
blessing.' Truscott managed to squeeze out a solitary
tear. 'You will not allow conventions to stand in the
way of the wishes of a dying woman?'

'No!' she said quietly. 'It shall be as you promised.' She felt ashamed that even in the midst of her
pity for him she'd felt a sudden lightening of her
heart at the thought of a possible postponement of
her marriage. In the usual way there would be at least

a year of mourning for a close relative, but it was not to be.

She crushed the tiny flicker of hope which had flared, however briefly, in her heart. She was being selfish. Now, when Charles was most in need of her, she was thinking only of herself. In a gesture rare with her she took his hands and pressed them warmly.

Chapter Thirteen

Truscott almost fainted with relief. In his play-acting, he had overlooked the possible consequences of his news.

The stupid girl might have upset all his plans with her foolish notions of propriety. Left to her own devices she would probably have gone into black for at least a year. Any postponement of his marriage would be sure to finish him, for Margrave would not wait.

His throat felt dry, and when he looked down at his hands he saw that they were trembling. It was no matter. Judith would attribute his pallor and his inability to speak to a natural distress. He glanced at Mrs Aveton for support.

'Our dear Charles is right,' she said at once. 'His filial sentiments do him the utmost credit.'

She wanted to laugh aloud. Truscott thought himself so clever, but this time he had overplayed his hand. She'd been alarmed herself, but he had made a swift recovery, twisting the situation to his own advantage. She could only admire the speed with

which he had extricated himself. It hadn't made her
like him any better.

Now he stumbled to his feet and took his leave of
them. There was much to do to prepare himself for
Margrave's visit, but he'd had a shock and his nerves
were still on edge. He forced himself to walk more
slowly, drawing in deep breaths. He must be calm.
If his plans for the forger were to go well he needed
a cool head.

Judith returned to her own room and sat down at
her desk. Since her return, and after the confrontation
with Mrs Aveton, she had felt curiously detached
from the world about her.

The only reality was her book. In writing it she
could forget the sad thoughts which beset her. In her
unhappiness she'd been convinced that she would
never write another line, but it wasn't so. She'd learnt
to leave a sentence unfinished when she put aside her
work. To complete it led her into the next, and soon
her pen was flowing swiftly over the pages.

Bessie eyed her doubtfully. She was deeply troubled. Lost in a world of her own making, her young
mistress was at peace, but in company there was a
certain brittle brightness in her manner which was
out of character.

Bessie stole quietly from the room. Then she sta-
tioned herself beside a window which overlooked the
street. Taking out her handkerchief she waved to a
figure opposite. The man turned quickly and walked
away.

She returned to her vantage point at the same time
on the following day. This time the family carriage
was waiting at the door. As Bessie watched, Mrs

Aveton left the house accompanied by her daughters, intent upon an outing to the Park at the fashionable hour of five o'clock.

Bessie opened the window slightly as the carriage rolled away. Then she beckoned to the watcher in the street. Silently she stole downstairs and let him in by a side-door.

Then, with a finger to her lips enjoining silence, she motioned to him to follow her up the back stairs.

Bessie had chosen her time well. Freed from the demands of their importunate mistress for an hour or so, none of the other servants were about. She guessed that they would be resting, or playing cards in the servants' hall, glad of the respite before the bustle attendant upon the evening meal.

She paused before Judith's door and tapped, but there was no reply. Throwing caution to the winds she opened it and departed, leaving Dan to enter the room alone.

Judith didn't raise her head. It was not until he stood behind her and laid his hands upon her shoulders that she turned.

'You!' she cried in disbelief. 'You must be mad! What are you doing here, and how did you get in? The porter has orders never to admit you.'

'Judith, I had to see you. Why did you run away?' Dan was very pale, but the blue eyes held her own.

'Need you ask?' she said coldly. 'You had best go at once, before my stepmama returns.'

'Not until I've had my say. Oh, my dear, I tried to tell you of my love. Why won't you believe me?'

'I judge by actions, not by words, and I will have no arguments. Will you go, or must I call the servants?'

Dan stood his ground. 'Only if you wish me to break their heads. Judith, you must listen to me, if only for the sake of our past friendship—'

'You presume too much upon it, sir. What am I to hear? Another tirade about the man I am to marry?'

'I didn't intend to speak of him…only of you.'

'And what of me? You have a curious notion of friendship, Dan. Do you care nothing for my peace of mind? I won't be worried in this way. Heaven knows I have enough to bear without your constant pestering! How can I make you understand?'

'You'll never do so. Judith, you don't love this man. Will you lie, and tell me that you do?'

'Love, so I'm told, is not a prerequisite for marriage. Is it not said to come much later?'

'You don't believe that, and nor do I!'

'I wonder that my feelings should concern you. You have no right…no right at all to question me!'

'Once, long ago, you gave me that right.'

'All that is past, but you won't accept it, will you? Dan, I have grown up. I'm not the girl you knew. You mentioned friendship? If you still wish to be my friend you will respect my wishes.'

'I'd be happy to do so if I believed that this marriage is what you wish with all your heart.' He moved towards her, intending to take her in his arms, but she put out a hand to fend him off.

'No!' she cried sharply. 'Please don't touch me!' Judith could not trust herself. Once in his arms, with his mouth on hers, she would be lost. And lost to what? To a man who had offered for her only out of pity? She could not bear it.

Dan's face grew ashen. She had recoiled from him so fiercely that his arms fell to his sides.

'Forgive me!' he said simply. 'I won't trouble you again. May I offer you my wishes for your future happiness?'

Dan's spirits were at their lowest ebb. What happiness could Judith hope for with a man whom he knew to be a villain? Without proof, there was no way to convince her. Her determination to wed Truscott seemed unshakeable.

Judith rang the bell for Bessie. She did not look at her maid.

'Show this gentleman out!' she ordered coldly. 'When you have done so you may return. I have much to say to you.'

Dan lost his temper then. Wild with frustration, he spun round.

'Don't take your anger out on Bessie, please. The fault is mine, if fault there is. Believe me, I have no wish to repeat it.' With that he strode towards the door. 'Bessie, you need not trouble yourself. I'll find my own way out—'

'Not that way!' Judith flew after him as he started down the main staircase. 'Someone is sure to see you.'

Her warning came too late, though she had a restraining hand upon his arm. At that moment the front door opened and Mrs Aveton entered the house, accompanied by her daughters and Charles Truscott.

The sight which met her eyes robbed her, for the moment, of all power of speech. Judith, scarlet with embarrassment, was in much the same condition.

Then Mrs Aveton found her voice. 'Why, you little trollop!' she hissed viciously. 'You should be whipped at the cart's tail!'

Ignoring Truscott's warning look, she turned to

Dan. 'Out!' she ordered. 'Or must I have you thrown into the street?'

Truscott thought it time to intervene. 'My dear ma'am, are you not a little overwrought? Judith, I'm sure we are agreed, is welcome to receive her friends at any time.'

'In her bedroom?' It was a scream of fury. 'Oh, the disgrace!'

Truscott became aware of the sniggering girls beside him. He bent a stern look upon them. 'Your daughters must be tired after their drive, Mrs Aveton. Doubtless they will wish to retire...'

It was clear that the girls had no such wish. Judith had been caught in the most compromising circumstances and the scene which must surely follow was far too good to miss. They longed to defy him, but there was something in his dark gaze which sent them scurrying away.

He turned to Judith's stepmother, jerking his head in the direction of the goggling porter. 'This is hardly the place for a discussion, ma'am. May we not go into the salon?'

'Not him!' Mrs Aveton glared at Dan.

'But certainly this gentleman shall accompany us. My dear sir, I well remember you. You are Lord Wentworth's adopted son, I believe?'

Dan murmured something unintelligible in reply. His thoughts were in turmoil. Due to his own folly he had placed Judith in an impossible position.

He dared not look at her, but he knew how she must be feeling, and the thought of her present agony of mind almost broke his heart.

What a fool he'd been to come here. He'd forced himself upon her, though she'd made her feelings clear that night in Mount Street. Why could he not accept that she cared for him no longer? In his arrogance he'd succeeded only in compromising her reputation.

'Perhaps a little refreshment, ma'am?' Truscott suggested smoothly.

For Mrs Aveton this was the last straw.

'How can you sit there speaking of refreshment, sir? Have you no notions of propriety? This girl deserves her fate. Mr Truscott, pray have no regard for my own feelings. Since all must be at an end between you, I shall excuse you if you wish to leave my home.'

'I had no such thought.' The preacher smiled at her, but there was no amusement in his eyes. 'In less than a week, Judith will become my wife. Her conduct is now my concern, not yours, I think. Nothing she might do or say will give me a poor opinion of her. I trust her implicitly.'

Judith lifted her head and looked at him in amazement. Another man might have placed the worst construction upon the situation.

'I...I'd like to speak to you alone,' she whispered.

Dan sprang to his feet. 'Then if you will excuse me?' He bowed to the assembled company and left the room. Judith was lost to him for ever. He knew it now.

Once in the street he looked about him blindly. Then he began to walk though he was unaware of his surroundings. For all they meant to him he might have been wandering on another planet.

His thoughts were all of Judith. He couldn't have made matters worse if he had tried. Now Mrs Aveton would humiliate her with all manner of vile accusations, and there was nothing he could do to protect her.

His fears were unnecessary. Truscott had seen at once that his bride-to-be was at the limits of her endurance. Her nerves were as taut as bowstrings. One false move, and he would lose her. If Mrs Aveton persisted with her disgusting insinuations, Judith herself might break off her engagement, feeling that she was unfit to marry him.

He moved toward her and took her hands. 'Your stepmama will excuse us, dearest one.' Over her head he cast a warning look at Mrs Aveton. It was a clear dismissal and she obeyed him, though she was loath to do so.

'My love, this has been most unpleasant for you,' he murmured soothingly. 'Won't you sit down, Judith?' He attempted a little joke. 'Now, you shall not look at me as if you are a guilty schoolgirl!'

'I do feel guilty,' she admitted quietly. 'What must you think of me?'

'I think as I always did...that you are true and good. I could never doubt you.'

His kind words tested her self-control, but she forced herself to speak.

'I owe you an explanation,' she whispered. 'I did not know, you see, that Dan would come here—'

Truscott placed a finger against her lips. 'No explanations, dearest. None are needed. Now let us forget the matter. We shall not speak of it again.'

'You are very good.' Close to tears, she fled. Now she was confirmed in her belief that he was a man of generous spirit. If she didn't love him, at least she could admire him.

Truscott helped himself to a glass of wine. He was

well satisfied with the way he'd handled her. In his apparent charity he had done his cause no harm at all. He had her now. There would be no further difficulty in the wooing of this witless creature.

He permitted himself a smile. He knew her well enough by now. There would have been no romping on the bed with his rival. Had they quarrelled? Either way, it did not matter. But how had the man gained access to her room? He thought he knew the answer. Bessie must be dismissed, but not until he was safely wed.

His spirits began to lift. It was high time he had some luck. That day he had awakened in the worst of moods. Margrave had let him down the night before, though he had waited for the forger until long past midnight.

Had his quarry grown suspicious? He went over their conversation, but he could think of nothing which might have alerted him.

Still, time was growing short. Cursing the necessity, he took himself back to the parish of St Giles.

There was no sign of Margrave in the gin shops. Then he bethought himself of the inn. To his relief Margrave was sitting in the corner, but he was not alone.

Truscott bowed to the bold-eyed wench beside him.

'Getting worried, were you, Charlie?' Margrave's look was sly.

'Not in the least!' Truscott seated himself and signalled to the waiter. 'Ma'am, may I offer you something, and you too, my dear sir?'

'Quite the gentleman, ain't he, Jenny? I said that you would like him.'

'Oh, I do!' The girl leaned forward, giving Truscott a full glimpse of her magnificent bosom. 'He's just the sort of gentleman as appeals to me.'

'My dear!' Truscott raised his glass in tribute to their fair companion. The girl had possibilities, unless, of course, she was Margrave's doxy.

'My niece!' the forger said mendaciously. He might have admitted that she was his insurance against treachery. With Jenny keeping an eye upon the preacher, he felt he might be safe.

'The dear child turned up last night,' he lied. 'I couldn't desert her. She knows no one here in London town.'

'And no work, nor a place to stay,' the girl confided. Her plump thigh was pressed close to Truscott, and he felt a stirring in his blood.

He pretended to consider for a moment. 'That need present no problem,' he said at last. 'I own a house at Seven Dials. As it happens, I'm in need of a housekeeper for the place. Have you any experience?'

'Plenty!' she leered. 'I wouldn't disappoint you, sir.'

'I'm sure of it.' His hand strayed beneath the table and lifted her skirt. Her face remained unchanged as his fingers wandered.

'Well, then, perhaps you'd care to meet me there tomorrow?' Truscott gave her the address. 'Shall we say at noon?'

'Right then, Jenny, be off with you!' Margrave waved her away. 'We have matters to discuss!' He turned to his companion. 'Tonight?' he asked.

'Leave it until Sunday. That is when I preach again.'

'We're getting short of dibs,' the forger told him.

'Then you should have come to me last night. I waited long enough…'

'Couldn't be done!' Margrave felt it unnecessary to explain that he had, in fact, been among the congregation on the previous evening. He knew that Truscott was a ruthless man, and he had feared a trap.

Now he was satisfied. In that milling throng of worshippers no harm could come to him. Jenny had been an afterthought, an insurance for the future. Truscott, he knew, had a weakness for the ladies.

It was a weakness he despised. In giving way to his lusts a man might expose himself to danger. Women were unpredictable creatures.

His face betrayed nothing of his thoughts.

'Then Sunday, for certain?' he suggested.

'For certain!' Truscott hurried away. Today he must get rid of Nan. The girl had been a thorn in his flesh for long enough.

Yet he was surprised by her tenacity. Even his beatings seemed not to have deterred her.

'I won't go!' she'd cried. 'You can't turn me away. How am I to live? How am I to pay for the child?'

'You should have thought of that before.' His tone was brutal. 'I told you to get rid of it.'

'But I didn't! She is your flesh and blood! How can you abandon us?'

He'd been deaf to all her pleas. Taking her keys he'd thrust her from the door. Spineless, that's what she was! In her place he'd have stuck a knife in his tormentor.

He'd locked the door against her, summoned a hackney carriage, and returned to the West End.

* * *

When Mrs Aveton came to join him in her salon he didn't rise to greet her.

'Well?' She was still in a towering rage.

'Very well, no thanks to you! You fool! You couldn't hold your tongue if it should hang you!'

'Don't use that tone with me, sir! What of you! Perhaps you've no objection to taking damaged goods?'

'Save your lies for those who will believe them.'

'Such nobility!' She gave an angry titter. 'Judith does not know you—'

'And nor do you, apparently. Do you suppose that it was her virginal purity that persuaded me to offer for her?'

'I know it wasn't.' Mrs Aveton glared at him.

'Then for God's sake, woman, use your head! We are too close to lose her now. You might have ruined all our plans...'

'What was I to do? You think yourself so clever, sir, but suppose I had said nothing? Judith is no fool. Her suspicions would have been aroused at once. Would you have her guess that we had come to an arrangement?' Her look grew crafty. She thought she had him there.

'You had no thought of that when you spoke out. Let me remind you that I'm not one of your feeble-witted friends...' Truscott paused. 'Even so, you've done me a service. Judith now believes that I'm a model of all the gentler virtues.'

Mrs Aveton began to speak again, anxious to justify herself still further, but he waved her to silence.

'Your ill temper is a serious threat to us. I'll have no more of it. Judith must expect to be punished.

You will confine her to her room until the wedding. Send up her meals and do not speak to her again.'

Mrs Aveton bridled. 'You shall not give me orders in this house!'

'I shall, believe me!' There was so much menace in his tone that she backed away from him.

'I'll do as you say,' she promised hurriedly.

'You would be well advised to do so. What's more, you must keep a sharp eye on the maid.'

'On Bessie? What has she to say to anything?'

Truscott looked at her in pity. 'How do you suppose that Ashburn entered this house?'

Mrs Aveton's colour rose once more. She sprang to her feet and tugged at the bell so hard that she almost broke the rope.

'I'll turn her off at once,' she cried.

'You will do no such thing. Have you learned nothing, you stupid creature? I'll deal with Bessie in my own good time.' Without further ceremony he left the house.

Unaware of the fate in store for her, Bessie was at that moment enduring a most unpleasant interview with Judith.

'How could you be so underhand?' her mistress demanded sternly. 'You have surprised me, Bessie.'

The maid stood her ground. 'I ain't sorry, miss. You may turn me off without a character if you like, but you won't make me sorry for helping Mr Dan.'

'You haven't helped either of us. In fact, you have made matters very much worse, to say nothing of distressing me...'

Bessie's face crumpled. 'I didn't want that, but, Miss Judith—'

'No! I'll hear no more excuses. You may leave me now. I'd like to be alone.'

Still and composed, Judith turned away. She felt drained of all emotion. Her sufferings that day had been severe, but now she felt nothing. Perhaps there came a point where the mind would accept no more.

She wished to speak to no one, but Mrs Aveton would certainly wish to see her. It didn't matter. The expected tirade of abuse would wash over her like a stream across a rock.

She stayed in her room until the light began to fade. Then she heard a tapping at the door. It was Bessie with a tray, and her reddened eyes told Judith that she had been weeping.

'Don't distress yourself,' she murmured. 'I was too hard on you. I know you thought you were acting for the best.'

'Oh, miss, it isn't that. I was to tell you that you ain't to leave your room before your wedding. Madam don't wish to see you.'

Judith managed a faint smile. 'You think it a punishment, Bessie? I could wish for nothing better.'

Bessie set down the tray. 'Then you'll eat your supper, miss?'

'At present I feel that food would choke me. Take it away!'

This brought a further flood of tears from Bessie. To cheer her Judith took a few mouthfuls of the food, but it gave her a feeling of nausea.

'I believe I'll go to bed,' she said at last.

She stood in silence as the girl undressed her, though she was distressed to see that Bessie's tears still flowed.

'Don't worry!' she said gently. 'In four days' time we shall be gone from here.'

Bessie was too overcome to speak. With a hand pressed to her mouth she fled.

Judith lay on her bed in a trance-like state. Only four days to her marriage? It didn't seem possible that she would then become Charles Truscott's wife. She had a curious floating feeling, as if she were detached from everything about her. It was comforting, and she prayed that this sense of unreality would last. Whilst it remained, nothing more could hurt her.

Wisely, Truscott did not attempt to see her for the next two days, though he sent her flowers and messages.

Jenny was now installed at the house in Seven Dials and, as she'd promised, she hadn't disappointed him. The wench had all the experience which he craved to satisfy his lusts. He left her on the Sunday morning with reluctance, promising to return as soon as possible.

'But you're to be wed,' she pouted. 'You'll tire yourself with your new bride...'

'You think so?' His eyes glowed as he looked at her. 'I'm more likely to tire you!'

'Never, Charlie! I'm a match for you!'

He was still laughing as he strode away. He'd rest that afternoon, recruiting his energies for the evening service.

He always preached at night, well aware of the theatrical nature of his setting. With the side aisles in darkness, and the body of the church lit only by four massive candelabra, he could sense the power he wielded over his congregation.

A single lantern hung above his pulpit, placed carefully to shed its light upon his face, throwing into high relief each plane and contour, and emphasising the hollows in his cheeks. It gave him a fanatical appearance, and he was pleased with the effect.

He might have been some latter-day Savonarola, he thought with satisfaction. The Italian monk had achieved the pinnacle of success with his preaching. A pity that he'd overreached himself at the last, and had been executed. Truscott ran a finger around his collar. Strangling wasn't a pretty death. He thrust the thought aside.

That night he was at the peak of his own powers. He'd never preached better and he knew it. Taking as his text 'What doth it profit a man if he gain the whole world, and suffer the loss of his own soul?', he launched into his sermon. When he paused for effect there was total silence in the church.

He spared his listeners nothing, and was rewarded by the sound of an occasional moan. When he drew the sermon to a close his garments were clinging to him. He had given his all that night. The only thing lacking was the sound of wild applause.

As was his custom, he moved into the church porch when the service ended, greeting his parishioners with a grave face, and accepting their congratulations upon his forthcoming marriage with great dignity.

At no time did he acknowledge by the flicker of an eyelid that he had seen Dick Margrave standing by a pillar, but he felt a fierce spasm of pleasure. His quarry was within his grasp.

He waited until the last of the crowd had left by the lych gate. Then he turned to the forger.

'Satisfied?' he asked cynically.

'More than satisfied, Charlie. You've got some prime ones there. I've said it before and I'll say it again. You're a blooming marvel.' Margrave began to laugh. 'That text! I thought it must have finished me! I had to go outside.'

'I thought you'd appreciate the irony. Now what do you say to a drink? My throat is parched...'

'No, I don't think so. This ain't a social call. Give me the money, and I'll be gone.'

'It's in the vestry,' Truscott told him smoothly. 'If you'll follow me...?'

Margrave laughed again. 'I ain't such a fool. I don't know what little surprise you might have rigged up for me. I don't stir a step from this doorway. You can fetch the money to me.'

'Still suspicious?' Truscott shook his head in apparent sorrow. 'We must learn to trust each other, Dick, but if you insist... Wait there! I shan't be above a moment.'

When he returned he was carrying several leather bags, and, unknown to Margrave, a heavy cudgel beneath his flowing robes.

'Will you count it?' he said carelessly.

'No need! You won't trick me if you know what's good for you.' Margrave held out his hands for the money.

Somehow, in passing over the bags, Truscott contrived to drop one. He'd tied it loosely, and the gleaming coins began to roll in all directions.

'Gold?' Margrave was transfixed by the sight. He bent, picked up a coin, and weighed it in his hand.

'What else? These people wouldn't insult me by offering pence.' Truscott fell to his knees and started to collect the gold. 'Give me a hand!' he cried impatiently. 'Unless you're satisfied with what you've got!'

'Nay! I'll not leave this!' The forger's eyes were glittering with avarice. The sight of the money had driven all thought of danger from his head. He began to crawl about the flagstones.

'Let me get the bag!' Truscott rose to his feet, withdrew the cudgel and brought it down with sickening force. One blow was enough to fell his enemy.

The preacher stepped out of his gown, folded it, and wound the cloth about Margrave's head. He'd no desire to leave a trail of blood. Then he seized a leg in either hand and dragged the inert figure into the churchyard to where a mound of fresh-turned earth rose above the surrounding grass.

He'd hidden a spade behind a nearby tombstone. Now he worked fast to toss the earth aside until he'd made a shallow excavation, thankful that the moon appeared only briefly from between the scudding clouds.

It was the work of a moment to roll the body into the hole and pile the soil above it. When he'd finished he surveyed his handiwork with satisfaction. Next week the family of the original occupant of the grave would erect a handsome tombstone, sealing Margrave in the cold earth for ever.

He was unaware that his every move was being watched. The Bow Street Runner was hardened to all kinds of villainy, but even he could not repress a shudder. He remained in hiding as Truscott returned to the church, gathered up his gold and locked the doors. Within minutes he was gone.

The Runner decided not to follow him. His quarry

wouldn't go far, believing himself to be safe. It was more important to mark the exact position of the grave. Now Lord Wentworth should have his proof. Truscott had not removed his cassock from about the head of the dead man. That alone was enough to link him to the crime.

The Runner moved closer to the grave, and then he froze. The earth was moving. With his bare hands he tore wildly at the mound of soil. If the man was still alive he'd have a witness. Then a dreadful figure rose towards him and iron fingers closed about his throat. He knew nothing more.

Chapter Fourteen

On the day before her wedding Judith had a visitor. She hadn't left her room for days, but when Sebastian arrived she was summoned to the salon.

He took her hand and gazed into her eyes, troubled by the dark, bruise-like smudges beneath them. Yet Judith was perfectly calm, standing before him with a grave, contained stillness.

He longed to shake her, to bring some life into that gentle face. If only he might have saved her from what could only be a miserable future. Now, he feared, it was too late.

'I am come to make arrangements for tomorrow,' he murmured. 'At what time is the ceremony?'

She looked at him without expression. 'At noon, I believe.'

'Then I shall take you in my carriage. Shall we say at a quarter to the hour?'

Judith nodded, not daring to ask the question which was uppermost in her mind. She was praying with all her heart that Dan would not be in the congregation as she made the vows which should have been made to him.

Sebastian understood. 'Prudence sends her love,' he told her. 'And Perry and Elizabeth will be there.' There was no point in distressing her with the news that Elizabeth had at first refused to go until Perry had insisted.

A silence fell as the unasked question hung in the air between them.

'Dan sends his regrets,' Sebastian continued. 'But I have some news which I know will please you. Nelson has sent for him. Dan left for Merton earlier today.'

He had all her attention then. Judith raised her head, and for the first time her face grew animated.

'The Admiral is pleased with his work?'

'We can't tell yet, but it seems likely. We must wait until Dan returns before we can be sure.'

'I'm sure! Oh, I am so very glad for him. You will tell him so?'

'He will know it, Judith. Until tomorrow, then?'

'How kind you are!' Judith gave him her hand, and even managed to force a smile.

She must be glad for Dan. She must...but if only this news had reached him earlier. It might have made all the difference. Then she remembered. Dan no longer loved her. Her heart was breaking, but no one must guess. She went back to her room.

As Sebastian returned to Mount Street he found himself regretting the impulse which had led him to offer to give Judith away. It had all the overtones of leading a lamb to the slaughter. Judith appeared to be in a state of shock, but it was nothing to the shocks which were likely to await her.

Damn the Runner! Where on earth was the man!

It was now a matter of hours before the wedding. Was there still time to stop it? At this late stage it was folly even to hope.

Later, Judith could remember little about the morning of her wedding day.

She had a vague memory of Bessie pressing her to eat something, however little, but she pushed the tray aside. When she tried to speak she seemed to have lost her voice.

'Drink your chocolate!' Bessie ordered. 'If you go on like this, Miss Judith, we'll have you fainting at the altar.' Even as she spoke she wondered why she was insisting. Privately she considered that to faint was now Judith's only hope of escaping the clutches of the Reverend Truscott. Yet her mistress, she knew, would not collapse. Judith's face was set. She would go through with the ceremony.

Bessie choked back a sob. This should be the happiest day of any woman's life. No bride should look so pale and listless. She drew the curtains about the old-fashioned bed and summoned the waiting footmen to remove the boxes and portmanteaux which contained her mistress's possessions. They would be sent on ahead to her new home.

Within the curtained bed, Judith lay inert. She had the oddest sense of looking down at her own body from some point far above. The fantasy would pass, together with this feeling of unreality. Soon she would begin to be aware of what was happening to her.

It was strange. She'd expected to feel a pang of regret at leaving this shabby room which had been her sanctuary for so long.

In this room she had wept for her dead father, found consolation in her books and her writing, and on occasion had managed to escape the cruel strictures of her stepmother. The months after Dan had left were far too painful to remember, but it was all so long ago.

When Bessie drew the curtains back she looked about her, willing herself to feel something. Anything, even the pain of loss would be preferable to this dreadful feeling of inertia. Now the room looked impersonal. Her pictures, her books and her few trinkets had gone. It might have belonged to a stranger.

She bathed in silence, hoping that the water would refresh her. Then, statue-like, she stood obediently as Bessie dressed her in the unbecoming gown of dull lavender which had been Mrs Aveton's choice.

Even the matching bonnet with its tiny clusters of flowers beneath the brim did nothing to improve her appearance. In Bessie's eyes, her mistress looked like a ghost.

'Miss, don't wear this!' she begged. Then she remembered. The rest of Judith's gowns were packed and gone.

'It will do!' Judith closed her eyes. 'I think I'll sit down for a moment.' She walked over to the window-seat and rested her cheek against the cool glass. It was difficult to decide if she felt hot or cold.

She knew that she must pull herself together. She was being unfair to Charles. He deserved better than to wed the marionette which she felt herself to be that morning.

It took a supreme effort of will to force herself to think about him. She tried to bring his face to mind, but she could see only a pair of bright blue eyes beneath a crop of red-gold hair. Memories followed each other in quick succession. Dan teasing her, laughing, entering into all her hopes and plans with the eagerness peculiarly his own.

Then the picture changed to a vision of his stricken face, pleading, angry, and finally despairing. She wouldn't think of him. It was just that she couldn't seem to recall the face of her betrothed at all.

It was madness. Charles had been so good to her. Always pleasant and courteous, his kindness was unfailing. She'd always be able to rely on him, and she would not soon forget his staunch support in a situation in which most men would have thought the worst of her.

And yet she could not love him, she thought despairingly. What did she want of a man? The answer to that lay only with Dan. Never again would she feel that leap of the heart whenever he walked into a room, and the joy which filled her soul. She closed her eyes, remembering his smile, the thrill of his touch, and even the very scent of him.

What had he called her? 'My best of friends'? There was more to it than that. Beneath the friendship there had once been the bonds of a love so passionate that it promised to last for an eternity. That love had vanished, and with it all her hopes and dreams.

A tapping at the door recalled her from her reverie.

Bessie answered it, returning with the news that Lord Wentworth had arrived.

'Oh, is it time?' Judith asked quietly.

Bessie wiped away a tear. Her young mistress might have used just those words if she'd been summoned to the tumbrils in France, and on her way to a dreadful death by the guillotine.

Judith pressed her hand. 'Don't look like that!' she pleaded. 'Charles is a good man, and he will care for me.'

With that she took Bessie in her arms. They clung together for just a moment. Then Judith disengaged herself. With her head held high she left the room.

There were four people in the salon, but it seemed to Judith to be excessively crowded, due to the fact that Mrs Aveton and her daughters were *en grande toilette*.

Judith looked at them in wonder, amazed by the profusion of lace, satin, feathers, ribands and jewellery which graced the persons of the three ladies. The purple satin turban of her stepmother was crowned by an immense aigrette, and the spray of gems sparkled and shook each time she tossed her head.

Now Mrs Aveton hurried towards her, conscious of Sebastian's penetrating eyes.

'Dear child!' she gushed. 'How beautiful you look today!' She'd intended to embrace the bride-to-be, in an effort to convince Sebastian of her fondness for the girl, but Judith turned away. Such pretence disgusted her.

Sebastian took her hand and kissed it. Then he turned to Mrs Aveton with a significant glance at the clock.

'If you leave now, ma'am, we shall follow you,' he said. 'You will wish to arrive before the bride.'

'Why, yes, of course! How like you to consider me! I hope that our dear Judith appreciates your condescension in giving her away, my lord. So good of you, and far more than she might expect!'

'Judith is a dear friend.' There was something in his tone which silenced her. Her colour heightened as she hurried her daughters to the waiting carriage.

Sebastian looked at his companion, noting her grave, contained manner.

'Judith?'

'I'm ready,' she said quickly. 'Shall we go?'

In silence he offered her his arm. There was nothing left to say. He longed to beg her to change her mind. It was not too late. His carriage would take her to Mount Street and to Prudence, but the tension in her slight figure warned him against such a suggestion. All he could do now was to lend her his support throughout the coming ceremony.

She would need it. He thought he'd never seen another human being quite so close to breaking down completely.

In an effort to divert her thoughts he began to speak of Prudence.

'Your visit helped her, Judith. The doctor now believes that her time is closer than we thought. The child could arrive within these next few days.'

'Oh, Sebastian, should you have left her?' Judith turned to him at once in her anxiety for her friend.

He patted her hand and smiled. 'These things don't happen in minutes, my dear. I offered to send Perry in my place, but Prudence would have none of it. She insisted that I kept my word to you.'

'But—?'

'No buts, Judith! Elizabeth has stayed behind to be with her. She will send word if anything should start to happen. I have no fears on that score. Our beautiful hot-head can be a tower of strength upon occasion, as I'm sure you know. Elizabeth won't lose her wits.'

Judith smiled for the first time. 'I know it! She has so many of the qualities of her aunt. Miss Grantham has left for Turkey?'

Sebastian nodded. 'Two days ago. Perry swears that she'll return with a Mameluke or two in tow.'

'He's teasing you. Will you give my love to Prudence? You will all be so relieved when this is over and the babe arrives.'

'I should be used to it by now, but I suffer through these times almost as much as Prudence. At least I'm not as bad as Perry. He was like a man demented on both occasions when Elizabeth gave birth.'

Judith squeezed his hand. 'All will be well, I'm sure of it.' She looked up as the carriage stopped, and paled a little.

'Are we there?'

'Yes, my dear.' Sebastian gave her his hand and helped her from the carriage.

She hesitated only once, as she saw the open doorway of the church. Then she straightened her shoulders, lifted her head, and together they walked slowly down the aisle.

Heads turned towards her as she passed, but Judith was oblivious of the sea of faces. Her eyes were fixed upon the altar and the man who stood before it, awaiting her.

As she reached his side he gave her a tender smile, but she did not respond. She was still possessed by a sense of unreality. This could not be happening to her. The girl who stood beside Charles Truscott wasn't herself. It was some stranger taking part in a ceremony which meant nothing.

Truscott then gave his full attention to the bishop, and Judith became aware of the opening words of the marriage service.

'Brethren, we are gathered together in the sight of God and this congregation to join this man and this woman in holy matrimony…'

The bishop paused. Then, as church law required, he asked if any knew of the existence of an impediment to the marriage.

It was a formality, but a silence fell for what seemed to Judith to be an eternity. Then, as the bishop was about to continue, a faint voice reached him.

'This man is the father of my child!'

A gasp like the sound of the rushing wind across a sea of corn seemed to ripple around the church, and beside her Judith felt Charles Truscott stiffen.

When he spun round to face his accuser she heard him curse beneath his breath. Then he regained his self-control and walked towards the figure standing in the aisle.

Judith recognised the girl at once. This was the frail creature who had accosted her in the street, and later had given her the mysterious message from Charles.

Now he disclaimed all knowledge of her. 'The woman is demented,' he announced. 'Tell me, my dear! What is the name of the father of your child?'

'It's you…Josh Ferris! Will you deny your own flesh and blood?' She drew aside her shawl to reveal a puny child which lay within the crook of her arm. The little creature seemed too weak to cry.

Truscott looked about him with a sad expression,

anxious to dispel the astonishment in the faces of his guests.

'Pitiful!' he murmured. 'The girl has lost her senses! I am not Josh Ferris, my dear. My name is Truscott...the Reverend Charles Truscott. Now let me get some help for you...' He looked towards the ushers who had hastened down the aisle.

The girl pulled away from the restraining hands.

'You shan't deny me!' she cried wildly. 'I don't care what you call yourself. The child is yours!'

Truscott turned to Judith. 'I am so sorry, dearest, to have you exposed to this. I do not know this woman.'

Judith answered him then, and in the silence her clear voice carried to all corners of the church.

'That isn't true!' she said quietly. 'This girl brought me a message from you.'

There was another gasp from the assembled guests.

Then Judith moved towards the young mother. 'This is no place for you,' she said. 'Let us go into the vestry.'

Suddenly, Mrs Aveton was tugging at her sleeve.

'What are you about?' she hissed. 'The ceremony must go on. Let them take this creature away. She should be in Bedlam.'

Judith looked down at her. The contempt in her grave grey eyes might have caused a lesser woman to shrivel, but Mrs Aveton was undeterred.

'Suppose this child is Charles's by-blow?' she murmured in an undertone. 'What has that to say to anything? A sensible woman would ignore it.'

'Then perhaps I am not sensible.' Judith removed

the clutching fingers from her arm, and turned to the bishop. 'My lord, I must have the truth of this.'

'Of course!' he agreed. 'We shall break off at once in order to investigate these allegations.'

'No!' Truscott's face was dark with rage. 'Judith, this is no impediment. You must believe me!'

'Even so, the lady is entitled to make enquiries.' Sebastian found it almost impossible to hide his relief. Now he took Judith's arm. 'The vestry?' he said quietly. 'You won't wish for a public scandal.'

'Leave her!' Truscott shouted. 'How dare you interfere? You and your family have done your best to give her a dislike of me. Now, I suppose, you will persuade her to believe these lies?'

'Judith wishes only to discover the truth, sir.' Sebastian's voice was cold. 'If you are innocent you need have no fear—'

'Guilty? Innocent? Who are you to judge? You with your money and your arrogance? My wife shall end her connection with you from this moment!'

'My dear sir, you are making a spectacle of yourself. Have you no consideration for Miss Aveton?'

'Miss Aveton is it, now?' Truscott attempted to seize Judith's arm. 'Don't listen to him. They are all against me...'

At this point the bishop was moved to intervene. 'Lord Wentworth is right. This is a most unedifying scene. It should not be taking place in public.' Frowning, he strode away.

'No, my lord, don't go!' Truscott hurried after him. 'Am I not entitled to defend myself...to refute these allegations?'

'You may do so, and I will hear you out, but not

before the altar. Later, if you can explain yourself to the lady's satisfaction, the ceremony may continue.'

Truscott returned to Judith's side, attempting to thrust himself between her and Lord Wentworth. With the dashing of his hopes all his composure deserted him. Now he was babbling wildly.

Judith ignored him and moved towards the girl.

'What is your name?' she asked.

'It's Nan, miss. Please, you must believe me. I wasn't lying. Josh turned me out. I had no money for the child. I think she's dying...'

Judith looked at the tiny figure lying in her arms.

'Don't give up hope!' she said. 'You shall have all the help you need. This man you know as Josh? He is one and the same as the man I was about to marry?'

'Yes, miss. Does he claim to be a preacher?' Her eyes grew bitter. 'He ain't no Christian gentleman. He would have left us both to starve.'

'I think you are very tired,' Judith said gently. 'Let us go to a more private place. There you may sit down.' She looked up at Sebastian and he nodded. Then he raised a finger to summon one of his servants, despatching the man for food.

In a last desperate effort, Truscott tried to intervene.

'No!' he shouted. 'I'll help! I'll give her money, but, Judith, you must listen to me!'

'I'm quite prepared to do so.' She slipped her arm about the girl, leading her through the door into the vestry. She was followed by Sebastian, and the frantic figure of Truscott.

Standing before his bishop, the preacher changed

his tactics, adopting a bullying demeanour towards the girl.

'Wench, you will burn in hell!' he shouted. 'That is the fate of those who lie before God!'

'Spare us your threats!' Sebastian turned on him. 'You will keep a still tongue in your head. My lord bishop, will you question the girl?'

Nan looked terrified, but encouraged by Judith's gentle manner she began to tell her story.

'Seven Dials?' Truscott cried at one point in her tale. 'I don't know the place.'

'Strange, considering that you have a house there!' Sebastian studied his fingernails with interest. 'You have been seen entering and leaving, and so has Nan. It is Nan, isn't it?' He smiled encouragement at her.

The preacher's face took on a ghastly hue, but he tried to recover his position.

'I might have guessed it,' he said savagely. 'You have set men on to spy on me. Much good may it do you! As a man of God my work takes me to all parts of London upon errands of mercy. I don't always know the names of the places which I visit.'

'Nor, apparently, are you able to recall the faces of those you tend.' The bishop's face was stern. 'Why did you claim not to know this girl?'

'Why, my lord, I can't be expected to remember all those who come to me for help. There are so many...' Truscott cast a pleading look at Judith.

She didn't glance at him. Memory had come flooding back. Here, in this very church, she had caught him beating a small child. Nausea overwhelmed her as she realised the truth. She had been mistaken in him all along.

Sebastian hesitated, but not for long. Judith must now hear the truth, however unpalatable it might be.

'Do your duties require you to stay overnight upon these errands?' he asked quietly.

A purple flush stained Truscott's face. 'I may have stayed on one occasion…but it was by a sickbed.'

'Ah, yes, these sickbeds! There are so many, are there not, and all at the house in Seven Dials? I'm told that your presence was required there for several days at a time.'

'Judith knows about it,' Truscott said defensively. 'My mother has been suffering from the smallpox—'

'You are lying, sir. Your mother lives in the parish of St Giles, in that salubrious part of London known as "The Rookery". To my knowledge she is suffering from nothing more than neglect on the part of her disgraceful son.'

Judith rose to her feet. She did not look at Truscott. 'I have heard enough,' she said with dignity. 'My lord bishop, this marriage will not now take place. What you choose to do about this man I will leave to your own judgment. Sebastian, will you take me home? Nan and her child shall go with us.'

'Judith, you can't!' Truscott ran after her into the main body of the church, empty now, except for Mrs Aveton and her daughters. 'It's lies, I tell you, naught but a pack of lies. They'll stop at nothing to take you from me.'

'Nay, Charlie, it ain't lies! Who knows that better than you, you murdering devil!'

The voice came from the shadowy porch. It was low, but so chilling that it stopped Truscott in his tracks.

He fell back, all colour draining from his face.

'Who is there?' he cried fearfully.

'A dead man, who else?' Margrave stepped into the light, and as he did so, Mrs Aveton screamed.

The forger was a terrifying sight. His face had the pallor of the grave, except for the patches of scarlet blood which seeped steadily from the cloth about his head and trickled down one cheek.

'Thought you'd killed me, Charlie? I ain't so easy to get rid of. Now it's your turn. Did you think I'd let you live to enjoy this lady's fortune?' He raised his pistol and levelled it at Truscott's heart.

'Wait, Dick! Hear me! It was a mistake! I fell against you. Then I thought that you had cracked your head. What was I to do? I couldn't have you found here...'

'So you decided to give me a Christian burial?' The forger's laugh struck terror into those who heard it. 'Lucky for me that there wasn't a tombstone handy. I'd never have left that grave.'

Judith found that she was trembling, but it was Sebastian who spoke.

'Sir, will you be a witness? If this is true, you may leave this man to the authorities—'

'Nay, I'll not do that. Lord Wentworth, ain't it? My lord, the authorities are no friends of mine. I'll handle this myself. I'm sorry, ma'am, that you are to be soon a widow.'

'I am not married,' Judith whispered.

'Really? Ah, I see!' He looked at the girl beside her. 'Our little Nan got there before me!'

Judith moved to stand in front of the shrinking girl.

'You are making a mistake!' she said steadily. 'Will you commit murder in this church? Please do as Lord Wentworth has suggested. You cannot take the law into your own hands.'

'Count your blessings, ma'am, and stand aside! I know what I'm about. They won't catch Dick Margrave!' As he raised his pistol once again, Truscott grabbed Judith to his breast.

Holding her as a shield, he thrust her ahead of him towards the porch. She felt the pricking of his knife against her ribs.

'Don't struggle!' he advised. 'I have nothing to lose.'

'Let her go!' Sebastian's voice was calm. He was almost within touching distance. 'This is naught to do with Judith. Your quarrel is between you and this man...' Imperceptibly, he moved closer.

'Back!' the preacher shouted. 'Unless you wish to have her blood upon your hands!'

Judith was terrified, but she kept her head. Truscott should not find it easy to drag her from the church. Apparently on the verge of collapse, she leaned heavily against him. Then she felt what seemed to be a sharp blow as he pulled her upright.

'No tricks!' he ordered roughly. 'Move!'

Now he had an enemy on either side. Margrave was ahead of him, blocking his exit from the church, and Sebastian was behind.

'You first!' he told Sebastian. 'Walk ahead of me!'

He cast just one brief glance at the horrified faces of Mrs Aveton and her girls, the bishop, and finally at Nan.

'You'll pay for this!' he promised. 'I'll be back!' His face was a mask of evil as he looked at her, and none of his listeners dared to move.

Then, thrusting Judith ahead of him, and using

Sebastian's tall figure as a further shield, he began
to edge his way towards the porch and freedom.

Margrave had moved to one side. As his enemy
passed it would give him a better shot, but Truscott
sensed his purpose.

'Out!' he ordered.

For a long moment Margrave hesitated and Judith
closed her eyes. She meant nothing to the man, and
there was murder in his face. In his desire for ven-
geance he was more than likely to fire through her.

Sebastian's murmur was audible to no one but the
forger.

'No!' he said. 'Not yet! You'll get your chance.'

It seemed at first that Margrave would disobey
him, and for Judith it was the longest moment of her
life. Then the man walked out of the church.

Judith felt the sunlight warm upon her face. Again
she felt a sense of unreality. Could this frightful
scene be taking place here, in the quiet surroundings
of the churchyard?

Sebastian's carriage was already at the lych gate,
ready to bear him home.

'Summon your man, my lord! If you wish this lady
to live you will obey me. He is to open the carriage
door, let down the steps, and stand away. Then your
coachman must drive off at speed when we are safe
inside.'

Sebastian stopped suddenly. 'You can't be meaning to take Judith with you?' he exclaimed in horror.

Truscott ignored the question. 'Do as I say!' he
shouted.

'No, listen to me! She will slow you down.'

Judith felt the prick of the knife, and she gave a
tiny gasp of pain. 'Do as he says,' she pleaded.

Sebastian's lifted hand brought a groom running to his side. The man's eyes widened as he realised what was happening. He was a burly fellow, and with his arms spread wide in a wrestler's stance, he started to move forward.

'No!' Sebastian was quick to stop him. 'Do as I bid you! This lady is being held at knife-point.'

'Very wise, my lord,' the preacher mocked. 'Now stand aside.'

Judith's view was partly blocked by Sebastian's massive figure. Then she heard the sound of running feet.

'Seb, am I too late?' Dan came tearing around the corner of the church. 'The Runner has news. I've brought him with me. Pray heaven we are in time!'

'Indeed you are!' The preacher's voice was a paean of triumph. 'In time to bid your lady-love farewell. Now, sir, his lordship has been most amenable. I trust that you will follow his example and do nothing foolish?'

As Sebastian stepped aside, Dan took in the situation at a glance. Beside him, the hand of the Bow Street Runner strayed towards his pistol. Then Dan saw the terror in Judith's eyes.

'We shall do nothing foolish,' he agreed. 'You are free to leave, but you shall not take Judith with you.'

'And how are you to stop me?' Truscott jeered.

'I fear that we cannot.' Dan paused. Then he looked at Judith. 'Why, my dear, you have forgotten the pearl necklace...'

'Pearls?' Even Truscott was startled. What was the fellow thinking of to speak of a necklace at this time?

Judith raised her head, and for a long moment grey eyes locked with blue.

'Yes,' she murmured. 'I had quite forgot.' She bent her head again. Then, with a sudden movement, she thrust it back with all her strength, catching Truscott full in the face.

He gave a cry of agony and staggered back as Dan ran towards him, twisting Judith from his grip.

Two shots rang out in unison, but Truscott had already dodged behind a tombstone. Then he began to run, zig-zagging between the graves.

The Runner raised his smoking pistol and took careful aim, but Margrave thrust him aside.

'He's mine!' he said with great deliberation. He fired one more at the running man, and this time he did not miss.

Frozen with horror, Judith watched as the preacher's head exploded in a red haze. Then Dan hid her face against his coat.

'Get her out of this!' Sebastian muttered. 'I'll see to matters here…'

Dan needed no urging. With the aid of the groom he half led and half carried Judith to the waiting coach.

'Back to Mount Street!' he ordered briefly. Then he gathered his love into his arms.

'Why, Dan, you are trembling!' Judith murmured in wonder. 'I am unhurt…'

'Then what is that?' With a shaking hand he pointed to her skirt.

Judith looked down to see a long rust-coloured stain creeping from the bodice of her gown down towards the hem. 'It's only a graze. He…he pricked me with the knife.'

'He might have killed you. Oh, my darling, I

thought you lost to me for ever.' He covered his eyes and turned away to hide the agony in his heart.

'Dan, look at me!' Judith pleaded. 'I must know! Can you ever forgive me?'

'Forgive you? For what?' he groaned. 'I should be asking your forgiveness for exposing you to danger.'

For answer she took his beloved face in both her hands.

'You tried to warn me,' she said tenderly. 'Don't blame yourself! I wouldn't listen. How could I have been so blind?'

'You weren't alone, my love. Truscott deceived everyone—'

'Not you! Nor any member of your family.'

'Prudence and Elizabeth had seen another side of him.'

'Oh, my dear, if they had only told me the whole…'

'Would you have believed them? Besides, Sebastian insisted that they must not meddle. He was unconvinced until quite recently.'

'But you?'

'I hated him on sight,' Dan told her simply. 'But I was mad with jealousy.'

'You hid it well.'

'I had to, Judith. In the end we came to believe that you were safe only as long as you remained betrothed.'

Her eyes widened. 'I was in danger? Why did you not warn me?'

'We had no proof until today. The Runner arrived as I returned from Merton. He'd seen Truscott's attempt to murder Margrave.'

'Margrave was the man who shot him dead?'

Judith closed her eyes as if to shut out the memory of that dreadful scene. 'He is dead, isn't he?'

'He is, my darling, but he was a man who lived by violence and in the end it killed him.'

Judith began to shudder. 'I'll never forget it. It was a frightful ending...'

'Try not to think about it, dearest.' Dan turned her face to his. 'It's over. Now we shall think only of our future.'

He kissed her then, and as his mouth came down on hers the long years of their separation sank into oblivion. They were still locked in a passionate embrace when the carriage came to a halt.

Judith felt light-headed, and when Dan tried to help her down her limbs refused to obey her. She looked down at her skirt and saw that the ominous stain was spreading rapidly.

'Don't tell Prudence!' she said in a queer, high voice. 'I'm sorry, but I think I'm going to faint.'

She fell towards him, and into darkness.

Chapter Fifteen

Judith awakened as the first grey fingers of dawn began to creep across the sky. She looked about her in bewilderment. This was not her room.

She tried to move and winced with pain. Cautiously she touched the firm binding around her ribs with her right hand. Her left was held so tightly that it was impossible to disengage her fingers.

In the corner of the darkened room a single candle was guttering low, and by its faint light she could distinguish a figure sitting by her bedside.

Dan seemed to be asleep, but he stirred as the door was opened.

'You must get some rest,' Elizabeth whispered. 'You've been here all night. Go now! I will stay with Judith.'

'I won't leave her!' came the obstinate reply. 'I want to see the surgeon.'

'So you shall, my dear, but he won't return at dawn. I promise to call you the moment he appears.'

Dan shook his head. 'He thought there might be a fever. I must stay in case she needs me.'

Judith felt a cool hand upon her brow. 'She isn't

feverish, Dan. Do go! At present you look worse than Judith. You mustn't frighten her. When she wakes she will wish to speak to you.'

'I do!' Judith opened her eyes. 'How long have I been here?'

'Since yesterday, my love. You fainted in the carriage...'

Dan's haggard face alarmed her, but she managed a weak smile. 'That was foolish of me. It must have been the shock.'

Elizabeth bent over her. 'Judith, you were stabbed. Do you not recall?'

Judith shook her head. 'I was pricked by the knife at first. Then I felt a sort of blow...more like a punch to my ribs.'

'You received a deep cut, Judith, but it isn't serious. By some miracle it missed the vital organs.'

'But you aren't out of danger, my beloved.' Dan was beside himself with anxiety. 'There is the risk of fever.'

'I shan't get a fever,' Judith promised as she laid a loving hand against his cheek. 'But I do feel sleepy. Won't you rest, my darling? Come back to me later...'

It was only with the greatest reluctance that Dan left the room, with so many instructions to Judith not to excite herself, nor to worry, and most especially to get some sleep, that in the end Elizabeth seized his arm and thrust him through the door.

'He's been like a man possessed,' she said ruefully. 'You gave us such a fright! That villainous creature! We should have warned you. Then we might have spared you this experience—'

'How could you, when I wouldn't hear a word against him? Oh, I have been such a fool!'

'No more than the rest of London, Judith. He was a cunning devil, and old in the ways of evil.'

'But he paid in the most horrible way...' Judith covered her face with her hands, as if to shut out the hideous memory.

'It was quicker than a hanging,' Elizabeth said briskly. 'Don't waste your pity on him, love. He got what he deserved...and to stab you as he did? We may be thankful that the surgeon was already here when you arrived.'

Judith looked up quickly. 'Prudence?'

'Prudence gave Sebastian two fine daughters not an hour ago. Her pains had started before Sebastian left but she didn't mention it to him. That was why I stayed behind. You didn't wonder why I was not at the church?'

'I was in a daze, I think. I didn't notice anyone. But twins? Oh, my dear, what a night you must have had!'

'It wasn't dull!' Elizabeth began to smile. 'Perry went for the surgeon as soon as Sebastian was safely out of the way. Wait until you see them, Judith. They are adorable...'

'And Prudence?'

'She's tired, but very happy. As for Sebastian?' she threw her eyes to heaven. 'Between them, he and Dan were most in need of the doctor's services.'

Judith caught at her hand. 'Sebastian should not have left her.'

'My dear, she wanted him to be with you. She felt that you would be glad of his support.'

'How like her! She was right! I was so glad to

have him with me. I still can't believe what happened. It seems like some frightful nightmare. But didn't Sebastian wonder why you stayed behind with Prudence?'

Elizabeth blushed. 'Not really.' She looked a little conscious. 'I had been behaving badly, you see.'

'In what way?'

'I made a dreadful fuss about your marriage, Judith. I didn't wish to see you wed to that monstrous creature. Sebastian thought I'd seized on the excuse when the doctor said that Prudence was very near her time.'

'I wish I'd listened to you.'

'You are not to think about it. Now you must try to rest. Is there anything I can get for you?'

Judith shook her head. 'I just want to sleep.' She closed her eyes.

Later, the doctor's visit was a trial, but not a sound escaped her lips as he changed the dressing on her wound.

'May I not dress and go downstairs?' she pleaded. 'I promise to sit quietly, but I'm making extra work for everyone whilst I am up here.'

'What's all this?' Dan was standing in the doorway.

'Why, sir, this young lady has her own ideas about her convalescence. I'm trying to persuade her to follow mine.' He turned to Judith. 'Miss Aveton, you have been fortunate. Your wound will heal quickly if you take my advice. Otherwise you may go down with the fever.'

'Miss Aveton will obey your orders to the letter,'

Dan said sternly. 'I will see to that.' He bowed the doctor out.

Then he strolled over to the bed, sat down and took both of Judith's hands in his.

'Goose!' he said fondly. 'Haven't you given me enough cause to worry about you? I've aged ten years in these past few weeks.'

Judith peeped up at him from beneath her lashes.

'I can see no sign of it,' she said demurely. 'Your hair has not turned grey.'

'It was white, my love. I was forced to dye it.'

'More play-acting, Dan? You have certainly deceived me—'

'With my red hair? Oh, dear, and I thought it looked so natural.'

'Of course not! Don't joke,' she pleaded. 'I thought you didn't love me. That was why I wouldn't listen to you.'

Dan took her gently in his arms and kissed her tenderly. 'Do you still believe that I have changed?'

Rosy with pleasure, she rested her head against his shoulder. 'I should never have doubted you. Oh, my darling, there has never been anyone else for me. I, too, have never changed in all these years. I used to think of what we had, and our parting almost broke my heart. I felt that my life was over. Nothing seemed to matter. That was why...'

He silenced her with another kiss. 'All that is past. We shall not speak of it again.'

'But we must, my dearest. So much is left unanswered. I cannot rest until I know.'

Dan looked at her with loving eyes. 'It may be best,' he agreed. 'But then you must lay the ghosts to rest. Will you promise me that?'

She nodded, tucking her hand within his own as he began to speak.

He skirted as lightly as he could over the beginning of his tale, mentioning Truscott's mother only briefly. He said nothing about the murder of Nan's brothers. There was no point in distressing her with that, though Margrave's cronies had betrayed him and given a full account of the affair.

Judith tensed when he told her about the house at Seven Dials.

'So Nan was telling the truth?' she whispered.

'She was, my love. The child is Truscott's.'

'Oh, the poor creature! Where is she now? I promised to help her.'

'She's here, my darling. Sebastian brought her with him. The servants are making a great fuss of the little one, and the doctor holds out hope for her.'

'Thank God!'

Dan patted her hand. 'I knew you'd be relieved. Shall I go on, or have you heard enough? The rest of the tale is unfit for your ears, I fear.'

'Oh, Dan, I have the right to know.'

'Very well. We had our information from a Bow Street Runner. Sebastian set him to follow Truscott several weeks ago. His discoveries were disturbing, but there was no proof of actual wrongdoing.'

'He could explain his visits to these places?'

'Sebastian did not challenge him. He thought it best to wait until... Oh, Judith, I should never have agreed. When I think that we might have been too late!'

Judith pressed his hand. 'Don't blame yourself, my dear one. This man—Margrave, do you call him— he was intent on murder. I knew it when I looked into his eyes. I should have been a widow before I was a wife.'

'You could never have been Truscott's wife. He was wed some years ago.'

'To Nan?'

'No, I believe the woman lives in Essex. Frederick sent word this morning.'

'The Earl of Brandon? He, too, was involved in this? I can't believe it!'

'Elizabeth pressed him into service. She was so sure of Truscott's villainy, and Frederick has sources which are closed to lesser mortals.'

'How shall I ever thank you all?' Judith murmured.

'Well, my love, you might begin by kissing me again.' Dan slipped a finger beneath her chin and his mouth came down on hers. In that passionate embrace all the bitterness of the past was washed away, and Judith's heart was filled with an overwhelming joy.

Then he held her away from him. 'I was warned that you must rest,' he teased her. 'This can't be good for you.'

'Nothing could be better,' Judith whispered. She was blushing furiously.

Dan was tempted to kiss her again, but with admirable self-control he managed to restrain himself.

'Temptress!' he accused. 'You are driving me to distraction. Just listen to the pounding of my heart!' He took her hand and held it against the fine cambric of his shirt. 'Would you have me faint with happiness?'

'No, my love.' Judith's eyes grew misty.

'Well, then, allow me to continue with my tale.

Sebastian was right. Truscott decided that before his marriage he must rid himself of his worst enemy. He tricked Margrave into meeting him, and then he tried to kill the man, burying him in a recent grave.'

Judith grew stiff with horror, and he slipped an arm about her, drawing her to his breast. 'He didn't succeed, my darling. The Runner saw it all, but when he tried to help, the forger attacked him, thinking, perhaps, that Truscott had returned to lay a tombstone over him.' Dan glanced down at his love in some concern. 'Judith, I should not have told you.'

'I'm glad you did. Now it is all clear to me. It all seemed so unbelievable, but now I see why Margrave killed him. Did he get away?'

'No! He was taken in the street. He was a wanted man, my dear. Forgery is still a hanging matter. Now murder must be added to his crimes.'

'I'd call it judicial execution!' Elizabeth had come to join them. 'The man deserves a medal, not a hanging.'

'Bloodthirsty wench!' Perry tugged gently at his wife's dark curls. Then he walked over to the bed.

'How are you feeling, Judith?'

'Oh, Perry, I'm so much better. There's really nothing wrong with me—'

'Apart from the odd stab wound?' he observed with some amusement. 'You ladies are a hardy lot. You put us all to shame!'

'Now, Perry, you shan't tease!' his wife reproved. 'Judith, do you mean it? Will you take a little broth? It will help you to regain your strength…'

Judith nodded, smiling, and Elizabeth whisked away.

'What a pair you are!' Perry sank into the nearest

chair and stretched out his long legs. 'Never a dull moment! What's this I hear about some necklace? Sebastian couldn't believe his ears when Dan mentioned it at the church...'

'It must have seemed strange,' Dan admitted. 'But it was all I could think of at the time.'

'Well, I've heard of defeating one's enemies with swords and pistols, but never with a string of pearls. What on earth were you about?'

Judith began to blush. 'Dan reminded me. It was just a story which I wrote some years ago.'

Dan's eyes began to twinkle. 'It was your first.' He turned to Perry. 'Judith was an admirer of Mrs Radcliffe, and her tales of Gothic horror. *The Mysteries of Udolpho* persuaded her to try one of her own.'

'I'm no wiser,' Perry said blankly.

'Well, in "The Pearl Necklace", the heroine escaped her fate by doing exactly what Judith did yesterday.'

'Ah, now I understand! That was quick thinking, Dan. I doubt if I'd have remembered it myself.'

'I haven't forgotten anything.' Dan took Judith's hand and squeezed it fondly. 'Dearest, I can't tell you what it means to have you safe at last, and here with all your friends. You shall never leave me.'

'Mrs Aveton?' Judith murmured. 'Has she been asking for me?'

Perry gave her a grin of unashamed delight. 'When she'd finished drumming her heels and tearing out her hair she closed the house and scuttled off to Cheltenham with her charming daughters. Sebastian persuaded her that it would be for the best...the scandal, you know.'

'Is someone taking my name in vain?' Sebastian put his head around the door. 'Judith, should you be holding court, my dear? You must be very tired...'

'No, I'm not! Oh, do come in! I so wanted to congratulate you. Prudence and the babes are well?' Judith held out both her hands to him.

'They are fine!' Sebastian's face was radiant with delight. 'And you?'

'I feel wonderful! Oh, my dear, I am so happy for you. Now you have got your heart's desire.'

'I think I am not alone in that.' Sebastian looked at Dan and Judith. Then he bent and kissed her. 'Welcome to the family,' he said softly.

'Great heavens!' Elizabeth walked into the room accompanied by Bessie. 'Judith, are you holding a reception? It won't do, you know.' She frowned at the circle of gentlemen seated around the bed.

'Off you go!' she ordered. 'Our patient is supposed to rest.' Her smile robbed her words of all offence.

As Perry and Sebastian left, Dan rose as if to follow them, but Judith clutched his hand.

'Don't go!' she whispered. 'I don't want you to leave me.'

'But, dearest, you must eat,' Elizabeth protested.

'Dan won't stop me. Oh, please, don't send him away.'

'No chance of that if you want me here, my love.' Dan took the tray from Bessie. 'I am quite capable of handling this.'

Elizabeth threw up her hands. 'Come, Bessie! Let us leave these love-birds. We are not needed here.'

'She was right, my darling,' Dan murmured when they were alone. 'Our need is for each other. Tell me again that you still love me.'

'I never stopped.' Judith gave him a misty smile and suddenly she was beautiful. 'Just hold me, Dan.'

The soup was forgotten as he stretched out on the bed beside her and cradled her in his arms. His tender kisses rained down upon her brow, her eyelids and her cheeks, until she sighed with rapture.

'Can it be true that we shall never part again?' she whispered.

'Never, my dear love. Shall you mind if we don't live in London after we are married?'

'No, I will go anywhere with you, but why do you ask?' She sensed that he was chuckling. 'Are you keeping secrets from me?'

'Just one, but you may hear it now. The Admiral will order frigates built to my design, but it will mean that we must move to Portsmouth.'

'Oh, Dan, as if that mattered! I am *so* happy for you.'

He cradled her head against his shoulder. 'Judith, that is the least part of my joy. I have you...'

He bent his head and found her mouth in a kiss that sealed their love.

* * * * *

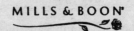

MILLS & BOON®

Historical Romance™

Coming next month

A BARGAIN WITH FATE
by Ann Elizabeth Cree

A Regency delight from a new author!

Michael, Lord Stamford needed a pretend fiancée to keep
his family at bay. Rosalyn had to accept Michael's
proposal if she was to regain her brother's estate.

DRAGON'S COURT
by Joanna Makepeace

Intrigue at Henry (the Welsh dragon) VII's court

Anne Jarvis has watched her father pay fines to the king,
and she wanted a husband who would give her a peaceful
life—Dickon Allard wasn't that man!

On sale from 6th November 1998

*Available at most branches of WH Smith, Tesco, Asda,
Martins, Borders and all good paperback bookshops*

FIND THE FRUIT!

How would you like to win a year's supply of Mills & Boon® Books—FREE! Well, if you know your fruit, then you're already one step ahead when it comes to completing this competition, because all the answers are fruit! Simply decipher the code to find the names of ten fruit, complete the coupon overleaf and send it to us by 30th April 1999. The first five correct entries will each win a year's subscription to the Mills & Boon series of their choice. What could be easier?

A	B	C	D	E	F	G	H	I
15	16	17	18	19	20	21	22	23
J	K	L	M	N	O	P	Q	R
	25	26	1	2	3	4	5	6
S	T	U	V	W	X	Y	Z	
7	8	9	10	11		13		

4	19	15	17	22
P	E	A	C	H

15	10	3	17	15	18	3
A	V	O	C	A	D	O

2	19	17	8	15	6	23	2	19
N	E	C	T	A	R	I	N	E

4	19	15	6
P	E	A	R

4	26	9	1
P	L	U	M

7	8	6	15	11	16	19	6	6	13
S	T	R	A	W	B	E	R	R	Y

3	6	15	2	21	19
O	R	A	N	G	E

15	4	4	26	19
A	P	P	L	E

1	15	2	21	3
M	A	N	G	O

16	15	2	15	2	15
B	A	N	A	N	A

C8J

Please turn over for details of how to enter ➜

HOW TO ENTER

There are ten coded words listed overleaf, which when decoded each spell the name of a fruit. There is also a grid which contains each letter of the alphabet and a number has been provided under some of the letters. All you have to do, is complete the grid, by working out which number corresponds with each letter of the alphabet. When you have done this, you will be able to decipher the coded words to discover the names of the ten fruit! As you decipher each code, write the name of the fruit in the space provided, then fill in the coupon below, pop this page into an envelope and post it today. Don't forget you could win a year's supply of Mills & Boon® Books—you don't even need to pay for a stamp!

Mills & Boon Find the Fruit Competition
FREEPOST CN81, Croydon, Surrey, CR9 3WZ
EIRE readers: (please affix stamp) PO Box 4546, Dublin 24.

Please tick the series you would like to receive if you
are one of the lucky winners
Presents™ ❑ Enchanted™ ❑ Medical Romance™ ❑
Historical Romance™ ❑ Temptation® ❑

Are you a Reader Service™ subscriber?   Yes ❑   No ❑

Ms/Mrs/Miss/Mr ....Initials ....
(BLOCK CAPITALS PLEASE)

Surname...

Address ....

....

....Postcode.......................

(I am over 18 years of age)   C8J